Airport Reading

GW00691418

Ivie Lindig

Published by Ivie Lindig
Publishing partner: Paragon Publishing, Rothersthorpe
First published 2016
© Ivie Lindig 2016

ISBN 978-1-78222-484-6

Book design, layout and production management by Into Print
www.intoprint.net
+44 (0)1604 832149

Printed and bound in UK and USA by Lightning Source

Contents

The Magnificent Three

"Shit! Shit! Shit!"

This very loudly from the woman opposite me at the wobbly airport cafe table. She follows it up by banging a fist and dropping her head onto her arms, at which my just-bought coffee slurps and spills into a determined stream, edging towards the overpriced sandwich I have also just bought.

Mind you, I do know what she means. Watching those announcement boards flicker and roll their blanked out eyes through one destination and another is depressing, to say the least, and as this airport and that in turn goes down there are various accompanying groans of despair, mine among them.

"Hey, I'm sorry."

She looks up, sees my half-ruined snack; a rueful smile.

"No problem," I lie. That sliver of smoked salmon, caged in its synthetic brown bread, is the fourth mini-meal I have got through since arriving, and I'll soon have to take out an unsecured loan to finance myself if this goes on. And go on it will, as we are now treated to an audial update, though I wouldn't go so far as to say it's a human voice.

"All flights to Australasia, the Middle East, African continent and Far East cancelled until further notice. Passengers please wait in the lounge and shopping areas for further information." About half the world, then. Great.

Together, we mop at the brown trickles, together we sigh at one another; together we are washed up, stranded on this beach of eternal flight delays. We have a bond: boredom.

"Freaking volcano," she says now. I grunt in acquiescence, contemplate the dregs of my coffee left to me. It does not look inviting

"Look," she says, suddenly, "I should go get you another coffee."

By now, I have picked up on her accent. American. North. Boston area, I think? And here's unexciting me from Bedfordshire UK. I refuse the coffee – I'm swilling with the stuff – and we swap details. She's en route to Australia. Melbourne? I ask? Sydney? Darwin? No, she smiles, and names some small outback place I've never heard of. Ah.

"And where're you bound?"

"Um. Thailand."

"How nice."

She's being polite. Thailand is where everyone and anyone goes on a winter package holiday. The package for safety, the Far East 'cos it's a bit exotic, even if most of your street has been there, will most likely be there when you are, and winter because you get a bit of a tan to show off in the staff room. But I admit, I've been before, the first time on vacation; it was predictable and pleasant, if anodyne, and I had a good time. I even had a sweet little holiday romance. Well, I was shagged a couple of times, at any rate. And here I am, going out there again; a last minute arrangement, this time, though in a hurry. How was I to know another flaming – pardon the pun – volcano was going to get all narky and pump its innards up into the stratosphere?

Especially as, this year, I have another and far more challenging reason for going there.

"Well." She leans forward. Her long, tousled hair extensions fall onto the table, and this close up I can see the faint streaks where her fake tan has started to fade. Bitch. Her, not me, I mean: despite the artifice, she still looks bloody good. Luminous deep blue eyes, and of

6

course, she's slender, tall, I would say, and those elegant legs in their well fitting pants actually do go right up to her armpits; well up to mine, anyway. But then, I'm short and ginger, and what nice men call 'pleasantly rounded', and the not-so-nice ones describe as 'plenty to get hold of'.

"So what are you going to do? Wait it out? Or give up and go back home?"

I bite hard on my nails. This is taking me the other side of anxious, right into fear, dread and paranoia country. What will happen if we're trapped here for weeks? What will he think? That I've not honoured my promise? Not done what I said I would do? And the consequences of that would be... I *have* to get to Thailand – and soon.

"I don't know. I had thought of trying to get a hotel room. Last time this happened, UK airports were shut for days, weeks even."

"You and the world," says the fake-tan-false-hair-enhanced one a little unkindly. "Watch the stampede."

Sure enough, there is a whirlwind of fellow travellers pushing, shoving, swearing and gesticulating at the exits, presumably heading for the nearest Travel Lodge/Holiday Inn etc. We Brits are a stingy lot. We like our airport hotels right next to the aeroplanes and we like them cheap.

"So," I retort, "what are your plans?"

"Dunno." A shrug of a finely hewn, bronzed, satiny smooth shoulder. *Cow.* "I don't have any place to go. This is like a transit stop for me."

And now I feel sorry for her, and a bit ashamed of myself for having been nasty, even if it was only in my thoughts. Isn't it said that to think horrible things, or to imagine evil deeds, is as bad as actually saying or committing them? Or is that my bible-bashing girls' school coming up to slug me again? *Bugger off,* I say to it, and from her bewildered expression I realise I have uttered this aloud.

"Not you!" I laugh, and break the tension in my own

head and something between us simultaneously melts and re-forms, like steel dissolving and turning into gossamer, incredibly tentative yet binding, strong. "Just banishing demons from the past. You know?"

"Oh *Gahd*, do I know that one! Hey, what's your name, little lady?"

The bristles on the back of my neck resurrect themselves. Anyone who calls me *little* is dead meat.

"Lucy." Through stiffened lips.

She doesn't seem to notice the frost in the air, leans back, smiles.

"Aw," she says, softly. "I have a friend with a kid called Lucy. Nice name. Pretty. Suits you."

Damn the manipulative crittur. Now I'm blushing. Okay, I confess, you can't win with me. Take the piss and I'll bite; compliment me and I'll go right back inside my flimsy hideaway and hiss at you. Still, I suppose she's trying to be friendly. *Make an effort, Luce...*

"So what's your name?" The lips have thawed a bit and I think I sound half-way civil.

"Princess Faren," says the golden girl, promptly.

"Eh? You're a Princess?"

"No way! In name only. It's like Prince for boys – popular in the States. I guess here it sounds just – plain silly."

"Not at all, no, really, it's – erm – very striking."

Actually I think it is a dumb moniker, and if I were this woman I'd have throttled my parents as soon as I got out of nappies. Come to think of it, perhaps she has? That's the thing about sudden intimacy with strangers in airports; you don't know a thing about them. The person mopping up your coffee spill could be a mass murderer. Or a bank robber. A great musician. Sex maniac. An embezzler on a grand scale. Chess champion. Someone from the CIA. The list is endless.

She's smiling at me now, this not-princess, screwing up her beautiful eyes and regarding me with a suddenly very intelligent expression.

"Come on, it's a bullshit name, and I hated it for years, but I've kind of come to terms with it. I quite like 'Faren' – it means adventurous. You can call me that, or you can call me PF like my friends do."

Whoopee. What a choice. Wickedly, I go for PF, which, in suitable moments, could be translated into something rather ruder.

"Great," says PF, still with that annoying smile. "So that means you're a friend, yeah?"

"Yeah," I mutter, slightly ashamed. She spots this too. Not so dumb, this blonde, bottle or otherwise. (I think it might actually be her natural colour. *Double triple bloody cow.*)

The DTBC stands up, and I see that her legs do go on for a long way, but not forever, which is to her advantage as there's plenty of interest beyond crotch level, and that she's about five eleven. Which means she is giant-sized and towers over me. She stretches honey coloured, toned and lightly muscular arms languidly over her head; there is a crashing sound as two men in the cafeteria queue collide and white crockery splinters on the tiles. The only time I have that effect on blokes is when I'm totally rat-arsed and staggering into them at the bar.

"Listen," she says, "there has to be some place a tad more comfortable than this. Let's go find it, and then you can hear a story I'd like to tell you."

* * *

After half an hour and several miles of trekking the maze of Heathrow, we have managed to grab ourselves a few square metres of best airport carpeting. We further

9

congratulate ourselves on being seasoned sojourners; we have both brought inflatable cushions – two, in PF's case – and along with jackets and light sweaters and our luggage, not yet checked, we are able to construct a limited but cosy nest against the adjacent wall. I dare say that after a few hours – days? – it will not feel so soothing, but for the moment we are grateful for this makeshift haven.

"So." I jab PF gently on the forearm. "What's this story, then?"

"Mm. Well, in order to tell it, I need to make a tryst with you."

"A what?" This is alarming. Is she – could she be – oh Lordy – coming onto me? I've never been into the Sapphic arts (what some would, vulgarly, call rug munching, but let's not lower the tone) and I don't wish to learn them right at this point in time. Or ever.

"Yeah. You know, A kind of promise, an arrangement of faith. I have an idea, and it could be a good one, but it needs you to be *completely trustworthy*. Oh, I don't have any reason to think otherwise, Lucy, but let's face it, we don't know each other from Adam."

"Or Eve?" I suggest, and PF grins appreciatively. "Okay, I take your point. But I have to know what you're suggesting first."

"I guess."

I am still wary, and she can see this.

"Right. Here's the deal. We neither of us wants to leave the airport – me because I can't, you because your flight might be reinstated any time in the next twenty-four hours. So, apart from needing to sleep, and the occasional pee, and some trips over there for coffee and their lousy food, what have we got to do? Huh?"

And the blue, blue eyes peer into mine with dismaying intensity, and again I draw back, mentally if not literally. Surely she *isn't* propositioning me, in such a public place and all? And in any case, even if she is that side of the fence, I would've thought she could do better for herself than fat, freckly old *moi*.

"So Luce? Shall we go for it?" I remain silent, and, somewhat impatiently, she continues, "Chaucer. Heard of him?"

"Of course." My national pride is stung. I mean, I might have done Chemistry at University, but I have heard of the guy. "He – er – wrote some stories, didn't he? In old fashioned verse. Some of them were a bit, um, cheeky?"

A swash of hair extensions whip my cheek and rattle against the partition wall, and her raucous bellow gives me a front-row of her perfectly veneered or capped, straightened and whitened teeth. A quick calculation adds another ten thousand to the cost of her appearance to date. And that's pounds we're talking, not dollars.

"You are something else, Lucy girl," she finally splutters. "One of your own literary treasures and you – "

"All right, all right."

Americans. They take over everything don't they? Our early warning stations, our women (in war time), our language and shopping habits and now even our ancient dusty old poets. I mean, America wasn't even born, as such, or heard of in the fourteenth century, or whenever it was that Chaucer scribbled his opus. The world had to wait, breathlessly, another hundred years or so before Columbus and his mates put their invaders' hooves on American soil. And then it was only the southern part, to begin with. (See, I was good at History. Facts. I like 'em.)

"Okay. Okay." She's sobered up; the extensions fall back into place, meekly, and she leans in confidentially once more. "Let's say that we each tell a tale – like Chaucer's pilgrims did – and, if we have to wait another day, or two, we should tell another. And then we'll judge which tale was the best."

There's a long pause. Chaucer. Me. Me and Chaucer. Brilliant and world renowned medieval author meets Chemistry teacher from Oakley, Beds. Some match! I also have a suspicion that any tale of PF's will be way more interesting than anything I have to reveal to the panting public.

"I – don't have anything to talk about."

This is lame in the extreme, and I well know it. It earns the flashing contempt it deserves; the oceanic eyes sweep my face like a lorry's headlights, and I actually flinch from the impact like a wounded sparrow. I even mix my metaphors horribly, and if this had been lab chemicals I was chucking together we'd have been blown sky high already.

At this very moment the boards flicker into new life. Another pronouncement is rapidly printing on the screens. Oh-oh. It seems that we are likely to be stuck for about three or four days. After that, the ash cloud being a rather more puny affair than the last one, and it being centred solely over the UK, wouldn't you just know it, we get the crappiest weather in the world and now we get the crappiest ash cloud that's too damn lazy to get its butt moving over to Russia or somewhere sensible. I mean, I'm not anti-Ruski or anything, but there is a lot of space in their country, and our ash cloud would seem like a pocket handkerchief in all those Siberian wastes, whereas in weeny Britain it blots out the lot... Lost my thread there; syntax gone haywire. (My old English teacher – and I do mean old, as the hills and all that – used to complain relentlessly that my essays 'wandered like a starving rabid homeless dog'. Thanks, Miss Viner.) Where was I? Yes, after that, the board scrolls to announce, proudly, like a parent reporting that their child has the highest score in the recent tests, that after about four days the weather system is due to change, and a kindly old uncle of a wind

12

will blow the bloody thing away from us and out over the Atlantic. Never to return.

Well, that's some good news. As the Priest in Romeo and Juliet says, "I do spy a kind of hope". There, we Chem. Majors aren't totally ilittarate. Illittarete? Iliter— oh, what the fuck. You're up with me, yeah?

In the meantime, though, we have another three days and around nineteen hours to get past, and in the light of this, PF's suggestion doesn't seem so loopy. With enough bottles of wine, it could even be fun. And we're never, never, ever going to see each other again,, so we can say what we like, *let it all hang out* as my old dad says, trying to be *trendy*. We can lie, we can invent, we can adopt a totally different persona –

As if reading my thoughts, PF frowns and says, "One thing, Lucy. Our stories have to be true. Nothing made up. No fantasy. We tell it like it was, we tell it like we are."

Oh great bouncing fisherman's bollocks. Oh steaming mile high heaps of dog-poo. Oh humongous double M cup knee-length *tit*.

"And I would know," continues this clairvoyant, soft but ruthless, "as I am sure you'd know if I didn't tell the truth about myself and my life."

You have to be joking, I think, sourly. I could believe absolutely anything about you, puss-cat.

"You agree, don't you?"

I am not to be able to get out of this so I nod, somewhat sullenly, and PF puts out a long, slender but well formed hand. I reluctantly clasp, and we shake on it. She's surprisingly strong. I should not mess with her.

"Great. Good girl!" (I *will* assassinate her at some point.) "Now I'm going to get some wine. What d'you prefer, white or –"

"Red," I say, firmly, wanting to haul myself up to something like knee level, so to speak, in the decision

13

making. "I like a good red, myself."

"Good choice," she says and I find myself turning like a fish finger under the grill in the warm glow of her approval. "Okay, I'll go buy a couple of –"

"Sure, and wouldn't you be much better with water or fresh juice now? The wine will only dehydrate you, and this place is going to get good and stuffy."

This is a new voice somewhere above our heads, and we squint upwards, against the lights of the airport lounge. All I can make out is a shipwreck of dark, wildly curly hair, partly dragged ineffectually back into a little knot, and beneath it the rather curvy figure of a woman. Quite a young woman.

Without so much as a by-your-leave, she continues,

"And you have a wee space here I see. I'll just be putting my things down, then, and sitting alongside youse."

It's an Irish accent, Irish as in Ireland, not the bit at the top that we roped off. The real MacCoy, then – or should that be O'Malley? You might have noted that I'm good on accents; something I got from my dad, who can place a person within ten miles of his or her town or village. We don't know why we have this weird talent, and it is of course, completely useless; there are no job ads for highly paid employment which go "Must be able to distinguish dialects to within half a kilometre". But I digress. Again.

Before I can home in further to this woman's hamlet, street or hovel, she plumps herself down in the remaining empty few millimetres of carpet between us with her two admittedly cabin-sized, neat cases. Immediately I feel defensive of PF and of myself. We are a team. We found this place. We planted our flag here, as it were. *Land ours.* I can sense the stirrings of primeval territorial ancestors in my blood. Where's my spear?

"Ah now, I can see youse don't like me crowding you, but gosh, I'm tired, and there's not an inch of comfy floor to

14

be had except this one. Sure, and I'll be no bother. And I'll buy the teas and the water and the juice for us all. Deal?"

"Mmm." PF is surprisingly languid, considering how this woman has gatecrashed our party. "But we really wanted wine"

"As I said, dehydrates. Not the wisest choice, " says our shamrock girl, quick as a flash, and smug with it.

I cannot hold back. In the pecking order of our strange trio, PF is Alpha Female, and I am def. not in third place.

"Who the fuck asked you?"

I see the dark, rather fine brows arch sharply; she's not going to say, "Language!" is she? But no, she simply settles herself and smiles.

"You're right," she says. "Sorry. If you want wine, you go and get it, but I'll provide tea and all, for when you're thirsty."

"Thanks," I say, grudgingly, and my team-mate nods. We both know that she's right. At least partly. "We'll hold you to that. No slithering out of it."

"Right y'are. Sure. What do youse take me for?"

An Irish interloper, I think, and then slug myself hard with that danged old RE lesson on Alternative Cultures again for (a) further uncharitable thoughts and (b) falling into ethnic stereotypes. The girl – for now I can see that she is rather young, younger than PF or me by some years – beams, and her firm, round face is brighter than a sunny morning, sweeter than spring flowers. (Hey, I didn't know I could write such beautiful things. Miss Viner would've been proud of me. Maybe I should hang out in air terminals more often.) There's a kind of freshness about her, even in this hothouse, a kind of – innocence? I privately put her at about twenty four. And yet, she seems confident of herself, at home in the world. Certainly in our little scrap of it.

We can't help ourselves, PF and I; we crumple into slightly apologetic smiles, and we lower the barrier, knock it down like a heap of egg-boxes in the wind, and welcome our new member into the tribe.

"So what're you called?" I ask, a mini-second ahead of PF.

Some unpronounceable Gaelic-Irish name, no doubt, with 'BH' combinations that sound like V, or Blathnaid that's 'Blawnid'. Something weird, way out and strange.

"Ann," she says, with another dazzling flash of small creamy teeth. "My name is Ann."

We are settled, we three – what? Muskatresses? – and PF is about to start her tale. A bottle of red wine nestles between my knees, opened – the bottle, that is – to let it warm up and breathe. Sharp, cold red wine drunk too soon is abominable, and I won't bore you with a chemist's reasons for that. Ann nurses what looks like a flagon of fresh spring water. I observe that her skin is flawless, even for a twenty-something year old, innocent of any kind of cosmetic as far as I can detect. And *no freckles*.

There's a silence.

"Are you sitting comfortably?" I murmur. "Then PF will begin…"

The other two look at me as if I'm nuts. Not that I'm old enough to remember Listen With Mother, but my mother passed on this saying to me when I was small, and it kind of stuck. It irritates the hell out of me, but you know the sort of thing; once you internalise a saying, you can't stop yourself repeating it – a bit like a hamster getting fixated on turning that flipping wheel, I suppose.

"Sorry," I mutter, fumble through some kind of explanation, and sit on my hands to stop me from slapping myself.

After another curious stare, PF leans back against her massive suitcase, bolstered with one of the pillows, takes a long, slow breath, lowers her smooth eyelids and opens that wide, full, perfectly pouting mouth on an out breath; closes it. And repeats the process. I have to say it, with her silver-blonde hair tumbling around her, she looks like some kind of saccharine angel in heavenly meditation. When I close my eyes, all colour leaches from my pale, speckled face, and I just look like a sleeping rice pudding. I know, 'cos I've had holidays snaps taken when I was dozing on the beach. Not, as they say, a pretty sight, especially as my hair, rather than falling in some tousled, seraphic fashion, looks like lumps of orange marzipan. In the photos, that is; in reality, it looks rather better. Red hair is not photogenic.

I have time for this unflattering introspection as PF is still doing her Zen inhalations, or whatever, and shows no signs of launching into her story. I can't imagine that Chart – er, Chaucer did any of this stuff – more likely downed, *quaffed*, even, another yard of ale. Good old Geoff. Man after my own heart.

"Preparation," whispers Ann, knowingly. "Getting the inner spirit ready, finding inner calm, centring down."

She has been introduced to our pact, and has agreed to be part of it. I am intrigued to hear what kind of account she will delight us with. Groping encounters in fields of sprouting potatoes? A quickie behind "The Green Leprechaun" after closing time? I rebuke myself for this stereotyping, but not too harshly; the logical, practical and totally rational stuff between my ears that I like to think of as *brain* reacts, and a snort of derision leaves my nose before I can stop it. I simply can't abide this 'good karkma' rubbish. Everything in this world, in this universe, has a scientific explanation, and I'm firmly on the side of evidence, proof and good old fashioned common sense. Ann looks at me in reproach.

"Shush!" she mouths. "Give the wee girl a chance."

Wee girl? Wee? Does she need glasses? Or is it a matter of complete lack of spatial awareness? Ann herself is not much taller than me, is shapely without being fat, though might run to it in middle age if she doesn't watch it, and has hips that are what some people called 'child bearing', though attractive enough on her perky frame, I have to say. Rather than the blonde tangles of Our Glamour Girl, Ann has tightly curled, positively bouncing hair, in a mass of black, probably reaching just below her shoulders; not an extension in sight. I doubt she'd find anywhere to put one. Her eyes are slanted, like a cat's, a luminous hazel-green, and her mouth quite a cute little Cupid's bow, though bare of lipstick or gloss, I notice. Nose-wise, not so great; it's a mite big for that dainty chin, and has a bit of a hook in it. She's 'bonny', as my grand-dad would say, rather than classical, and no way is she beautiful. But then, nor am I. We are in the same boat there, a somewhat ordinary fishing vessel, whereas PF is the sleek, luxury yacht of this outfit, if not to say the legendary barge of Cleopatra, a Quimquimire... As you see, I do remember some things from school; not that they ever come in useful.

"Okay," says PF languidly leaning back on her large travelling case and the blow-up pillows. "This is just a trivial little incident I'm going to tell you about. It's nothing very dramatic, though I guess it could have been. I have a much better and more interesting story to recount to you for my second turn, but this will get us going."

PF has opened those brilliant eyes of hers now, and is searching our faces for our reaction, or perhaps just to make sure we're paying attention. *Yes, Miss*, I think, irreverently, *we're listening.*

Rather unexpectedly, she then says, quietly,

"It's nothing much; I hope you won't be disappointed with this one."

Like good little girls in class, we shake our heads in unison. *No, no, PF; you could never disappoint us.* I have a strong feeling this is true.

"So why am I telling you it? Well, it's something I did when I was quite young – around twenty or so – and which won't take long to tell. It's, like, a message of how harebrained we can all be when we're that age, and how we think we're untouchable. Immortal, y'know?"

We nod, solemnly, looking like those daft dogs you get in the backs of cars. I can sure identify with this one. The bit about being naïve and cocksure when you're twenty-something, that is, not being a nodding dog.

"Yes," says PF, slowly, almost dreamily. "I find it interesting, in fact, to look at how I was then – how life was then. When there seemed no real clouds in the sky, and things were simple, and all you had to do was just keep on going, keep truckin', the way you always did, and it would be okay."

Without meaning to, I utter a curt half-laugh, half snicker, and the other two look at me curiously.

"Sorry," I mumble. "Go on, PF."

"Mm, then, " says PF, though still eyeing me carefully, "as I said, I was only just on the edge of my third decade; the world was indeed my very own pearl-producing oyster at that time. I was a student," she adds, "but not taking my studies very seriously. There were reasons – but that's another story."

And one, I think, that we're not going to hear? But I say nothing, and wrap a jacket around my knees, and curl up against my own pillow and prepare to listen. PF as a student is an intriguing thought: was she even more beautiful then? Or was she an ugly duckling? And what was she studying? Or not? Everything is possible with this woman. Everything and anything

"So, then. Here goes. It happened when I was at College – oh, way back. I used to travel a fair bit. You know – just kicking about the place for the sake of it. The US is one big old country, as you know, and even a small state on the map in America is a lot of land when you get to journey in it. I hadn't a heap of money, that goes without saying, so along with buddies, I used to hitch rides."

She pauses; scrutinises our faces again. I don't hitch hike myself, but I know some people still do and I know it was the way students got around in my mother's generation, or so she told me. To my left, I sense Ann tensing up; she's looking worried already, with a funny frozen look that might be shock, disapproval or worry, or perhaps all three.

"Go on," I say. "So you got rides."

"Yes. Dodgy. Dangerous, stupid, foolish. Clod-brained. Call it what you will. Every parent would have ten thousand fits if they knew their daughters were standing out on the highways with their thumbs out, waiting for some truckie to stop and give them a ride. Sometimes we'd hitch in pairs – never more than two, it puts drivers off, and anyhow they don't have room, usually, if you have kit bags with you; and hitching with a man, well, you'll wait a long time, in my experience. No," she goes on, looking at Ann's expression, "not because the driver wants to rape you; no, more that he, or she, is afraid of being attacked by the male hitcher Danger works both ways, you know."

And she stares meaningfully at the Irish colleen, whose tongue has been very quietly and I suspect involuntarily clucking throughout this.

"I believe it does, now," Ann says in an undertone, and subsides in a *phlumphff* of her own cushion.

Having silenced us, her audience, PF takes queenly command and sits up more straight, puts her strong, elegant shoulders back and launches into her tale.

"On this particular day, I started off very early in the morning; I wanted to go visit some friends in the next state, and it was a long way, but by late afternoon I was still nearly – oh, maybe fifty miles short of where I wanted to be. All the rides had been good – decent people, sometimes couples, sometimes guys, but all willing to help and actually concerned that I should be safe. I should tell you that I mostly hitched alone. I'm tall, I'm strong and I don't think I looked like a weak little thing you should easily mess with."

21

We'll go along with that one, then. I suppress a smirk. "So I wasn't afraid. Cautious, yes. Wary, sometimes. But never scared. You might think that was dumb, and at this distance of time I might begin to agree. At the very least it was – let's say immature. But there you are. At that age you imagine you know it all, that you rule the world, that it will do as you want."

"Ah, yes, right you are."

A sigh, and this unbidden and out of the blue, from my left. I don't know why I'm surprised by this reaction, but I certainly am. Connections of this kind between Golden Girl and Irish Innocent seem unlikely, but...

Before I can go further with this thought, PF firmly continues.

"And for a long time I was completely lucky. Drivers were not only kind, they were also, as I said, concerned. 'I have a daughter back home,' they'd say. 'I'd hope that if she hitched she'd get a safe ride, like I'm giving you.' They'd even buy me a meal sometimes, and some of them went out of their way to drop me off nearer to where I wanted to be. It was great. All that free travel – I got to see the length and breadth of three states, in big wagons, sitting high and getting this fantastic view of the land and the wide open sky, in luxury autos with the top down, with the sun and the wind blowing my hair in all directions and a radio or disc on full blast. And all I had to do was sit there and enjoy."

And Ann and I sit here, and also enjoy. We like the picture painted: a young, fresh, blonde haired girl with tanned skin dangling one long, slim arm out of the window, incredible legs stretched out in front of her, relaxing in the heat of an American landscape. In our vision it never rains or snows, nor is it cold or in any way other than heavenly. PF would have us see it so. It is how she sees it herself, of course, and it is how we – or I, at any rate – want to see it. The drivers are shadowy figures: big gnarled truckie with a baseball cap slung backwards on his grizzled hair, a kindly face and huge, meaty hands on the wheel of his juggernaut thundering across the Yankee plains with the honey-sweet PF beside him... A well-heeled business man in his stretch limousine or American style sports car, designer sunglasses screening benevolent eyes and a philanthropic disposition as he tenderly conveys Our Princess to her destination, possibly via an upmarket roadside eatery...

"Then," says PF, so sharply that we both jump. "Then, naturally, the bubble of good fortune burst. After all, I was trading on my luck and wearing it out. Had about six or seven of my nine lives, if you like. On this late afternoon, as I told you, with a lot of miles to go and nightfall coming fast, I got stuck on a highway – it doesn't matter which, or where, it wouldn't mean anything to you if you've not been to that part of the States – and I knew that if I didn't get a ride soon, I wouldn't make it to where I wanted to be."

A pause. Dramatic effect, or what? The faintest of smiles from our Golden One, and then she takes up the tale. She certainly knows how to tease...

"So I was mighty glad when a middling kind of motor pulled over, some yards ahead, and a hand came out of the window and beckoned me to get in. I sure ran down that tarmac, and hopped into the car without really looking at who was driving it – a thing I had told myself I should never do. You can get quite a good impression by looking at someone's face in that situation"

"Such as?" Ann breathes the question, agog. As am I.

"Oh, you know, if he or she – and it's usually a he, by the way – looks relaxed and smiling in a nice, ordinary sort of way, you can tell they're gonna give you a ride with no trouble. If they look a little – what you could call furtive, or embarrassed, as if they don't want anyone to see you getting in, then back off. I always made it a rule to linger a while, arm on the window frame, so that if the driver thought better of it, or was a bit suspicious they could make an excuse and drive away. Or I would have had a little precious time to assess, and refuse. It's a rough and ready rule, but it worked for me. I also took the view that ninety nine point nine recurring per cent of people are good, and harmless, and mean to be kind. A view, as I can see you're about to ask, Lucy, that I maintain to this day."

"Good for you, PF!"

Ann treats us to her wide, Irish smile, and showers it especially on the fair and generously minded Princess Faren. I'm not sure I agree, so I keep *schtumm*.

"Sure, and though we're all sinners, aren't we all God's creations too, and have that goodness in us? Isn't it so, sure?"

"Yes," says PF, suddenly thoughtful. "I do believe that, Ann. I do indeed. The vast majority of folk are just average Joes, or Janes, honest and sincere, trying to live their lives. Though one can be disappointed."

For some obscure reasons her gaze swivels round to me. WTF? What have I said or done to deserve that? Huh? However, I'm more interested to hear how the story goes than analyze what the beautiful, perma-tanned lanky one thinks of me right now. Or why. I hold my tongue.

PF takes up her thread. "It didn't take me more than a few minutes to realise, that for once, I'd picked a bit of a bad 'un. Not that he made any physical advances, or touched me, he didn't even say anything that I could call outright worrying. It was his manner. He kept asking me the same things, over and over. Where was I going, exactly? What route did I want to take? Did I know that it would be completely dark in just over half an hour and that the place was hard to find? That the minor roads would be pitch black, with no lighting? What was I doing there, at this time of night? And on and on, until I ran out of answers, and just stayed quiet."

And there's a quiet amongst us now; all I can hear is Ann's slightly husky, open-mouthed breathing.

"And...?" I say. "Go on, PF. Go on."

"Well, we travelled in a kind of awkward silence, for about ten or fifteen miles more, and then he suddenly said that he was going to turn off down another road, not the one that would lead to where I wanted to go, but to his own home. It was far too late now, he said, to try and find the place in the dark, and anyhow he was tired and needed to get back after a long day. He did tell me what his job was, something that meant a lot of driving around. I think he was speaking the truth. And what about me, I asked him. Could he drop me off there and I could walk back to the turn off? No, he said, he wouldn't leave me on a dark highway, and I could stay the night at his house. His wife wouldn't mind."

Another pause. Time for us to assimilate the picture... the pitch black road, trapped in a car with a stranger... yikes. I hope my mother doesn't have anything like this story to tell. No, she couldn't have; not my comfortable, middle aged mum in her pleated skirts and M and S sweaters... Could she? But PF is speaking again. Listen!

"Now I began to really panic. Not something I do very often, as you might have reckoned. The car was going much too fast for me to jump out, and unless we came to some cross roads and lights where he had to stop I couldn't get away. I only hoped that when we reached his house I could run for it and go bang on someone else's door. On the other hand, he might be driving me off into the middle of nowhere, and then... "

Ann's plump white hand is over her mouth; her eyes are wide with horror. For once, I cannot blame her. For all my foolhardiness, I would never have put myself in such a situation. For some reason, this does not make me feel superior to this goddess in human form. Strange.

"But he didn't," says PF, placidly, "and I think I knew even then that he wouldn't. I guessed he was regretting having picked me up, and that he just didn't feel like driving out of his way and maybe getting lost, and then having to find his way back home, and that he didn't really know what to do with me. I did wonder what the wife would say, though, and how he'd explain – me."

There's a lengthy pause. I contemplate backwoodsy American homestead, with its wooden stoop, and I try to visualise the bemused housewife in her hessian pinny standing, hands on wide hips, with an *Aw gee Hank, what yah done gone done this time, huh?* But she won't appear, and all I see in my imagination is a dark, threatening space.

Suddenly, my mind clicks. Light bulb ON.

But there was no wife, I think. *There wouldn't be.* But I don't say it. I don't want to spoil this tale.

"Of course," continues PF, quite serenely, "there was no wife. There was a house, sure, that was obviously his home, and in the inky dark he let us in, and took me into a back room and pulled all the drapes. But no wife. Not another soul or creature in the place – not a dog, a cat, a bird, or anything that lived."

Ann is now clutching my arm, and it hurts, but I don't shrug her off; I am picturing the scene, and already some possible outcomes are forming in front of my eyes. Short of murder or grievous permanent injury – PF is right here and looks all in one stunning, incredibly well formed piece – all manner of terrible things might be coming next.

But PF lowers the tension slightly, as she says, "It was a drab little house, but clean enough, and looked lived in. He explained that his wife was away visiting with her sister. There were photos around of him with a woman, and him, younger, with kids, so again I guessed I was getting the truth here too. Not that it made me any less freaked. By now, I wished I'd bolted the moment we got out of the car, but he kind of hustled me in and I couldn't see anything much in the darkness, though I could tell that there wasn't another house anywhere near. It wasn't that late, but there were no lights."

Ann's other hand has released its grip on me and crept to cover the first one, and her skin has drained of colour, only her red mouth standing out like a slash of blood.

I am sidetracking now to take my focus off the ghastly image that I have swimming before me: PF at the mercy of some axe murderer, only escaping after some terrible event, such as her grabbing the weapon and slicing his genitals, or pushing his face down onto a hot stove plate, so that the face sizzles and the eyeballs melt and run in hideously gooey tracks... And yes, I have thought of writing horror fiction. Maybe I should give it a go? Another unexpected possibility that's emerging from this little oasis of ours?

But the truth, says PF, interrupting my wanton fantasies, is a lot more ordinary than you might anticipate – though less than pleasant..

"He made me a cup of chocolate, and gave me a cookie. Normal as can be. He didn't talk much, and it was kind of awkward, but I began to think there was nothing to fret about, and that by morning I'd be gone and all this would be like a bad dream. He showed me the spare room, neatly made up; and said I could use that. And there was the bathroom, et cetera, et cetera. All so, so harmless.

"Then..." There's a distinctly deliberate pause here, and we hold our collective breath. Or should that be breaths? Miss Viner? Never an English teacher around when you want one, is there? But I'm distracting myself from my goosebumps, and I'm actually relieved when PF starts to speak again.

"Then – he went out of the room and came back with a camera. One of those old type ones, with film, and a huge phallic stick-out lens; a good one, by the look of it. But I *didn't* like the look of it, and sure enough, he asks me, have I ever posed as a model for photography? He's a keen amateur, himself. Would I like to pose for him now? He'd only take a few snaps, wouldn't take long. If I'd just like to take off that top?

"All this while he was coming closer in to me, wielding the camera in his pudgy little hands, and I reckoned that if he'd wanted to hit me with it he could have done some real damage, so I just kind of yelped and said no, I hadn't and wouldn't, and then he put the camera down and – and – "

"*And? And?*" says her audience, collectively. "And what?"

"Well, something that weirdos like to do. Unzipped himself and stuck his big dick right out at me, and started to rub himself with one hand whilst he grabbed his camera with the other, and came even closer in, getting right up to me, and all the time just massaging that thing of his and staring, staring into my face – "

"Oh dear Lord, oh blessed saints," says Ann on a half sob and a long, exhaled breath.

"'Kinell," is all I can mutter, and now have a very unwelcome image slap bang before me that I wish would go away. Was PF raped? Forced into some unwanted sex act, as the papers say?

She reads our minds again – probably not difficult as our brains are probably hurling out signals for anyone to pick up, not to mention our horror-stricken faces that say it all – and she sighs, like a relief.

"No, it didn't end as it might have done. He was kind of fixated on what he was doing, and I – well, all my senses and muscles were on red alert. I just shot as fast as I could into that little spare room and slammed the door shut, and dragged a wardrobe and a bedside chair up against it, and then the bed, so that he couldn't get in. After that there was just this – like, silence. I had no idea where he was: outside my door, peering through the cracks? Jerking himself off in the passageway? Tiptoeing to the kitchen, to his own bedroom? Outside the house, coming round in back to my window?"

Our Princess grimaces slightly, continues.

"You can bet I made sure that was fastened tight, that the curtains had not the tiniest gap, and lay down on the bed in my clothes, hardly breathing. I kind of sensed, though, that I'd foxed him; he'd been a bit timid in the asking, and I'd rebuffed him pretty plainly, so perhaps he'd admitted defeat. All the same, I didn't sleep much. Oh, a bit, as I was dog tired after all that travelling, but in snatches, and listening – listening for every sound."

"You would be, so," says Ann, breathing out long and slow. "What you girls put yourselves through, indeed. Risking your lovely bodies and your sacred souls."

My now automatic irritation with Ann rises, but immediately I know that, in my heart of hearts, I agree with her. We do risk our lovely, or unlovely selves, never mind the souls, if there is such a thing, and if I seem a bit confused as to whether we should, or should not do such things. Put it this way: equality for women – whatever – hasn't really worked it out yet. 'Bout time it did, I say. But PF is resuming, and we stay subdued.

She laughs, softly.

"You needn't get all riled up," she says. "It ended quite tamely, you know? He didn't try anything more, and at six o'clock, or a bit before, when it was not even light, he came with a cup of tea for me, and knocked ever so politely at my barricaded door, and said he would give me a ride to the turn off, as he was getting on the road again. Nothing was said about the night before, not a single reference to the camera, or taking photos, or any of that flasher stuff, and it was all as if nothing had happened except that he'd had an unexpected family visit. This was like absolutely surrealistic, bizarre, but it didn't strike me at the time; I was just keen to get the hell out of it."

"Indeed, indeed, so you would," murmurs Ann, and I can only agree.

"Well, you'll not guess what he made me do? I had to climb out of the window in back, out of my room and he came round with a short ladder – we weren't very high up – and clamber down so that nobody passing the front would see me. Then he had his car ready, with the engine running, and all the doors wide opened, so that I could sneak into the car quickly, keeping my head down low, and then he made me lie on the floor, and he shut the doors, and off we went."

She laughs, softly.

"I have to say that if I was a neighbour – and in the thin grey light I could see there were a few other houses a way off – I'd have wondered what the hell was going on with him starting the car with all the doors open wide, but it sure wasn't my problem, and I wasn't about to get ants in my pants over that. I was just glad to be awake, alive, unmolested, unexploited, and on my way back to the high road."

There's another few moments of quiet as we digest this further image: the Golden Girl crumpled up on the floor of the back of this car, probably under some dingy blanket; it's a diverting scenario.

"And he tried nothing else?" I ask, at last. "Like, in the car?"

And I'm not sure whether I'm hoping she'll say yes, or no. This isn't a very healthy idea, really, so I squash it, stamp on the little fucker at once. But if she says no, it makes the story a bit of a damp squib; all that build-up and it fizzles out. Whereas if it's a yes… my principles take a nose dive, right down to the bottom.

But she says no, there was nothing else to it, just that after a good few miles he let her sit up, and then dropped her, quickly, and without a word, a hundred yards short of the turning, disappeared into the brightening day, she says, at high speed and without a backward glance.

"I don't know which of us was the more relieved – he or I."

I note the correct grammar here: I'd have said, *him or me*, and got a right bollocking from the in-my-head Miss Viner. Hm. Our PF, for all her States-side drawl, is educated, is litter – litar – is yes, highly intelligent. I wonder what her real story is? And if I'll ever find out.

"And the point of this tale would be?" I say, rather more maliciously than I might. "Just asking."

"The point is," says PF, patiently, as to a slow five year old, "that we should now be asking whether we women should expect to remain safe under any circumstances? Whether we can blame the man for coming onto us if we make ourselves what some might call 'vulnerable'. Whether, in other words, women can ever have complete equality, where no woman need ever be afraid of a man, whatever she does. In theory, I shouldn't have had to be worried about little Mr. Porn Pix; having refused his come-on, I should have been able to feel safe. In fact, I shouldn't have had him come onto me in that way at all. He had no right to assume I'd pay for the ride with dirty pictures of my tits or helping him jerk off. As it turns out, I was safe enough – maybe he heard me yanking the furniture in front of the bedroom door – but I didn't feel totally secure even then. And given that I felt I had reason to be scared, was it my own fault?"

We look at each other; PF is searching for an answer to her own question too, that much is clear. We all want to say no, I think, that it wasn't her fault; she didn't ask him to take her to his home. But she was on a darkening road hitching rides with strangers, so...? But then again, a woman should be able to do this. If people can hitch hike – and there's no law against it – shouldn't they be able to expect, not ninety nine point nine but one hundred percent goodwill, whatever their gender? Would a man be at risk to the same extent?

I'm rather afraid that we might come down on the side of yes, you brought it on yourself. Certainly Ann will opt or the Big Yes. No doubt about that. A lot of crap about girls having to be the goody goody ones to stop men being evil, and all that nineteenth century shit.

"Hey," I say, lightly. "You've set us quite a little conundrum there, PF. To be honest, to be perfectly frank, I can't answer you definitely one way or the other."

PF nods.

"Yeah," she says, ruminatively twisting and untwisting a long braid. "Oddly, I'm with you on that one, Lucy. I can't give you a straight yes or no. And I've always thought of myself as a free twenty-first century woman."

And Ann? To our utter amazement, she says in a firm, clear, strong voice,

"I think it is quite disgraceful that a man should think he can behave so towards a young woman. It's my opinion that men should grow up, and behave honourably, and that we should not be the ones to bear the burden and the blame. And at times," she murmurs, "all too often, the consequences."

This is a shock, and even PF looks at a bit of a loss. It is enough, certainly, to unhinge the strongest jaw.

"However," continues Ann, "we all also have to live in the real world, and we have to realise that if we challenge the status quo we could end up in bother. So it's a matter of compromise – either that, or continuing to challenge

32

and put ourselves out there and taking what comes – but *then*, girls, then putting the blame where it surely belongs. It's a difficult thing to balance, isn't it so?"

"It sure is." PF is evidently disconcerted. There is another lengthy quiet.

"I thought you said this was going to be light hearted," I protest. "It turned out to be pretty serious after all, didn't it?"

PF laughs.

"I guess. Yeah. Sorry, ladies. Until I started telling it, I don't think I'd realised the implications myself. It was just meant to be a story of how silly we were when young, and can ever be – I've always considered it quite funny. I wasn't harmed, and I'm still here, and perhaps I learned a bit from it. And," she adds, looking thoughtfully at Ann, "I've learned more from the telling of it this evening."

This sinks in. Nobody says anything for another while. Only I hope we'll tell some funnier stories than this one – I mean, it was interesting, but I could do with a laugh. A good few laughs, come to it.

Time for more wine. I wend my way to the wine shop, which is doing good business. Gaps are appearing on the shelves already. Two more of the red stuff find their way into my hands, and as the harassed assistant puts them tenderly into tissue paper, and then a carrier, I am aware of the increasing heat in the terminal. It shouldn't take long for this lot to reach room temperature. Out of some unbidden fellow feeling, I even get a takeaway cup of tea for our Irish friend.

Back at the ranch, PF and I concentrate on the little ritual of getting the bottle open, de-corking it, sniffing it, tasting the aroma – all the crap that would-be wine buffs go in for. Screaming, scarlet infants and exhausted, hot and bored children are sweating restlessly on their makeshift beds. It is getting towards midnight, and already everyone is well fed up. The screens have gone totally blank, as if the ash cloud has somehow seeped into their inner mechanism, and a greyness of information blackout and mood descends. Times passes, and the bottles empty.

"Perhaps we should try to get some sleep?" I slur unenthusiastically. "No use trying to stay awake for nothing."

"Yeah, guess you're right," PF concedes. "There won't be any news until tomorrow anyway. Well, 'night, girls."

I note, even in my bleary state, that she seems utterly unaffected by the considerable amount of wine she's sunk in a short time, whereas I – there's no other way of putting it – am well on to totally pissed, and Ann, who has overdosed solely on water and the occasional tea, has slumped slowly to the carpet and is snoring quietly, her head on my feet.

The terminal lights begin to lower, and all grows eerily hushed. A whimpering child grizzles itself to sleep; PF shuffles into a sort of graceful, snake-like curl, and sleeps. I lie awake for a few moments, and then think of something that all at once seems terribly important to ask.

"Why did you say you were going to Australia?" I prod PF in her fleshless side. I can feel ribs. Bugger the woman. I lost track of mine years ago.

"I didn't," she answers, sleepily, and her breathing starts to deepen again.

"Well?"

"Well *what?*"

"Why are you going to – wherever it is in Oz?"

"Oh. Didn't I say? I'm going to stay with an aunt and uncle for a while. Always wanted to see Australia. Can I go to sleep, now that I've answered that critical question that will pull your country out of recession and solve the problem of world peace?"

Sarcastic vixen. However, she has a point. Did I really

34

need to know that, right at this moment? *Yes*, replies my tired brain, before it folds itself up for the night. *Yes, you did. Don't ask me why right now, but you did and do need to know.* And with that I am certain, beyond a doubt, that there's something more to PF's trip than just visiting relatives; call me intuitive, or call me intuitive, but she's concealing the truth. But then, she's not the only one.

Somewhere, some way away, a couple start a row. Their voices are like stage villains, hissing and spitting. Probably fighting over floor space, or who gets the blow-up pillow, or whose frigging idiot idea *was* this holiday? There's a sharp slap. Another. A few sobs. Nothing more.

Doziness overtakes me; my mouth grows slack and I have those lovely confused thoughts that precede deep sleep. Then a lonely, flickering neural connection alerts my torpid intellect to a single thought – probably all that it's capable of post-booze, post-travel fatigue, post-stress and sheer bloody panic.

"PF?"

A rustling amidst the blonde tangles.

"Mmmmmffff. Mmmfff?"

"PF, were you … even in the least bit turned on by what happened in the house?"

"For Gadsake. Go to Goddam sleep, will ya? I'm sure not going to talk about that right now."

"Sorry. Sorry, PF. I was a bit swayed by the way Ann was looking – kind of out of her depth at that point. As if maybe it was all too much."

"Yeah, I saw that. She could a bit of a drag at times, don't you think?"

I hate myself for agreeing with this, and hope Ann hasn't heard, even subliminally in her loudly snoring state.

"Mm. Don't think she can help it, though. Just a young girl straight from her Irish family. Probably never seen much of life."

"Yeah, right, but she did come up with that surprising stuff about women not taking the blame. And what's she doing travelling long haul on her lonesome, then? We don't even know where she's going. You thought about that?"

I haven't, of course. More puzzles, more riddles to work through. I have the sudden thought that none of this, nothing during the next few days, is going to be straightforward. And I have things to keep to myself, too; secrets.

"It's bizarre," I muse, more to myself than to Princess Faren. "Not being racist, or whatever, but the Irish are known to like their drink. Nothing wrong with that – they're great people, and their cailighs are fantastic. Yet Ann won't touch a drop."

Now my disobedient grey matter is stirring, the single active synaptic connection nudging its switched-off mates, hollering at its neighbours, *Hey, wakey wakey sleepy heads, there's good stuff coming down the line!*

"PF?"

"Forchrissssake!"

"Will you tell us – um – another story some time? A funny, sexy one?"

"Not right away." The last on a huge, extended yawn. "Your turn for Listen With Mother, or whatever. Now get outta my face."

"Okay. Sorry, PF." I must stop apologising to the bloody woman. She started this thought train. An enormous yawn overwhelms me. "Goo-night."

No answer. Only long, slow breaths from the PF side of our cave, and the snuffling of Ann's beaky nose on the other. The rogue connectors in my head, thwarted, begin shutting themselves down, but just before they do, there is this startling thought, which has been struggling to make itself heard: PF told this not very outrageous story now instead of her other one because she's not sure of Ann and how she would react. So any other story she tells must be ... must be... something very much ... much more...

But now the brain is sending its offline garbage into oblivion, firmly telling me that it's not going to give me another blink of anything tonight. The airport is utterly silent, and someone – presumably the last – has turned out the main lights, and we are cast into a dim, warm fug which would send the most raving insomniac straight into dreamland in half a minute.

The shadowy dark and the stillness take over. I find a bearable position, dislodge Ann's head gently, and finally fall asleep.

Dawn breaks. Is breaking. Somewhere, I suppose – only not here, in this windowless, artificially illuminated airport. So how do I know it's morning? Well, I'm one of those peculiar folk that wake up regular as clockwork at six every day. Doesn't matter how much, or how little sleep I've had, my stupid old body clock chimes merrily and says, hey, Luce, it's morning time! Let's hit the road!

Actually I don't mind. It's a tad tiresome if I've had a good night out, naturally, but I get over it, and yes, I do make use of every moment of the day. That's why I prefer to travel and go on holiday alone; I'd drive – have driven – vacation companions insane jumping out of bed at what is to them still deepest, darkest night, squeaking open the wardrobe door, swishing water in the shower, rustling through what to wear... Equally, they drive – have driven – me barmy with their slug-a-bed (howzatt, Miss Viner, for a humble Chemistry teacher? Eh?) lazy habits of not getting up till half the day is gone and wasting all that loverly sunshine, all those sightseeing hours.

Yep, I'm a travel bore. But I'm happy that way. And I get to see a lot, if not ever a real sun tan. (Those freckles.)

So now I sit up, perhaps not quite as limber as at home in my superbly comfy bed under my feather and down quilt, indeed there is considerable stiffness and a nasty cramp developing in one leg, but I am upright at least; unlike the other two Babes in the Airport. PF is sprawled languorously across most of our little encampment, her long legs even in unconscious repose elegant, her blonded tresses tumbled round her slightly flushed face... No, I'm not going that way, I don't fancy the woman, but I have to admit she is your actual, real life Sleeping Beauty. I don't see any handsome princes around, however, so it's touch and go whether she will ever wake up.

As for Ann: little piggy snout buried in the carpet, making little piggy grunting sounds, her mouth slackly open and a wee trickle of dribble sliding down her chin. The hair, in her case, does not fall artlessly but is frazzled into a wild jungle of black threads like wire, and her short-waisted frame does itself no favours hunched up like that.

I expect I looked just as bad. Worse. Which is one further advantage of being the first to wake up: you can put right all the wrongs that a night's snoozing has done to you. With this in mind, I head to the toilets, remembering to dig out my travel washbag. There is only one other woman vertical, and we smile at each other, like survivors of a battle as we pee, ablute, brush, powder, apply mascara, straighten, tug and primp No words are necessary. We are guardians of the Morning, Sentinels of the Dawn, Watch Keepers supreme; yea, natural leaders amongst all those wimps and weaklings still wrapped in their indulgent slumber.

Well, whatever.

Back at the ranch, I have a a coffee and sip it slowly, savouring the freshness; it's coming up to half past six and by some miracle of compassion and efficiency the cafeteria has opened a bit early. I hope they're paying them overtime. I also hope there's going to be some information coming through; but the boards are shuttered and veil their mysteries. Doesn't look as if the ash cloud is getting its butt out of the way, then. For something to do, I take out of my hand baggage yesterday's paper and start doing the Sodukos. I start on 'Fiendish', just for the hell of it, and I've only been going for a few minutes when a wail pierces the silence. A child. Has woken up. Has realised it is Not in its Own Room. Is distressed. Shushing sounds follow, and the infant howls louder, by way of competition. I sneak a look, and see the weary mother, deep circles round her sunken eyes, struggling to stay awake. Dad is snoring by her side, along with two other young ones. She definitely needs more rest than she's getting – and I don't mean just this last twenty-four hours. God preserve me from marriage. (Do I actually mean that? Probably.)

"Hi," I say, over to her patch before I know it. "You look whacked. Let me take – him, er, her? I'm good with kids. Oh, and I'm Lucy, by the way, and I'm a teacher."

It's then that it occurs to me that a strange woman with untamed red hair coming up to you in what is still really the middle of the night and offering to take your child might seem just a bit – suspect? But I smile, and squat down, and I think something in my peasant face must reassure her, as she murmurs something about gratitude, and shuffles the baby into my arms. Immediately it quietens; in shock, perhaps, at the horrible sight of undiluted Lucy, fierce hair and all those muddy sunspots, at close quarters. A small fist shoots out from underneath the baby blanket, grabs and pulls. Ouch! *Little sh —*

""Oh, little darling!" I am going to Hell for my disingenuous ways, that's for sure. ""Isn't she – he – sweet?"

I am destined never to know whether this miniature descendent of Genghis Khan is male or female, as Mum sinks down to the horizontal, leaning into her husband's belly, which is capacious enough, and back to the welcome land of Nod, whilst I take a walk round the airport with little Monster Munch, who is now trying to eat my hair, and point out things of interest, especially in bright colours.

Now you might think that there *is* nothing of interest in a deadly silent airport waiting hall. That's where you'd be wrong. There are loads of fascinating sights (and that takes me right back to school days: I was always being told off for writing 'loads of' instead of the more genteel 'a lot of', 'many', or, more ambitiously, and in the English top set, 'several', 'a great number of', 'diverse' , *myriad*, even. Bah, humbug).

So what can we look at? Oooh, baby, see that man over there? The one with the RED shirt and the GREEN tie and YELLOW socks? Do you think he's colour blind? Or did his mummy forget to put out his clothes for him yesterday? Sssh! Don't squeal, baby, he's fast asleep! And just LISTEN to him snore! Sounds like Big Ben winding up to strike, doesn't it? Now here's something nice: a SHOP. We like shops, don't we? Yes, we like shopping! This shop is a nice shop, isn't it? It's got lots of lovely bright things in the window, all sparkly. Which do you like best? Oh, *dat one* Hm. Yes, very nice. Diamonds. You've got good taste, baby! And a great future ahead of you. Now don't get your fingers – careful – caught in the mesh, will you? I don't have wire cutters in my pocket –

Oh my days! Look over there. What's that lady doing? What is the lady doing, children? She's taking off her skirt! Watch the lady. Is she taking off her blouse? Yes, she is taking off her blouse; it is a pretty BLUE blouse with PINK flowers on it. We've seen a lot of colours this morning, haven't we? Red, green, yellow, blue and pink! Let's make up a song about colours, shall we? Oh but wait. The lady is… No! No, lady! Don't! Don't do that...

And once again, Lucy flies to the rescue. This woman has by this time peeled off her bra, quite seductively as it happens, and is even now hooking her fingers playfully into her tights and pants to slide them over her undulating hips and down her legs. Her eyes are wide, wide open, but they have no expression, and she is standing on her own near a closed gift shop. A somnambulist! (My goodness, baby, I've been eating the dictionary today.)

Now you should not wake a sleepwalker, but somehow

I must stop her before she parades, as God made her, well, perhaps a bit more rounded than when she was first made, as I don't suppose she was born with those beautiful boobs... Baby is staring at her with interest, and points a small index finger at this intriguing personage.

"Tit!" says baby in a clear and fairly loud voice. Dear me. And I thought a child's first words were Dad, Mum, and possibly Cat, Dog?

A man in a nearby huddle of bodies and limbs stirs; if this goes on, and baby explores the full range of his/ her vocabulary, everyone will wake up and see this poor woman, and then she will wake up and see them seeing her, and boy, will she be embarrassed? As well as whoever is travelling with her, though this is by no means obvious in the muddle of humanity draping itself over the floor.

There's only one course of action I can think of, and I do it, putting my hand very gently under her elbow and sort of persuading her across the airport carpet, whilst she at least still has her knickers on, to our abode. What else can I do? When she comes to, we'll reunite her with her luggage and her family and friends. Just as gently, I ease her down onto the floor, and let her settle in the space where I slept only an hour ago; baby observes all this with bright infant eyes and tracking movements of the head. I wonder what happens to all such imprints, memories clicked into the brain's incredible store, as by a digital camera? Will this little scenario surface thirty years hence into a novel, a play, a screen script? Or will he/she just grow up thinking that people are really creepy and not know why she/he feels like this? You see what idiotic ideas ramble through my head? Express this sort of thing to a man you're dating, and he'll look at you sideways and say that he's going to be very busy during the next few weeks and he'll call you. Sometime.

And now there is Light! Someone's upped the low

wattage glow in which we have been bathed, and I realise that the woman I've just added to our menage is Asian; not very dark, but that lovely, even honey colour that would – hah! Will – make PF's fake tan look a mite tawdry. Bitch, Lucy, Bitch.

So? So? Wanna make something of it?

I cover our new inmate, if a temporary one, with my jacket, and wander off for more hot coffee and treat myself to a croissant, sharing its flaky warm fatty delight with baby, who seems able to cope with this and does not choke to death on the bits. People are moving; not yet ambulant, but twitching and stretching. Loud yawning. Groans. Ruffling of tousled heads of *myriad* hair. (Two fingers up to you, Miss Viner.) Vaguely coherent sentences begin, rather as Early Man must have started to articulate his bewilderment at his very existence on this hostile planet.

"Wa'ti'zzit?"

"U 'wake? Eh? U stilsleep?"

"Gerroffmelegfurfukssake."

A few figures shamble like lemmings towards the smell of roasting coffee and early breakfasts, and my secret world has ended. I am always regretful at this stage of things; getting up early – sometimes earlier, in the summer, when the light rouses me – it feels as if I'm the only one in the world, or the only one conscious and living. Then the ordinary business of the day kicks in, and the magic is over, and you're in a traffic jam with a couple of thousand other drones.

As it is now. Baby's mum is waking up, and before she can panic and think her child has been spirited away, I take baby to her. It is now nearly eight o'clock, and he/she/ it is drowsing against my shoulder. I must recommend the tip of warmed croissant to young mothers. Clearly it has soothing effects on the infant stomach. Mind you, it has had soothing effects on my stomach for years now, which is undoubtedly why I can no longer feel my ribs.

"Oh, thank you so much!" she says, and gives me a big, grateful smile. She looks less draggled, and much more rested for that extra bit of sleep, and I realise she is not as old as I thought – actually quite pretty.

"My pleasure," I say, smiling back, and indeed, I am not indulging in the sin of deceit now. It has been pleasurable, the surprisingly chunky small body tucked into mine, heavy, solid, but somehow soft like a bundle of play dough, emanating its own special heat and smelling of – well, of baby.

Oh yes, I like kids. That often amazes people. Just don't want the husband. Well, in my situation, as it happens, there'll be no need.

* * *

"Who the frig— ?"

PF delights us with this fragrant morning greeting, staring in some dismay, as well she might, I suppose, at the recumbent intruder lying on her shins.

Before Ann can fully awake, and hear more expletives, which somehow I know she doesn't like, I shush our Yankee girl and explain.

"Okay," says PF, resignedly, and shifts the stranger so that she can make her way to the Ladies'. Not that she has much need; with inner rage I note that the night has done nothing much to her but make her dishevelled hair more attractively bed-headed – a look that, apparently, men like. Her skin is still lightly tanned, and looks fresh. Maybe it's not fake after all? Bugger. The eyes are just as blue; no bags lurk underneath the long, curling lashes. Her clothes are not even particularly crumpled. I give up, especially as she comes back barely ten minutes later looking what I can only call radiant, with the hint of lip gloss and re-arranged hair, and a cup of steaming herbal tea.

"All I drink in the morning," she says, a little smugly. "Milk is not good for the digestion first thing."

We are silent for a few minutes while PF sips at this miraculous infusion. I think of my huge bowl of muesli back home, with lashings of the white stuff, and my mug of tea so strong it is virtually rigid. Followed by thick wedges of toast slathered with *delish* sugary marmalade. Ribs now heavily disguised. I stare at PF's sleek torso and despair.

"Now," she continues, "what's our plan for today?"

Plan? Is this woman mad? We could visit the toilets several times more, get drinks and food and, erm, visit the toilets gain and get a newspaper if there are any, and … we could restructure our little shelter, move it around a bit … call Llewellyn Bowen for some advice, maybe…

She's interpreted my expression, and laughs. The teeth, of course, are dazzlingly, sparklingly white and clean. Also perfect in shape. They might have been made for her mouth. Come to think of it, they were. *Miaouw.*

"No, I mean, who's going to tell today's tale, and when?"

"Ah," I say. "Yes. Right. Well, we ought to wait until Ann properly wakes up and I suppose we should sort out our visitor first."

PF looks dubious. "Actually, I don't expect Ann to be telling any stories somehow. She seems too – too –"

"Prudish?" The word comes out, rather too loudly.

"Ssh! Not exactly. But not very worldly. You know?"

I do know. But I still think she should be given the chance to join in the entertainment; she can always refuse. I take a peek at the subject of this dilemma. She has flung out an arm towards the top end of our den, her hand flat on the carpet. It is her left hand, and I notice something that either I was too tired or getting too pissed the night before to notice, but should have: she is wearing a solid gold wedding ring.

"Not that innocent," I say, poking my head in the direction of the hand.

PF's perfectly arched eyebrows rise.

"Wow!" she says, and I feel gratified to have outwitted her. "Now that does put a new spin on things."

"Meaning?"

"Meaning," PF continues carefully, "that she must have something to say. She hasn't lived her life in a glass case, at any rate."

"Maybe." I think about this. "But still, somehow I don't feel she'll be up to giving us a story about rampant sex, or any kind of – naughty adventure."

"And who said our stories have to be about sex?" says PF, very evenly.

At once I feel wrong footed She's right, dammit. I did assume this – probably because we were getting all girly and giggly and confidential, and what else do we women talk about when we're on the way to being rat-arsed? I don't think we discuss the Crimean question, or the prospect of a left wing Labour government, or the future of the Eurozone now we've left it, do you?

"So," says PF, smiling at me forgivingly, "we tell whatever interesting stories we want to. Then Ann can have no objections. After all, she muscled in on our camp, so she has to abide by the rules."

Again, the foxy minx. (Can you have a minx that is foxy? Miss Viner?) Anyway, she's mollified me by that use of 'our'. Huh, Lucy, hold on a minute. Could it be that PF actually likes me? It has been known.

At this precise moment, the would-be exhibitionist suddenly opens her eyes, sits up and yawns widely. I see that she, too, is a beauty. Okay, that's two and two

46

then. Teams: The Two Sleeping Beauties versus the Two Ugly Sisters. I'll leave you to work out which is which. This one has large, dark and what I believe they call in romantic fiction liquid eyes, slightly almonded, a nose that is a little prominent but not unsightly, a wonderfully full, sensuous mouth and cheekbones to die for. Likewise the legs, which is all we can see as she is still clutching my fleecy jacket. Her sensational boobs I have already had a glimpse of. The legs could challenge PF's, and that's saying something.

"Mmuh?" says our Asian peach. "How come I'm over here? And who are you guys?"

Her accent: now, let me place it. North East but not Geordie? County Durham? I'm just narrowing it down when she suddenly realises that she's half naked under the coat, peering under it at her unclad torso. I expect her to scream. Instead, she bursts out laughing, giving us a good ringside view of strong, brilliant, and I am pretty certain natural teeth. More competition here, then. For the Princess, of course; I'm not even on the starting block.

"What are you laughing at?" I ask stonily. After all, I did rescue her from Ultimate Mortification – otherwise those well formed knockers (and more) would have been on full display to the assembled multitude of bored travellers.

"Oh, I've done it again!"

What has she done again? In unison PF and I ask, at which point Ann finally joins the living world and scratches amongst the black wiry frizz in bewilderment. I give a brief account of the last hour and she nods, accepting the situation with amazing readiness. Well, I reckon the whole caboodle is pretty outlandish, and all we can do is get on with it. Go with the flow, as you might say. (Though I wouldn't. Unless I was really stuck for words. Similarly with "learning curve". Dopey expression. Am at one with Miss V. on that.)

The girl sobers up, stops heaving with merriment and says,

"I'm Samra. From Gainford, County Durham, via Pakistan."

Hah! Dialect-sleuth Lucy does it again!

We introduce ourselves.

And?

"Well, you see, I've been living in the UK since I was about five years old, but I was born in Karachi, and that's where I'm going – or I will be, when this ash cloud business gets sorted."

And? This still does not satisfy us on the point of her night-time sleeping strip-act.

"Um, yes. The stripping off. I dream about it, you see, and as I sleep walk from time to time I, like, act out the dream. That's all. Usually it's at home, so it doesn't matter. But that it could happen here, in a public airport lounge! Dad and Mum would die of shame."

This intriguing and apparently amusing thought sets her off again, and it is some time before we get to hear the rest of her account of herself – or all that we're going to know for the time being. It seems that she is going to Pakistan to get married. An arranged marriage? She doesn't say, and frankly I don't like to ask. It seems that she will then live in Pakistan as a good wife. For ever?

Samra assents, inclining her lovely head, and the long, shiny black hair slithers over one shoulder. This young man, whoever he is, is sure getting a prize.

"But," says Ann, rather carefully it seems to me, "but are you happy with that? I mean, is this your choice? It would appear," she adds slowly, "that you've lived a pretty westernised life here."

We take a glimpse briefly at Samra's fancy patterned tights, her high-heeled shoe boots in cut-out black suede and patent which for some reason she has slept in. Yes indeed, up with it in UK down to the last sexy ankle strap and buckle.

"It is both my choice and not my choice," says Samra placidly. "In a way it was not my choice to make. It is and was, has always been, my destiny. I have known for a long, long time that I would be marrying Faisal. If you like to put it this way, I have chosen my destiny."

Oh-oh, here we go again. All this rubbish about destiny and karma is going to come up again; can't be doing with it. We've only just met Samra, though, so I don't feel I can take her up on that; mind you, if I'd had a few glasses of red in the evening it might be a different matter…

"But, Samra, won't you be missing England?" Ann is like a terrier with a rat now, leaning forward with suddenly sharp, keen eyes.

"I don't expect to. I've had my fun here. I've worked, I've earned money – quite a lot of it as a matter of fact – I've had a good education and I'm ready now to to and do what I have known for – oh – most of my life that I must do."

An arranged marriage, then, by the sound of it. But again, for some reason I hold my tongue. The old intuitive antennae are in full ON mode; there's something more to this, they're telling me. Just you wait and see.

We wonder how old she is.

"Twenty-three. Which is ancient by Pakistanti bride standards. Faisal has been very patient."

Well, at least she is old enough to know her own mind. Kind of. That's a relief to the rest of us, I think. Even so –

"And what is – was your job here?" It is Ann turned interrogator again. Maybe the dark coarse abundant hair is Spanish? The Inquisition springs to mind.

"I was a night club pole dancer and stripper," says Samra, nonchalantly dropping her thunderbolt as one might discard chewing gum. "So you see, that's why I dream about it and act it out sometimes."

She was *what??* How on earth has she managed to do that, when, we assume, she is from an orthodox Pakistani Muslim background? How on earth will she enlighten the benighted Faisal, who presumably doesn't really know what he is getting? However, it does explain those fabulously toned thighs. Maybe I should give it a go? But the notion of dumpy fattish red haired Lucy straddling a pole in a night club is so ridiculous that I sweep it quickly right out of my mind. They'd pay me to go away.

"I worked in London, you nitwits." Samra laughs again, and I for one bawl out myself for my stupidity. Did I think she'd do that on her home ground? "Mum and Dad might have suspected, but we put it out that I was a secretary in a big London company, and nobody ever questioned it. That's the way in our family."

Ann's mouth is now open as wide as the Dartford tunnel. I've seen smaller jaws on a hippopotamus.

"And just how are you going to forget all that, and adapt to being a housewife in Karachi?" she demands, I think a bit more forcefully than is justified.

But Samra merely laughs.

"You think I'll regret giving it up? I tell you, after five years of sliding up and down and round a pole in a G-string, with men leering up my crack, and of taking off stupid bits of glitzy underwear so they can get off on me when they're home in the dark, I'll not even give it a thought," she says. "I've had all the freedom of a western way of life, and I can turn my back on it now and settle down."

"Ah!" A satisfied grunt from our Irish friend. This pleases her, obviously. Catholic, you see. Obviously she's got a hubby of her own, come to that. Kids? Looks too young, though; somehow I don't think so, especially as she's travelling solo. Back to the Secret Stripper.

"Jesus! That's quite a story." PF has been unaccustomedly background throughout this, and now it's her turn to probe. "Let me ask you something, Samra, if I may."

"Sure."

"Have you had boy friends? You know, like real relationships?"

"Of course I have. I told you, I lived a pretty cool life in London."

"So you're not – a virgin?"

A gasp of horror from Ann and almost one from me. There's nothing like the Yanks for doing the in-your-face stuff, is there? Is there? Although I have also to admit that P.F.'s question has made me curious. It's just that stone cold sober at half past eight in the morning I wouldn't have asked.

Samra takes it in her stride.

"Of course not. But that's all been fixed."

She means – ? Means – ? We know what she means. So poor Faisal will never know the whole truth about her past life in free-for-all UK, then.

"No. Why should he? It would only distress him. I want our marriage to succeed. I shall make him happy.

"You don't know him," I protest. "How can you say that?"

"But I do, you see – know him." Samra speaks very calmly. "In any case, Karachi is not out in the sticks, it's quite a modern city. And you know, marriage is something you both work at. It does not always start with 'falling in love', exactly – or at any rate not western style or like in the romantic Bollywood movies. I've done that, been there, got all the sparkly tee-shirts for that one. I tell you, it's moonshine. Fairy dust that falls from your eyes after a year or two. Marriage is real. It's an agreement, a contract, and love is what you build within it. If you try to understand the other, really understand them, then you will at least like them, and in time deeper love will follow."

There is a short silence here. Then, thoughtfully,

"Of course, it helps if love is there from the start. "

We mull this over, Ann nodding affirmatively and energetically. I can see that she is more persuaded by this than either PF or I are. I cannot help but think that this is an ideal, and that Samra is being very naïve. What if she loathes poor Faisal on better acquaintance (she hints that she has met him)? It is unlikely that he will abhor the stunning adult Samra on clapping eyes on her. What if he has some personality traits, some habits, something as simple as slopping his food all over his clothes, or belching in bed, or picking his toenails, or – well, anything that makes it impossible to love him; what if a fuller understanding of him – or he of her, for that matter – leads not to mutual respect but merely to dislike, or worse, contempt? He could be a wife beater, a covert homosexual... or just terminally boring.

It is time, however, to reunite our promised bride with her possessions and travel companions. To our astonishment, she is going alone. She does not belong to anyone in that morass of sleeping forms now brusquely separating themselves and finding things to do in the gift shops, the cafeterias and WH Smith's. It appears there is only one thing we can do to help this poor deluded young woman, for deluded I think PF and I concur that she must be: invite her to join us. As it happens, the little group next to us last night has gone, where we do not know, or care, and we gleefully claim their smidgen of carpet. We can now accommodate a quartet.

It has to be as I suspected, though; there is a lot more to this girl's true story than she's told us. The fact that she is travelling unaccompanied for such an important and, yes, life-changing event sets my radar on full alert, but for the moment, that doesn't matter. She's part of our tribe now, and we'll get on with it. Besides, I'm gagging to hear her stories about the strip joints.

"Okay, Lucy girl. Your turn."

This, of course, is La Princesse Faren, blast her awesome blue eyes. I begin a lame protest that my tale is not after all very engrossing, and that I am sure Samra's story would be far more worth hearing but La Faren is having none of it. This was our agreement, she says firmly, and fixes me with with her lighthouse-beam gaze. Sudden thought: does she wear contact lenses, the kind that enhance the colour? Probably not. They'd surely have dropped out onto the carpet during the night, and our glamour puss would have spent an ungainly half hour groping around for them, which is, naturally, not the sort of thing that would ever happen to her. I once thought of buying contacts, not that I need glasses to see or anything, just to pep up the shade of murky grey that I project onto the undeserving world, but –

"LUC-EE!"

Yes, I am rambling in my head again, and the two Beauties of the outfit are tapping fingers impatiently for me to Get On With It. I should explain that we have enlightened our newcomer, and clarified the idea for Ann, as she was at first a little unwilling to take part in all this, and more than a bit baffled as to why we're bothering when we could just have nice cups of tea and do a bit of reading, or knitting, which for Pete's sake she has dragged out of her bag (who was Pete, come to think of it? Anyone know?). They have both embraced the idea, Samra rather more enthusiastically than the homespun Ann, who rather than taking the story-telling fully on board is kind of holding it at arm's length, as you might a dead mouse you've found behind the fridge. She'll get there. Probably. A deep breath. Another. Come on, Luce, you can do it. Even it it does seem, in the cold light of day and lack of alcoholic support, a pathetic little episode. So, hesitating, fumbling for words, conscious the of the expectant air hovering around me, I make a start.

It was one summer, long ago, I explain, when I was – oh, perhaps twenty-one, and just finished my last year at Uni. Where I studied Chemistry. (This brings a glance of approval from the Irish one, a blank look from Samra and an expression of what I can only interpret as pity from PF.) Yeah, it's a plodding old subject, I continue, without the glamour of physics and the intellecterual – intalectu – well, the academic status of further maths, but it has its uses. Actually, when you go into it deeper, the Table of Elements is really quite astounding and has some challenging, well, elements...

"LUC-EEEE!"

A combined shout heads me back in notional handcuffs to my story. Obediently, I soldier on.

Okay, so after all that dry science stuff, it seemed a good idea to go on a vacation, to France in fact, along with a group of my friends. You know, sunshine, vineyards, wine and all those sexy French fellas with their sultry accents, all those romantic gestures and little suppers out in the balmy night air in the bistros? (Not to mention plenty of The Other.) So off we went, all five of us, on a cheap student flight to Paris, and then we hired a terrible old car and drove straight through the centre, to the Midi, and stopped when we were tired and slept at little pensions and farm houses, and once or twice out in the open, in a field, on beach towels and rolled up sweaters for pillows. What did we eat, Ann? Ah, ever practical, and and I can see you like your food. No, I don't mean you're fat, before you say anything, I just mean you have – a – a well fed look about you. I mean it as a compliment. Wholesome, home grown food. Oh, you were okay with it anyway? Good. Yes, PF, I am getting on with it.

I have to tell you it was all pretty idyllic. The weather did us proud, with long, hot days and those warm lazy nights we'd dreamed of. This was the France of painters and writers, the France that peeped tantalisingly through the pages of our boring text books at school, that said, there is more to me, La Belle France, than this asking for a couple of coffees in a cafe, or booking a train ticket to Lille *avec ma famille*. I could feel myself kind of expanding in the warmth, not only of the sun, but the whole experience. I'd expected the French to be a bit snooty, a bit precious about themselves – well, they can be in Paris, but in the countryside, it was hospitality and good nature all the way. We ate off fresh cheese, Ann, and put it with huge, ripe but still firm tomatoes, and wonderful crisp French bread, and got pots of olives, and some fruit each day, and we truly felt we were dining like kings. Or queens, rather. There were lots of those small, unpretentious bars in the villages we passed through, and we drank good, strong coffee, wine at night, and ate the house meal, which was always excellent. As well as cheap.

You're frowning, PF. Oh, where's the point of all this gastronomic detail? The point, my dears, the nub, the rub even, is that despite all this glorious weather, the fine food, the kindness of all the natives we met, one thing was missing: the sexy men. Where were they all? Could the whole lot of them be in Paris, we asked each other? Had the entire pin-up boy population emigrated to new lands and better things? The only males we came across were ancient – at least sixty – the *patrons* of bars and pensions, or the husbands of the concierges, and some land workers, true, traditional peasants with lined skin like old leather, bent backs and bowed legs from all that cycling carrying strings of onions. No, really, I mean it! The old men in the squares used to sit all day drinking coffee and smoking, and we got a few kisses blown our way, but it was hard to imagine them even mustering the wherewithal to get off their chairs, never mind swinging into action. So: we five young, frisky lasses, well, we did gradually get a bit fed up about this, and one night, under an amazingly starry sky, we had a Serious Confab. Like a high level summit conference to review the current situation.

Which went like this:

"God, I could do with a shag." Thus, Chaz, full name Charlotte, wafting a half empty bottle of vin rouge around her head.

"Trust you to lower the tone." Madge, so named because she bore a passing resemblance to the young Madonna, and everyone forgot her real handle. "Mind you, I don't disagree with the sentiment. Just the language." (Madge's father was a stockbroker in Surrey and they mixed with the *ton*, she'd have us believe. If not minor royalty.)

And when we'd finished sorting her out, and forced quite a lot more wine down her throat, she gave in, and agreed that a bit of the old *how's yer father*, a seeing to, a bonk, a screw, would be a jolly, jhollee, really really reallly good idea, but where in the name of Beelzhebub could we find shome?

As you can see, it didn't take much with our Madge. Truth to tell, we were all as out of it as pub-crawling newts. I guess this is why what happened, did.

Ann, you're looking away, you're not part of this, are you? Oh, I see. Well, just try and give me a hint you're mildly interested, would you? *God, I can hear myself going into teacher mode. Cut it out, Luce.* Sorry, Ann, you listen as you want to. I just hoped the language didn't – oh, you're not worried, you've heard worse before. Well, that's reassuring. *Actually, not very.*

So, to resume:

It wasn't very late, and we decided to go back to our pension and have an early night, as there wasn't much to do. French villages are lovely, but their entertainment value is limited, as we were discovering. After the riveting nightly boules challenge is over, that's it, in effect. Bar and bed. Or just bed.

"Ah, mademoiselles! Comment ça va?" Our concierge gave us a huge smile, beckoning us into the public area. "Il y'a quelques hommes qui visitent notre village..." and then she rattled off a lot more.

I rather lost this, but as it happens, one of us, Suzanne (or Suze to her friends), had a French grandmother, and she cottoned on: there was a party of men in the bar from northern France, who were some sort of part of some sort of cycling rally, and, affirmed the good Frenchwoman, they would be delighted to meet such "jeunes jolies filles" comme nous. Or whatever. Who cared about the grammar, the motives, the rally? There were MEN in the bar, French men, and they were not the local antique variety. Answer to five maidens' five identical prayers. Providing, of course, that there were five of them.

It so turned out that there were: precisely five. Would you believe it? Oh, you wouldn't, Samra? You think I'm making that part up? *No need to sneer, dear. This young woman is slowly creating an impression. A bit of a cat? From her tone of voice, I think the claws are coming out. Hm.*

I tell you, faithfully – and if you recall, PF and I made a tryst – there were just five men in that watering-hole. Not very young, not students, sure, but not aged either. And after all the gnarled locals, and the wine we'd put away, they looked to us like gods descended from Mount Olympus. Well, at first, at any rate. I mean, I bet even Johnny Depp starts to look downright plain and uninteresting after you've lived alongside him and watched him slurping his cornflakes and flossing his teeth for long enough. PF, that's made you laugh. Didn't know I could. Nice, though. Obviously, we had some more drinks – on them. Obviously, we went into that strange process of pairing ourselves off. It's like some old courtly dance, isn't it? First Chaz liked Gerard, then she sidled up to Louis, and when Madge made eyes at the curly-haired Gerard, Chazza goes right back and takes ownership of his arm, and that was that one settled. Madame whateverhernamewas was smiling away, and even her husband, Monsieur whatevertheirnamewas, with the glowering face, cracked a grin and winked at us, and put on some music, you know, the French sort that sounds like frogs with laryngitis crooning, and with stupid words, but it somehow pulls you in and makes you want to lean your head on someone's shoulder and sway with them to the rhythm. So we all swayed together, and soon it was midnight, and Madame changed tack, as if we were in some kind of Cinderella land, and said quite briskly that she was locking up, and that the gentlemen *doivent sortir*.

This was a bit of a shock; we'd assumed they were staying at our place but no, they were booked in at a bigger place, a swanky hotel some two miles away, and we had to go up to our rooms and say *Bonne Nuit*, and that was that. Or at least, it seemed that way. I'd insisted on having a single room, with my strange waking habits, and when the others found out that I would bounce out of bed singing on the dot of six, in the summer sun, they virtually shoved me into this small room on my own. The other four had two doubles. Thus it was – ooh, get that, I'm sounding almost Dickensian, okay, okay, Ann, I was being funny – thus it was, I sadly curled up on my bed, fuzzy with drink but not too fuzzy to realise that a good chance had slipped through my fingers. Claude, the shoulder on whom I had leaned and with whom I had swayed so delightfully, wasn't half bad, you see. But now he'd bunked off to that posh hotel without even asking me to go with him. No manners, these French men. Such a letdown. Sulking, I was. Like a kid. Okay, Samra, description coming up. Sorry I was boring you. *More claws. Hmmm.*

What can I tell you at this vast distance of time? He was tall, dark and handsome. Yes, he was. About six foot, which is way tall enough for Lil' ole Lucy here. Good, erm, physique. Nice firm buns. (All that cycling.) Dark hair, a bit longer than most Frenchmen wear it, but suited him, with his exceptionally smooth, tanned skin and dark brown eyes – at least, I thought they were brown; it was pretty dim in that bar. I'd say – I thought at first sight that he was around forty. Perhaps a tad more. Not bad. Would know what he was doing. And I'd had enough of the old Chateau wotsit to feel quite uninhibited, which always helps, don't you think? Oh yes, Ann, I realise you wouldn't know as you don't touch a drop. *Christ, how did we get stuck with her?*

You can see, then, that going up to my little cot on my lonesome was not going to make me feel very cheerful. It was completely blacked out too; Madame turned out all the lights, and the back of the pension faced open land without a street lamp for eternity. All I could hear was the crickets and occasional bark of a farm dog, way off. Plus the faint rumblings of my stomach which had had too much booze and not enough solid food. The others must have gone straight to sleep, as there wasn't a sound. Not that I would have heard much; my room was right at the back, in a kind of extension over the kitchen; the other rooms were across the landing, and the walls and doors in that old place were medieval.

There being no choice, I turned over and dozed and then fell into a heavy dream of being chased by large French cows across a meadow, and they were after the bottle of wine I was carrying, and there was no gate to the field, and the fence was high and –

Clatter!

Had I dropped the bottle? Was it the sound of hooves getting too near?

Tinkle! Clatter!

The cows! They're going to get me, I can't – oh God, I'm being attacked – I –

Wake up. Wake up, Luce. It isn't the cows, it's something on your window. Oh Crikey. Oh merciful heavens. THROUGH my window. Something is trying to get through my window. Is it a cow? Don't be so brainless, girl, that was the dream, and this is – oh shit, it's real. A big black shape poking at the casement. It's making a noise. It is speaking –

"Merde! Ouvre la fenêtre, pour l'amour de Dieu! Ouvre!"

It's Claude. Oh, God is good. Don't gasp like that, Ann. I'm not being facetious. I really had given up hope of my prayer being answered, and here he was: Claude. Beautiful, handsome, tall, charming, lovely Claude. Avec les tight buns.

So, listeners, I let him in. Well, it would have been downright inhospitable to leave him hanging out there, wouldn't it? It was a squeeze, as the casement was tiny and Claude was a big man. Mm, Samra, quite a hunk. Anyway, there he was, right beside me, and I didn't bother asking him how he knew which my room was, and whether he'd gone to his hotel and come back here, and how he'd climbed up, and all that totally irrelevant stuff, as who was bothered? We fell right to it.

The tearing off of the clothes – his, mostly, since I was in a long cotton tee shirt for bed and cotton knickers. I don't know why, but I always wear knickers in bed. Funny, isn't it? I mean, I put on clean pants in the morning, but I don't like sleeping nude at that end, so I have a stash of white cotton briefs for night-time wear, if you – yes, okay, PF, I'm wandering again.

So it didn't take long for us both to be completely starkers, his well-toned, brown body lying beside, then on top, then underneath my white skin, and I can tell you, I was in much better shape in those days. The Lucy you see before you now is but a larger shadow, a much larger one, I'm sad to say, of her former self. My hair was very long, too, even longer than it is now, pretty well down to my butt. I never thought a lot of myself at the time, but looking back, looking at old photos of me at twenty one, what was I worried about? I was a little cracker. Funny to think it was less than a dozen years ago.

Claude seemed to think so, anyhow – the little cracker bit. He kept stroking me all over, *all* over, and licking me pretty much all over too, and planting butterfly kisses on various parts of me that had never been kissed before. (Like behind the ears, in case you're thinking naughty thoughts.) This was the French lover I'd always heard about: romantic, tender, slowly building you up to the moment of fullest intimacy, and then, oh then, yes, it was stupendous, it really was. For about five minutes. Which is quite a long time for men, isn't it? But he'd got me well fired up with all that kissing and panting and licking and stroking and hurling me round the bed so that we landed up in most of the positions possible for two human bodies to achieve, and when the action proper started, I was steaming up and ready to boil. Oh yes ma'am. Ready, primed, willing and able. But then he stopped. At first I thought this was part of his game; you know, get you to that point, and then tease you so that you plead for more, beg and slaver for it. But no. He embarked on a long string of French which was mostly do do with my little love, my beautiful Eeeglish girl, my wonderful Lucee, how I love you, how I love your wonderful hair (he could wrap himself in it forever) your soft skin, your luscious breasts, and so on and so forth, and all the time he was gazing not at me, but at the bedside table. How did I see this in the dark, PF? Ah, forgot to say – I lit a couple of candles when we were trying to negotiate his entry. the one through the window, that is.

This went on for a while, and then he quite suddenly leaned over and blew out those candles. Eh? If I was so beautiful, why did he want us in darkness? Then a horrible idea flashed through my mind: he was going to strangle me. Knife me. Perform some unspeakable, perverted acts on me. After all, I didn't know this man at all. Ann, close your mouth. I know exactly what you were about to say. Yes, I do, so save it.

Clearly, he did none of these things, but I heard a funny sort of half choking noise, and then something being put down on the table. Maybe a watch or a ring? Dunno. I wasn't interested in that. More keen to get him back in the saddle again, which he did. and we romped on for another five or ten minutes, and it was great, and I didn't want it to end too soon, so I just gave myself up and enjoyed him threshing like a combine harvester on speed; can't say he was hugely endowed, but he wasn't bad either, and I liked clutching his lovely arse. The moans coming from him let me know he liked that too, so I gripped him even harder, and we rode together like wild horses on the gallop.

Then he bloody stopped again. This was a bit much and I said something to that effect, but his English wasn't so hot, and he just grunted and sat up, and turned way; he seemed to be rubbing his face, or struggling with his chin and under his hairline for some reason. Five o'clock shadow bothering him? And then there was something kind of floppy in his hand, which he also put on the table. Was he going to use a condom? (Which he'd tucked behind one ear?? Believe me, it has been known.) I didn't like that: I was safe, and I hate those darned rubbery killjoys. No. That wasn't it either. Off we went for another hummocking ride, and this time we got right into the swing of it. I had to bite my lips and swivel my head into the pillow to stop making too much racket, though God, it was bliss, and I was still just pissed enough not to care.

I could tell that he was going to come; men always speed up a bit at that point and kind of go away from you mentally, and I was clutching at him, anywhere, any place, and I sank my hands into his thick, longish hair and knotted it with my fingers, and shrieked with the sheer abandoned pleasure, and he gasped and groaned, amidst which I sort of half caught a *"No, no, Little Lucy, no"*, which puzzled me a bit as I'd have thought *Yes, Yes, Yes* would have been the better thing to say, but the moment passed, and I so yanked tighter at his long, rough –

W I G.

That youthful, sexy crop of tangling curls was but a commonplace hairpiece. A bloody wig. And underneath, I felt a perfectly smooth, perfectly bald head.

Right, Samra, you can stop having hysterics now. PF, sit up, you'll wee yourself. Ann, even you are trying not to giggle, I can tell. Girls, be serious. This was a Terrible Moment. No really. You can imagine. All the thrill drained away, just like that. He'd had his fun, and yes, I'd had mine but you know, girls, we like to go on a bit, not have it all end so abruptly. I mean, it had been good, I was grateful, but – well, just *but*.

I relit one candle, before he could stop me – he was a bit pooped by this time, poor old dear, as yes, I could tell, when I looked at what was on the table, and took a glance at his suddenly wrinkled face, and saw the top set of teeth lying there and a sort of thin, slippery synthetic stuff, that he wasn't a day short of fifty-eight. Must give him credit, though; the bod was excellent and I had no complaints in the performance department. Then I started to laugh, to howl, to bellow, and had to stuff my head into the pillow again; and he just slunk from the bed, put on his trousers and shirt, picked up those bits of him that were not attached, groping kind of blindly for what I think were probably some contact lens (in deepest darkest brown?) and silently let himself out through the window. I could could hear him painfully slithering down the old vines and the drainpipe – so mystery solved as to how he'd got up there – and the soft bump as he hit the ground. I did feel very sorry for him, poor old Claude, but I couldn't stop hooting, and then I fell right to sleep and didn't, for once, wake at six but snoozed on right through till half past seven.

I never saw hide nor – if you'll forgive the joke – hair of him again. We didn't see any of the others either, and I believe to this day that none of the other girls knew anything at all, or Monsieur et Madame. What was the plastic stuff, you ask? I heard afterwards that they were all working as actors for TV and film commercials, and weren't actual cyclists at all, though they were advertising the rally and some of the bikes, so I guess that's why old Claude had been given a nice young hairdo and some synthetic masking to put on his face – he would have been handsome once for sure – and that he wore them when he wanted to pull birds in the evening. I guess it's hard to come to terms with getting old when you're beautiful. *Well, I shan't have that problem, that's one thing to be thankful for.*

I look across at PF, and I can see that she is thoughtful, even a little wistfulness there. Have I hit home? Does she fear growing older too? Samra is too young, too confident, too set on her destiny, to fret about things like that, and Ann? I shouldn't think she could care less. And in any case that gold ring means that she's got her man, and I'm pretty certain she'll stay with him. And he with her. Maybe we'll find out about that when it's her turn.

But PF? I wonder that she's never mentioned a relationship, even in her first story, when she also told us about something that happened when she was a decade or so younger. Is she hiding something? Is there something about herself, her past, her love life, that she wouldn't want to talk about? But then, I suppose I haven't said much about me, either; haven't talked about a boy friend or partner, haven't gone into detail, except that I've shared an incident, a meaningless but funny one, from my younger self. It's early days, though. Perhaps PF's second story, if we get round to it, if the ash cloud doesn't all of a sudden get its clogs on and scoot away across the ocean, perhaps her follow up will tell us more about her.

Do you know, I'm almost beginning to hope the cloud doesn't move for another two days. That sounds daft, I know, but I'm becoming intrigued by these people, and I'm liking our little kingdom; and there's another thing. I'm getting time to think about where I'm going, and why, and what's waiting for me there. Who, that is. *Him.* Will it go well? Will they be angry with me? Not want to go ahead with our deal? When I booked my flight in a big hurry and dashed to the airport, I blotted out everything except getting there. Now the anaesthetic of panic is wearing off, and a new train of thought is unhappily bedding itself down in my brain.

Being trapped in this airport is like being in limbo. Quite an attractive one. I've decided I like limbo. Got fond of it, in fact. Limbo = no responsibilities. No yesterday, and in particular, no tomorrow. QED, Limbo = Good.

But going back to PF – I really do wonder.

There's a long silence after I've finished my tale. A mellow silence, with each deep in her own thoughts. I do not ask questions of anyone, as it would spoil the new sisterhood I sense. Even the unsophisticated Ann has put down her knitting (something light, white, small and delicate on thin needles, I notice: is she – could she be – ?) and is leaning back against the wall, a budding smile widening her sweet mouth. (I note this too, that she has fullish and rather soft lips. Maybe that man of hers is luckier than we imagined?) With that same gentle expression, almost but not quite a grin, she murmurs something to the effect of my tale being "Most instructive, Lucy", and for a wild moment I wonder if she was picking up hints for her – um – marital relations, difficult to think of it as a sex life where she's concerned, for some reason, but then I discarded this idea as *totally* absurd. Totally.

PF appears to be drifting into a contented sleep, but Samra-of-the-cat's-claws, if not the cat's whiskers, is wide awake and still giggling.

"Was it really that funny?" I ask, curious, but also rather flattered. "I mean – "

"No, but yes, well, no, but – "

"You're beginning to sound like a certain television character," I remark, mildly, and she laughs out loud this time, and blushes.

"Yeah, sorry. It's just that your story reminded me of something that happened to me once."

Oh, it would, wouldn't it? Now you're going to tell a much better one, something that'll outdo my miserable little account, and that will be utterly outrageous and witty, and make my

French encounter look like a –
Aw, cut it out, Luce! STOP IT. She's trying to be nice.
Yes, but she ain't succeeding.

Exasperated with myself, I brush off the two bothersome figures, wicked little imps, sitting on either shoulder and whispering in my ear, and stand up. I'm cramped and I fancy another wander round this old airport, see what everyone else is up to, how other folks are coping. Even if there's no real fresh air, as in outside, cool, rainy walking weather, I need a change. Hunter gatherer, me. Time we had some food, come to think of it.

"Well," I say, at last, "I'll look forward to your story, in that case." But it comes out stiff, non-genuine, and she spots it. We stare at one another, a meeting of eyes and a declaration of hidden agendas. So well hidden I can't for the life of me fathom out what they might be.

"All right," she says, abruptly. "You going for a walk round?"

Cautiously, I nod. She's not coming with me, is she? That's all I need.

"In that case," she says, calmly, "you won't mind if I use your space to stretch out a bit, will you? I need a bit more kip after all that restless sleepwalking. It leaves me drained, y'know?"

"Be my guest," I mutter, not believing the 'drained' bit for one moment, but thankful that I am going to have a while on my own, to dwell on and mourn my past youth, my golden years, and to beat myself up for ending up in the cul-de-sac that is currently my life. Thirty-something Chemistry teacher in city comprehensive, somewhat overweight, no boy friend, got a house but it's nothing to shout about and anyway it's most the building society's, Head of Department-ship not in sight. Chained to the whiteboard for ever more, or at least till I'm a crone of nearly seventy when the state will reluctantly cough up my meagre pension. And now this latest turn of events, the one I'm going to sort out in Thailand, the one that will change this dull existence for a long time, for ever, perhaps: am I capable of dealing with that? I'd better be. There's no way out now...

Leaving the fair Samra to luxuriate in my abandoned billet, I stroll across the lounge and decide to go further afield, into alien territory and beyond. People-watching is one of my hobbies, and boy, there couldn't be a much better chance than this. *Peoples* are everywhere. Bodies. Faces. Mouths open, snoring, being stuffed with food, closed, flapping, yapping, snapping... Quite a lot of this last. Tempers are running high as small children fret and screech and grizzle, bored out of their tiny trees with the hastily packed amusements-for-the-flight stuff, hot and constrained. Worn-out parents placate, stroke, soothe – and then snap, and occasionally slap. Provoking, inevitably, real hows of indignation and resentment. That's the upside of my situation: I'm on the outside of all of that. At present.

Everywhere, couples snuggle in tight embraces, getting in some good snogging – well, it passes the time – but in the increasingly tawdry setting of an overheated, over-populated, litter-strewn airport lounge, this is distinctly unsavoury and I don't want to witness any of the lip-sucking, tongue-flickering activities I see at far too close a range. *Jealous, Lucy?* I don't think so – mentally catapulting that little shoulder hugging demon into touch. I'd opt for something – classier. Yes, at long last I'm tired of all that – the lust and the lunging and the desperate searching. Telling that story about my time in France made me realise something – not before time. I want a grown up relationship, something steadier, *dignified*. Not a word I associate with myself as a rule, but what do you know? Could be time I did.

Maybe there'll be some dazzling fella in the airport, just on his lonesome, who, miraculously, has a yen for a slightly (erm, okay, very) chubby mature woman with bright red, untidy hair and freckled pallid complexion? Maybe he'll home in on me, lean on me, tell me I've saved his sanity in this dreadful experience, that he wants to spend a lot lot lot more time with me, and …

Yeah, right. And I'm the Queen of Sheba, Lady Gaga and Angelina Jolie all rolled into one.

"Hi there!"

A voice behind me makes me jump. I turn, and there he is. I don't believe it. No. Really. I don't. I just don't.

A BLOODY FINGER-LICKIN' WELL-GORGEOUS GUY.

I guess he must like flame coloured hair, 'cos he's smiling at me and doesn't seem to have leaped back in horror at the sight of my blebby visage with its squeezed up mucky dishwater eyes.

"Are you as fed up as I'm feeling?"

The accent is British, but not English. Ah, a bonny wee Scotsman we have here. And very bonny he is too. Light brown hair, sort of casual but trendy, tall-ish, about five ten and a half, good enough for pygmy me, light brown eyes too, and a face that looks as if it works out at the gym along with the rest of him.

Rrrrrrrrrraaaahhhh!!

Calm down, girl, He's simply passing the time. Nobody like him goes for girls like you. Be brisk. Be perky. Be the professional (Chemistry) teacher, captain of the sixth form hockey team. UGH. What?

"No, actually, I'm not bored, but I feel a bit hemmed in, you see I'm with three other girls and we have this little sort of, you know, like an encampment, and it's on a bit of carpet we took over, look, there, *pointing*, and it's become like our territory, and we have pillows and things so we can sleep, at least PF and I do, that's Princess Faren, yes, really, she's not a princess, she's American, you know what daft names they call their kids, and they're all quite incredible people, and we have this sort of pledge thing where we all have to tell two stories about ourselves, and they have to be true, and it's kind of like the Canterbury Tales, you know, Geoffrey, um, Charter, only more up to date, of course, and then we're going to judge whose story is the best, and then – then, well, I don't know what then, but it's great fun and I want to hear all the tales the girls have to tell and so I actually don't mind if the ash cloud stays for a few more days, y'know?"

I'll give him this: he hasn't blinked, or gone running, or done anything throughout this mad tirade except listen carefully and politely, the brown eyes fixed on me with a charitable expression, oh terrible thought, as one who is finding himself listening to a brain-damaged child.

Then he smiles, slowly, gradually, so that it fills all that beautiful face, OMG, and then he put out a long, well-formed hand.

"Fergus," he says. "And you?"

Swoon.

"Er – Lucy."

I wish I could have invented a more exciting, charismatic, erotic name, 'cos it doesn't matter, this is only a temporary meeting, a 'fleeting encounter' I think they used to call it, but too late. Lucy it is, then. Bugger.

"Well, Lucy," says Fergus, withdrawing that lovely fist. "How about a drink?"

"You're on." Jolly Chemistry teacher speaking. *Jolly hockey sticks.*

I can't quite believe this is happening, and am starting to revel in my luck when a horrid thought comes creeping into my defenceless mind, which is flapping wide open to the four winds, without any noticeable brain activity. If I have to take him back to our camp for any reason, or if the others come exploring, he'll take one look at PF, and then another at the pole-dancing one, and it's bye-bye whatever your name was, nice meeting you.

Right. I get a firm and determined grip on my dissolving grey matter. Tactics are my strong point. Good rehearsal, all that getting year nines to start calculating the electrons and protons in a molecular formation – well, I'll not bore you with that – which I manage by putting the chocolates I use (milk, white choc and plain) to explain atomic structures just out of reach until they get it right. Ho, ho, cunning or what? Funny that all my year nines end up obese, though.

"Let's go a bit further from here," I suggest, innocently. "I'm feeling as though my world has shrunk to about twenty metres of blue patterned floor covering."

He grins appreciatively. *Lucy: Score 1.*

"Know what you mean. Look, I have an idea. We could go to a hotel bar. And before you get worried, they are relaying announcements all the time about the status of the ash cloud and flights."

So who was worried about that?

"Oh, that's all right, then. Good."

Lying to innocent children about how useful Chemistry will be to them in their future with a bland face is also good practice. Lying really is a key Life Skill. Should be a core subject on the curriculum. And if Mr. Moron objects that his precious little Emily is being taught how to lie, just remind him that the blonde you saw him with last week was not his wife. You didn't, actually, of course, but it works every time. Every time.

But I must focus. Concentrate on this Wonderful Thing that has come as if conjured up by some kindly genie into my life. A truly splendiferous guy taking me, Lucy B., school teacher non-extraordinaire, for a drink. Maybe our

little scrap of carpet is a magic one? Maybe…
Now, Lucy girl. Don't get drunk and blow it.
Unless he wants me to, that is.

* * *

The drink went well. The conversation likewise. For some peculiar reason I didn't clam up like I usually do with men that are way out of my league. I suppose it was the relaxation of tension: this one isn't for me, couldn't possibly be, so just chat along as with a friend. It seemed to come off. We talked about work – me, briefly, as I know only too well that glazed look that comes over men's faces when I talk about Chemistry, and not the body kind, which is a pity, as I really do love this funny old science. Call me weird. A lot of my friends do. "Hi, Weird," they greet me as they pass me in the street. "How's things in Weirdsville?"

Now where was I? Yes. Work. I handed this one over to Fergus and was mightily glad that I did. He's an artist – a genuine, money-making, properly employed one, not one of these struggling daubers who sell something in one exhibition and think they've made it. To have a real job that pays you well means you're pretty good. Fergus works free lance but is paid by an agency, as they can always sell his stuff and give him lots of commissions. He's also thirty-five, which was a shock as he could pass for ten years younger. I don't have to tell you that he does work out regularly, runs, swims, plays squash and all that, but also spends a lot of time on graphics and advertising art, which is mostly what sells.

"But I have a real urge to get back to *painting*," he said. "You know what I mean? Just good old fashioned representational *art*."

I was so caught up in his lovely rolled R's – Western

Isles? – that I didn't completely hear what he said, but nodded sagely and hoped I looked at least part way cultured and intelligent.

And then he wrong-footed me utterly, shocked me to the core. Wherever and whatever my core is, I can tell you that it was frozen, rooted to the spot, leaving me open mouthed and speechless. The gang back home would never believe it. Lucy with nothing to say?

"Yes, oils, I think. Definitely oils. I'd love to paint you in oils, Lucy."

ME? Paint me? Was the man after all a lunatic? A handsome, fit, sexy nutter? Probably. That would be my option, I guess. No *normal*, handsome, fit, sexy –

"Would you let me paint you, Lucy?"

Oh-oh. Not a crazy, perhaps. This would be a new version on would-you-like-to-see-my-etchings. Hotel room booked for a few hours, huh? And if you'd just slip into this bathrobe… And mindful of PF's warning tale, I tell myself, *Well, no thank you Mr. Arty-Farty, I'm not that sort of girl.* Well I am, if I'm honest, but I feel so let down I wouldn't dream of it. Wouldn't dream of it, really not. Really.

Then it occurred to me that he could just be serious. Maybe it was those direct, unwavering, honest brown eyes; or maybe I just got the vibes. He actually does want to paint me, I thought. And then I blushed, most furiously in a confusion of wonder and embarrassment.

So I made light of it.

"You'd have a job to find a canvas big enough," I said.

"Luc-ee. Don't say things like that. You're a painter's ideal."

Eh? Huh? You what? I've never been anyone's ideal, certainly not my parents', for whom my older sister was a daughterly paragon personified – though they tell me they love me, amongst much heavy sighing, as if to say, *despite* – and I am most certainly not my own – ideal, that is.

"Why me?" is all I can think of.

"Pre-Raphaelite perfection," said the wonderful Fergus straight off.

Whilst I hunted in my meagre store of educational references, and dug up a couple of mistily-remembered portraits of slightly anaemic, droopy women with messy red hair – ah! I was getting it now – Fergus went on about my glorious auburn barnet, tumbling down my back from its hastily scraped up ponytail – "so free, so casually abandoned" – my milk white skin and my beautiful uptilted eyes the colour of a stormy winter sea... blimey. Next time I take my kids on a school trip I'll make sure we go to the seaside on a foul day in January, just to check up on this.

"But – but I'm fat," I said at last, when he'd finished eulogising. "You'd want someone a lot slimmer, surely? And taller? Weren't Pre-Raphaelite females kind of willowy and slender?"

Showing a mouthful of gnashers as flawless as PF's (does he live on porridge and celery sticks?) Fergus laughed a lot. Quite shook our table and slopped a bit of his drink.

"They weren't necessarily as ethereal as that," he explained kindly. "Painters – real painters – like women who are fleshy, with curves and rounded lines. You can always increase height, disguise a figure in drapery, soft clothing, for effect. In any case." He glared at me suddenly, quite alarming it was, like the sun sulking all at once behind a thunder cloud. "In any case Lucy, you ARE-NOT-FAT. You are curvy, and very much more beautiful because of it. So let's not have any more of that nonsense."

"But I used to be – " I began, and then stopped. I wasn't liking the memory of myself at twenty-three, and a stone and a half lighter.

"Forget what you used to be. Revel in what you are now. One lovely, unusual, striking, pale-skinned, curvaceous redhead. Oh boy, I can't wait to get you on canvas."

That's a new one. I mean, if I score at all with a man it's usually that he can't wait to get me into his big station wagon/home/bed/out of my knickers. This man wants me flat on a piece of starched linen. Well, go with the flow. It's a compliment, sure, and the things he said are just astounding, not that I believe him for a minute, but let's suspend belief, shall we and see what happens next?

PS: Do artists fall in love with their female models? Want to screw them? Make passionate love to them in their grotty attic studios? I rather think so. Oh, *goody*.

* * *

Back in the trenches, or so it feels after a civilised drink and good conversation in a half way decent airport hotel, I glide on air. Fergus, he of the Isle of Ross, and lately living in Glasgow and part of the arts community there (I wonder if they need chemistry teachers in that part of the world?) looked at me long and steadily when we parted and said, would I like to have dinner with him at the same hotel tonight, at eight? Oh no, I don't think so, I said, really I am *not* that kind of girl, and walked swiftly away.

Hahahahahahahaha. *Kidding.*

So now I have to rummage in my bags to find something nice to wear; this travel-comfort gear will never do. There's no chance of keeping such frantic activity secret from the gang so I come clean. The others haven't moved far, just been for a short stroll, a coffee, a spruce-up in the heavily over-patronised washrooms, and then back here. There are some briefs spread out on suitcases to dry, and a much larger pair which are surely Ann's; the troops

75

have been doing some emergency washing, as I must do before this evening.

"You mean you *pulled*?" This is Samra at her most sarcastic of course. "Already? Among – this?"

She waves her arms wide, to embrace the squalid chaos that is now our quarter, our 'hood.

"Is it so unlikely?" I try to sound haughty, though she has a point; this is not, on first impressions, the best pick-up scene in the world.

"Frankly, yes," says our exotic dancer looking me up and down and taking in, no doubt, my baggy sweatpants which bunch round the middle – and, yes, my bum does look very big in them.

Ann doesn't comment, though looks at me carefully. I think she's not wanting to judge, but is a little alarmed for my safety. I'm starting to like her. At least with her what you see is what you get. Or at least I think so. Whereas our night club stripper here is a sly one, and most of what she says could be taken two ways.

On the other hand, PF's reaction is downright odd. She frowns at me, as if disapproving, scowls, and mutters something about, well, if that's what turns you on, go for it, and subsides into a magazine. She cannot, simply cannot, be jealous; I mean, she hasn't set eyes on the fair Fergus and I might be lying about his pulchritude (I'm limbering up on the vocab for tonight at dinner), and anyway, if she wanted to pull a bloke all she'd have to do is stand up, toss that long, artfully rumpled golden hair, pull at her skirt, balance on my shoulder whilst she puts on her strappy shoes and *voila*! A queue has formed from here to Barcelona. She looks up, as if sensing my speculation, glowers again and buries herself in something called 'Time' magazine. That's strange too; not the sort of publication I'd think of her reading. Isn't that the one for especially clever people, the nerds who are interested in politics and world events? Hmm.

Well, thanks, girls for your undying support and lurve. I'll just choose some gear for tonight, then, and get out of your way. Fergus has said that if you pay you can use the showers in the hotel leisure suite, even have a swim if they're not too full. Now that is one good idea. I love swimming, and it would be a great way to unwind, forget myself and the dilemma I'm in vis-a-vis Thailand, and make myself look glowing for dinner. I might even lose a few ounces, particularly if I fit in a quick burst on the treadmill. I look at my watch. It's only half past two. I don't need to go to the pool until five so what is there to do before then? At which PF, who is rapidly becoming pigeon holed as a mind reader, puts down her periodical and says,

"Time for someone else's story before Lucy deserts us for for her swishy dinner date."

Sarcastic cow. I could go back to hating her just like that. But in fact this is a relief, it gets us back to where we were. When all's said and done, I'm having dinner with someone I don't know at all, and if the ash cloud lifts soon, won't ever see again, never mind being translated into latter-day Pre-Raphaelite beauty on canvas. And if we are back on schedule, then it's –

"Ann's turn."

Ann looks at me aghast.

"Ah now, I thought youse were joking when you said about us each telling a tale. Sure, and that was last night, and you'd had a wee old skinful, if youse don't mind my saying."

PF turns the stony blue headlamps on her, and she wilts.

"It's why we allowed you to join us, and you hadn't had a drop, since you don't touch the stuff and you agreed, stone cold sober." I get this in swiftly, and PF nods, and grins. I'm back in her good books. (But why do I care?)

"That's true. Now come on, Ann. We've noticed your gold ring – and you must have something in your life to tell us about."

Ann flushes at this; pales, bites her lip, looks down at her hands and twists them a little; blushes again. Then, firmly, she puts back her head, makes a vain, rather flustered attempt to tidy her hair with a band and some clips, sits up straight and says,

"Okay, then, but it will not be like Lucy's story. No, not at all. I'm not about things like that. I think you did say it didn't have to be about – about sex, Princess Faren?"

It's disconcerting to hear Ann call PF by her full name, but it does lend a certain authority to the situation, and PF merely inclines her regal head.

"Whatever you have to say will be well received, and you couldn't possibly do another Lucy – that story was unique, and hilarious, and cleverly told by a natural raconteur – even if I didn't quite believe some of it. We need something different now. The stories should be as varied and as different as we all are – very like Chaucer's characters, by the way, if you recollect."

Three faces look at her blankly; I realise that I called the brilliant fourteenth century bedtime story teller by the wrong name and this to the divine Fergus, who, I am sure, will have read not only The Canterbury Tales but everything else in English Literature besides; Samra looks bored – I don't think A Level English featured in her school career – whereas Ann just looks at a loss. But I am also left stunned, basking in PF's praise. From plump (okay, *not* fat) homely Lucy I have become a natural raconteur and Pre-Raphaelite beauty all in one day. Any time now I'll wake up and find myself at home in bed, having overslept my alarm for once and late for school…

Ann further fusses with her hair, puts away her knitting, now revealed as most definitely the beginnings of a tiny patterned matinee coat, takes a cotton, lace-trimmed hanky from her bag, and folds and settles her agitated hands. We wait in expectant silence. It dawns on me that of all of us Ann is, regardless of her open manner and simplicity, the least predictable when it comes to telling us about her life; it could be anything at all, or nothing.

So, now," she says at last, with a lovely lingering Irish lilt, "So, I'm going to tell you a thing that is true, and it did happen to me, and it was a few years ago, but I remember it to this very day, as indeed I should, for it was an important time in my life and one I learned from much. I'm going to call my story –"

A pause. The thick, humid air seems to curdle, and grow still. A muffled and incomprehensible airport announcement is saying something to the effect that owing to the stationary something something of the ash cloud, which is now something or other not expected to move for a further something at the least, more ablution facilities something something something, but we can't hear what, and where, how or when.

We're not bothered. We want to hear Ann.

A deep long breath from our girl. We hold ours, hardly daring to make a sound in case it puts her off. Then, softly but distinctly –

"I'm going to call it – 'Pure Passion'."

We wait for Ann to begin. It seems we will wait a long time, as she has retreated into some kind of dreamy trance, looking neither at us nor at anything in the airport in particular; I suspect that her eyes are fixed on the ceiling. Her face is as tranquil as a becalmed sea – wasn't it so in The Ancient Mariner? *A painted ship upon a painted ocean?* Clever line, that one, though, sorry Miss Viner, but I thought most of the rest of that overly long poem was crap. I suppose they had the time to write hundreds of pages of terrible verse in those days, without television, DVDs and the internet?

Stop waffling, Lucy, and get back to the moment. I note that she is playing with her gold wedding ring again. Ah! A tale of infidelity from our saintly one, I wonder? Now that is downright malicious, Lucy my girl. You're becoming a bitter and twisted harridan in your old age, and you've jut been asked to dinner by one fit bloke, so think Nice Thoughts.

Okay, I'll try. It can't be hard. Viz:

Ann is a nice woman. Really she is. Fresh from the Old Country and all. My red hair, I've been told, is more Irish than Scottish or Viking, with its shade of richer auburn. I'm sure Fergus will put me right on that one. There, now I've got a warm glow, so I can be sweet about Ann. She's one of life's innocents, a naïve young wife from Ireland, very inexperienced; I bet this is her first long haul flight – though I realise that we haven't asked her where she's going – and none the worse for that. Full of good intentions, and kind at heart, I suspect. Probably very good with kids. But then I remember, with a small jolt, so am I. A fragile bond between us, then, as well as my possibly part-Irish roots?

"C'm on, Ann," I find myself murmuring, as gently as I can, prefacing this encouragement with a little cough. "We're all keen to hear your story."

A moment passes, and stretches out. Time is kind of elastic, isn't it? Longer at some points than you'd like, and then, twang! It snaps back and five years have gone by. They have for me. Only what seems like ten minutes ago I was twenty-seven, and now – those years with all their awfulness have passed, and I'm where I am – but let's not go into that.

"Yes, come on, Ann," says PF lazily, but with a sort of firmness. "Who knows, this ash cloud thing might shift its ass all of a sudden, and then we won't get to hear what you were going to tell us."

I have the strong impression that neither PF nor Ann herself could give a baboon's bum if this turned out to be the case, but I, for one, and I can't speak for Samra, who is playing with her Tablet, am definitely intrigued. What kind of passion can be pure – a passion for music? Art? Science, even? Have I told you that I'm passionate about my subject? That I find molecular structures and sub-atomic particles, and their reactions and interactions so fascinating that I could just study them all day, going deeper and deeper in to their mind-boggling complexities? Oh, I have. And you think that's possibly why I'm – twang! – thirty two and not married, not even a steady? You're probably not wrong.

But I have Fergus! Who doesn't seem to mind my oddball fixation on Chemistry. Perhaps I could persuade him to paint me into a sort of Table of Elements composition? Yeah, okay, that's a really dumb idea. Come on, Ann! I need to take my mind off what will, or won't happen with Fergus. I'm quite nervous about dinner tonight. I guess I –

81

Ann starts to speak, at last. Her voice is slow, lower than normal for her, and suddenly quite melodic – hypnotic, even. I think I wasn't far off when I talked about a trance; she'll surely send us into one if she carries on like that. But I should listen. I have a feeling this is going to be some kind of revelation.

"It was some time ago," says Ann, "that a girl experienced a passion so profound, and yet so pure, that it took over her whole soul for some while, and in so doing it both scared and excited her, with the consuming nature of the obsession and all.

"She was young, but not too young to feel such things. She had not been out into the wider, wicked world yet, but she had her head on her shoulders right, and she knew that she would have a choice to make in the future – much as you have done, Samra."

Ann breaks off and looks across at our pole-dancing inmate, who is now giving Ann her full attention, with slightly open mouth and very brilliant eyes. Hm. A connection has been made there, then…

"So," continues Ann, "she knew that she must tread carefully – oh, so carefully, like when you walk through a forest and try not to step on the fallen branches, or she would ruin everything and be badly hurt. So many girls go that way – oh, so many, and then countless are the tears that fall."

I am beginning to be drawn into this already; Ann has a way with words that I think none of us expected, and her story, though she said it happened to her, is unfolding like a fairytale or a legend. I draw my knees up to my chin, tuck my feet neatly under my thighs, cross my arms and rest my head. This is, indeed, like the Listen With Mother I tried to explain to PF, but I'm not going to say it. I'm not going to utter a word, a sneeze, a hiccup, a single sound. Carry on, Ann. You have me now.

"This girl," continues Ann, "met a young man – just a year or so older than she herself." (Ah! So it is about a boy, not music, or art, or anything like that. Ah-huh.)

"He, like her, was not of the sophisticated world, but again, like the girl, he was wise, and would not be the cause of distress or pain if he could help it. In other words, he was pure of heart, as was she.

"However, even the pure in heart can be tempted, as you will see. There is no prize for being good and never straying into the path of sin if you don't get the opportunity. Rather the sinner that repenteth, and all that, you know?"

It strikes me that she's relying on bible knowledge here, but PF and Samra, who have succumbed to the oddly rhythmic voice, nod sagely. I guess it's not restricted to the Bible, that idea, or even to religion, for that matter. After all, don't I get more out of turning a bad kid around and getting her, or him, to work and achieve good results than in popping out starred A grades from my top set? Well, then.

"So," the soft, sleepy inflection takes up the narrative after a short, reflective pause. "These two met, as boy and girl will do, have done since Adam and Eve, and will do till the earth ends its life span and there is no being left on it. First, they used to walk home together after their college day had finished. Not even hand in hand, not touching, never touching. Except with their minds. Oh, they touched there, to be sure. Everything she loved – nature, the wonder of the world, books, music, beauty – he also loved, and they talked for long hours about all these things. It was by chance that they studied on some of the same courses, but that's not important. It wasn't the College, or what they were studying that drew them together like steel to a magnet: no, it was something else, deep in the soul, of the spirit. Even beyond the heart, that fluttery red pulsing organ that is so unfaithful and capricious! No, my friends:

true passion is of the soul. Does any one of youse know what I mean by that, then?"

Her clear eyes sweep from one of us to the other, and there's no escape. She's asking us, and she wants us to answer. After a brief silence, PF startles me by her reply.

"Sure I do. It's a bit like the Wuthering Heights thing, isn't it? *The* most romantic novel ever written, in my opinion; it really got to me when Cathy says, 'I *am* Heathcliff'. Not that she wants Heathcliff, or wants to be with him in marriage, or screw him… but that they are, like, one person and without him she is incomplete."

Ann smiles, a little lopsidedly, but still, a smile.

"I'll forgive you the coarse imagery there for a beautiful book, but yes, that's pretty much like the people I'm describing."

Another silence. Samra breaks it.

"I know exactly what you mean." We look at her in astonishment, PF and I. A pole dancer, a stripper understanding purity? Oh, pull the other one! But then,

"In fat, that's partly why I'm going to Pakistan. I'll tell you about it later, when it's my turn. I don't expect all of you to understand."

She glances very pointedly at me. I feel my face flush, though whether with anger or embarrassment I'd be hard put to say.

A quick approving gesture from Ann. Now it's my go.

"Well," I say, hesitantly, "the nearest I can get to that is my passion for my teaching subject. I see in it a kind of pureness, a simplicity in spite of the incredible complexity of physical structures. I can lose myself in that, forget myself and all my pathetic little worries and woes and just – just revel in the marvellousness. The – the miracle of it if you like…"

I don't feel I've explained this well, not well at all, and I expect some sniggers or at least glances of derision; but

84

I see PF look at me with a darkening and softening of the eyes, and Samra puts up a thumb and mouths, "Nice one!" whilst Ann herself quietly repeats, "Miracle. Yes, the miraculous. You're talking of the mind and work of God, Lucy."

Oh crikey Moses. Immediately I could cut out my own blabbing bloody great gormless tongue. I'm not given to belief, I'm a hard-headed scientist and I don't think that any super-being made any of this. It's simply physical and chemical reaction, a chain of reactions which have led to us – PF, Samra, Ann, lil' old ginger me, this airport and everyone in it and the bloody ash cloud – to where we are now. Miracle was an entirely incorrect word. Everything around us is just plain fact. Understandable. Discoverable. Quantifiable. Known. Recordable and –

"Now don't go resisting the idea," cuts in the slow Irish drawl. "Just allow yourself to go with it."

And before I can explode and tell her to go with it to Hell and back (in which of course I don't actually believe), she resumes her story and I quieten like a child given a dummy on mamma's lap. What is happening to me? What?

"Well, these two lovely young people continued like this for some while – a year, maybe more – and gradually they began to see each other not only on the walk home, but sometimes also in the evenings, or at the weekends, when he would visit her at home, in her bedsit in the town. She was living away from her parents, you see, she wanted to taste independence, and learn what she could from it. After all, how could she commit, how could anyone commit to another for life if they've always been tied to their mother's apron strings?"

"Too true." *Sotto voce* from Samra, and I glance at her sharply. There was real conviction in that.

"Well so, these two would spend two or three hours of

an evening, once or twice in the week, in her tiny sitting room with its one comfy chair and the kettle and the pots for a cup of tea, and a tin of biscuits, but plain ones, mind, nothing too fancy or expensive. For she was also trying to live the simple, good life, and he admired her much for this. Now where did he sit himself, you might be asking, when she relaxed in her one easy chair, which he insisted she have? They did not, you understand, resort to what some girls and boys might have done; he did not occupy the chair, and she did not sit on his knee. They had not, up to this time, even even held each other's hand, strong though the feeling was flowing between them.

"He would sit on the floor, at her feet, but not touching; very very close to her in mind and body, but never touching. And she would sit very very still as they talked, and then fall silent, and then talk again, so that she would not, by mistake, move a leg or an arm and make contact with him. The contact, you see, was between their minds, their souls. Must ever be so.

"This went on for another few months, but somewhere towards the end of that time their bodies began to sing different songs to them. Perhaps it was simply the proximity, you know, the fact that they were so careful, so extraordinarily careful not to touch that it seemed inevitable that, sooner or later, they would, just by accident if you like. Perhaps that woke up their senses so that their frail, weak hearts said to them, 'I want more than this'. Each kept these feelings to themselves for a while, thinking that the other did not feel the same but one evening –

" 'I want so much just to put my hand on your arm,' he said, and she jumped as if someone had let off a pistol shot. 'I'm sorry, I'm sorry,' he said in a hurry, for he had spoiled their time together, he thought. 'No, no, don't be,' she said in a rush, 'for I have imagined you doing that.'

"They stared at one another for a long long moment,

and then the tears began to run down her face, down the cheeks of that innocent yet wise girl. Oh, and then he yearned to fold his strong arms around her and bring her comfort, but he knew he could not , must not. She looked at him most tenderly, and dried her tears. 'It is going to be a test for us,' she said, serious now. 'A real test. And it is going to be difficult and hard, like climbing a steep mountain that isn't there.' This was a strange saying but he understood – for remember, their minds and souls were one.

"'Yes,' he said, 'We must be careful. I want so much to be nearer to you, to sit against you, to touch your lovely face, to stroke your hair, and then more, I would want more, and that is the trouble. Once you touch, there is no going back, so I have heard. You cannot undo that first link, and then it is not enough.'

"The girl nodded. 'We must not go down that way. You know it is not right for us. You know why.' Sadly, he inclined his head. 'I shall sit further away, in the future,' he promised, 'and thought the longing will still be there, it will be easier to put it out of my mind.'

"The girl rewarded him with a sweet, slow smile, and he felt blessed. She did not want to tell him how much she wanted the same as he did: the stroking of skin, the playful fondling of the hair, his beautiful long, dark hair, and all that would come as a result of that. But she guessed that he knew, and would not discomfit her by saying this.

" 'Our passion – for that is what is between us, is that not the fact? – shall remain pure, as pure as infants in their sleeping,' he said, and moved himself a good twelve inches further back, though till reclining at her feet. The girl looked down at his silken hair, and his young, smooth brown arms, and sighed. He was adorable just to look at, she reflected, and this would have to be sufficient. She could be passionate about his mind and his soul, and take pleasure in gazing upon him, and he likewise. They would manage."

Here Ann stops. There's a prolonged silence, of the kind I can only call pregnant, inappropriate though it is for the story we're hearing.

"Is that all?" demands Samra, rather rudely, I think, and PF jettisons a little frown in her direction. Ann sighs, lifts her hands in a helpless gesture, and takes up the tale.

"But of course," she says, looking down at her modestly covered knees, "it was not as simple as that. How could it be? These two were young, awful young, with the sweetness and the perfume of budding flowers, and after all, what are men and women supposed to do? The distance of a further twelve inches from her feet did not prevent the longing, the straining of her heart; he was so very lovely, though most lovely of all was his bright mind, his quick intelligence and his spirit. Yes, his spirit; this is what she loved most, and she must needs work hard to remember that the body is but a poor second to this. So she, and he, scolded the wanton calls of their hearts, and all the aching desire, the longing, the heat and the fast beating of the pulse they contained, until surely something would explode into small pieces, or one of them would give in, and make a clumsy gesture, and all would be lost.

"I can see," says Ann, meditatively, "that you're wondering what precisely would have been lost? And why would it matter? Well, trust for one thing. Each trusted the other to keep the earthly, bodily lust at bay; each felt it terribly strongly, but they were from decent, traditional families and knew they must not do that which leads so many onto the path of disaster, and one that would ruin her life forever. Such was their passion, yes, their pure love for one another that even the slightest brushing of a hand, an arm would trigger a cascade of such exchanges, each more intense than the last, until – "

There's another pause, and we three sit still as wax, hardly wanting to breathe. *Until?*

"Until," she finishes, curiously flat, "until there would be no going back, ever, to their beatific state of grace. To the innocence of the pure passion which was what they wanted to share. All would be spoiled – all – with that first touch."

"But..." PF speaks in an unwontedly subdued voice. "But – was there to be no more? Not ever?"

"Not ever." Ann's tone is brisk and final now. "They had to part, you see – him off to a university in the North of Ireland and she – well, she went to live in London, to take up her career. And one thing I have not told you; their families were from different churches. Catholic and Church of England marriages are not easy in Ireland, even now. And so, so, they said their farewells."

This is disappointing. A huge build up, then – nothing; though my earlier assumption has been proven correct. Ann is a strict Catholic girl, the young man in the story an Anglican. Problem. I echo Samra, without thinking.

"Is that all?"

She laughs, lightly.

"Ah, no, to be sure. This was a painful time for her, but she had to test herself more, to find out what was right, and see if she could survive out there on her own."

Again, a murmured affirmative from Samra, and I'm looking forward to her stories, more than I thought I would be. Funny how one person can have a knock-on effect, like touching hands round a circle, isn't it? Oh, you know what I mean. That's wasn't a very good image, but hey, I'm trying. It's a strange old situation we're in, and my brain feels as if it's being pulled about like strands of candy-floss and floating out of my head. Not in a bad way; it's good, it's all good, but it's a mite funny-peculiar as well. I'm so used to orderly thinking, organised days, lesson plans, books to mark, meetings, my days punctuated by bells, break duties, setting up the apparatus and all that school stuff; this feels what I'd think tripping might be like. (Now it might also surprise you to know that Luce doesn't dabble in drugs. She knows too much about the effect of chemicals on the old brainbox, see? Not to mention other bits of the body. Keep off 'em, peeps.)

"So," I venture, "did she survive? Did she – find out what was, um, right for her?"

"Oh indeed she did. After a few years of learning how to live in a big, unknown city, and doing a job she only half way liked, she was old enough to know herself, and then she was ready to commit, which she had not been before, nor did she know anything really about proper commitment. Which is why she had to say goodbye to that most loved boy."

"And? And? And?" Three voices, as one. She's a clever storyteller, this Ann; she pauses at all the right moments to get her listening worms wriggling on the hook.

"And she found The One. The One who was right for her, as she had always known, and then she could give herself cleanly, with no guilt, nothing hidden that might come out one day, heart and soul." The dreamy smile crosses her serene face again, and she puts back her head, so that a few disobedient black curls spring out of their clips and band. "She wears his ring. As you can see."

"So, at last, she met Mr. Right?"

"If youse want to put if that way – yes, indeed. She did."

Three simultaneous sighs greet this announcement. Despite everything you might have thought to the contrary – well, perhaps you didn't, perhaps you're a good deal smarter than me – we're all quite hopeless romantics. Then my mushed-up brain fires a random spark of rational thought.

"So, as this story is about you, Ann, where is your Mr.

Right? Why aren't you with him? And whilst we're asking, where are you going to anyway, and why?"

The dark frizz shakes with mock severity.

"So many questions, girls! Well, to take them one by one. The story: it could be me, but it could be so many young lasses I've known, y'know? But yes, as you're asking, I'm bound for Africa to a country called Mali. To work with the poor folks out there who need our help so much. Especially the children. Ah yes, the wee ones."

I have a sudden insight.

"As a nurse."

"Not exactly, but I shall be working in the clinics – and other places."

"And him? Where is Mr. Right in all this?"

Surely she's not – parted from him? After finding him? No, Catholics don't hold with divorce. Can't be that. And there's the matinee coat. So –

Ann laughs at this, merrily, and I feel a fool immediately. There is so much more to her than I imagined – and she's clearly quite a bit older than I'd supposed. Late twenties rather than early? The candy floss floats around in my head. At this rate I shan't recognise myself by the time I get to Thailand. *Jesus! I must make a phone call before he gives up on me and they become really angry...* But I want to hear the end of this, so I sit perfectly still, knowing there is just one thing more.

"Why, waiting for me to go and work with him, of course."

Wow. Lucky, lucky Ann. Lucky, lucky bloody Irish cow. Must have been born in a field full of bloody shamrocks or four leaved clovers, or whatever. I picture this man: hair blonded by the heat of the sun, tall, tanned, in a white doctor's coat, and Ann beside him, comely, bright, both of them gazing down at some malnourished African child whose life they are going to save; and I experience pangs of horrible, unworthy envy. She has a vocation, a real vocation, that takes her into the wider world, and a man by her side as dedicated, as committed as herself. Perhaps I should go out to Africa? Do they need Chemistry teachers there? I guess they must. But then, I come back to reality a jolt: I too have committed myself, I have to go to Thailand and carry out what I said I would do. Where does Fergus come in all this, or anyone like him? Where, indeed.

What a tangle, Lucy girl. What a rare old knot you have tied yourself up in.

* * *

Now, the moment you've been waiting for. Or at least, I have. My date with Fergus: it's time to get ready. We've treated ourselves, after Ann's story, to a short nap in the afternoon. There isn't much to do, and after the surprisingly intense and even, yes, *erotic* tale she told, we're fair worn out. We all keep thinking about weeks, months, years of loving someone, wanting them so urgently, and yet having to keep it at bay; it's positively gothic, like stories of knights longing for their lady, but always suffering unrequited passion. And I ask myself the question I wonder if Samara and PF are also asking themselves: is celibacy more sensual than a good old thrashing around in the hay, where nothing is secret, or forbidden, and therefore not so exciting after you've done it a few times? Think: The French Lieutenant's Woman. (See, I do read. Occasionally.) Think: Regency dresses, Victorian repression and tight laced up corsets. Know what I mean?

At any rate, we've all snoozed and dozed and snored and sniffled our way through a torpid hour or two, and I guess lot of others have done likewise, as the lounge quietened down for a very un-English siesta. I don't expect anyone slept that well or that long last night, and I'm not exactly mad about the idea of another bedtime on this floor. But now I must concentrate. What to wear? It means hauling my biggest case into the ladies' again and throwing out most of my gear onto the tiles before I can find one that suits. And is suit*able*. What about this? Green and white floaty above knee length? Hm. A tad see-through and quite short. Don't want him to get the wrong idea. Well, come on, be honest, Lucy, you do, but not the wrong idea coming from ME. Okay, that gets crammed back into the bag then. How about the LBD I brought just in case I get asked to some do at the Embassy? And yes, in case you're wondering, this could be on the cards, owing to the mission I'm on. Do I know people in high places, or do I know people – well, along those lines. No, LBD too formal. Back that one goes. Cotton flares and a pretty top? Make me look like a suburban mum, which I don't know why I ever bought let alone packed for this trip, though it might be useful if I want to look – staid and respectable. Def not how I want to look tonight. Stuff that, then. Oh, I just don't know.

"Hi, Luce." PF is suddenly right behind me. "Having trouble?"

For once, 1 don't sense any edge. For once, I'm glad she's here. I need some womanly advice.

"Hum," she says, when I've explained my dilemma. "You know something, Lucy? You look good in whatever you wear. Just go in whatever you feel comfortable in. Don't try too hard."

I'm positively gasping, gagging even. That this amazing gazelle-legged creature should say that *I*, short arse pasty redhead, look nice. I'm beginning to think the woman is on some substance that I wouldn't mind a share of. Forget what I said about drugs.

"Close your mouth," she says, grinning. "You'll catch

flies. And how about this?"

It's a skirt; silky, nothing special. Shades of fawn and beige, with white, fashionably pleated. Draped ties on the waist. With it she indicates a white lacy blouse, but not too revealing, simple fitted shape, tiny cap sleeves. I put them on. Find a pair of bronze ballerina flats. Ye-ess... Yes, I think we've got something here.

"Now, the hair."

I submit, mesmerised like the helpless rabbit-in-headlamps, to the deft touch of strong, long fingered hands. My hair assumes form. A pattern. A *style*. My God. This person is a genius. Clips are expertly inserted, sections pinned, curls left in little wisps.

"Pretty neck you got," grunts PF through hair grips. "You should show it off more. There."

And to be sure, as Ann would say, there I am. Groomed, stylish but not OTT, not at all over any top, just – classy. By a miracle, and sorry, Ann dear, but this is a bleeding miracle, I don't look so fat. Maybe it's the clever draping and swishy fabric? Or my hitherto undiscovered beautiful neck? Whatever, I am eternally grateful to PF, and throw my arms around her in an impulsive hug. She stiffens, her arms pushing at mine to get me off her. I'm puzzled. I thought she would be one of these touchy-huggy people, being American and all.

"Don't do that, Lucy!" she says sharply. "you'll ruin your hair."

Right, PF. Right you are.

Life is full of these sudden fleeting shocks, isn't it?

I'm looking at my face in the wash room mirror. The poor thing's a bit jaded, worn. My face, that is, not the mirror, which is painfully bright and reflects exactly every single minging open pore, flaky skin, threatening pimple – you know the story. Ah yes! I remember now: I was going to use the hotel gym and pool to give myself a nice glow for dinner.

Raking out a swimsuit – black, Olympic passion-killer style, leave the miniscule bikini for Thailand, if I ever get there – along with goggles and shampoo, shorts and a tee shirt, I head for the hotel leisure suite, pay my dues as a day guest, and get changed. I thought I'd have to fight for a place on the treadmill, snatch weights off fellow prisoners, weave my way in and out of the thrashing mass in the pool; but no, the place is quiet, as presumably my fellow travellers mostly choose to fill their faces with food outlet crap and lie about reading tabloids and gossip magazines (which of course I never, *ever* do). I complete my forty-five minutes' running, my routine of weights, twenty minutes on the cycling machine with hill stuff to tone up those muscles and hope they don't go south again by tonight, and then my equivalent of sixty lengths in the watery patch that passes for a swimming pool. You didn't guess I was an exercise freak, huh? Not many people do. Well, when you've got all those paintable curves like there's no tomorrow, it pays to keep them at least toned, otherwise they turn into straggling S-bends – with lumps and bumps as courtesy extras, competing with a lot of cellulite.

Right now I'm finishing off with a steam room session. Boy, it's good. I can feel all the nasties oozing out of my pores and a teeny little bit of fat melting, yes, melting away... Okay, so Fergus insists I'm not fat; but he's a man and *artist*, and everyone know they don't see women as ordinary people do. Now, what do I mean by that? The tyranny of the fashion world folk? The diet companies that make trillions out of our insecurities? The bitchy, cat-scratching celebrity circus of cool? Mm. Fergus has given me something to think about there.

Just a brief spell of the old legs-crossed-against-logic-and-anatomical-sense meditation, and it's time to get togged up and try to do my hair like PF did. I suddenly wish she was here now; not just to fix the hair, but for some sort of moral (or immoral, who cares?) support. Under that dazzling exterior, there are many other threads that make up the elusive Princess Faren. And she *is* elusive: one minute I think I've sussed her, then she says or does unexpected things that send me back to square one. Like brushing me off so abruptly after our matey-girlie clothes and hair get together; like reading Time magazine and so far as as I could see getting really into it; like her reaction to my having pulled a fella. There's also a strength about her, a calm stepping back from what's going on, taking it all in and not getting fazed by it. Yes, now would be good to have her here.

But she's not, so I struggle alone with the rampant not quite dried hair – if I waited for it to be completely dry I'd miss my date and probably the next week of my life – and the clips and pins. There, I have achieved a passable version, and the damp tendrils snaking into my (admired) neck don't do me any harm. PF was right about the outfit, too, and I was right about the exercise: I do kind of shine, and not in the wrong way, and my skin looks tighter. The simple outfit we chose whispers "natural, quietly confident" rather than shouting, "sexy, loud, in your face, dying for it", if you know what I'm getting at. I think you do.

Fergus's expression as he greets me affirms all of this.

"Wow, Lucy! You look wonderful."

"Yeah, I brush up nice," is all I can think of to say. I'm not used to such appreciation these days. But then, I'm not used to presenting myself like this either. Usually it's either end-of-the-day slob-out gear, when I've got home after a full day at school, meetings and preparation time, or the kind of tarty get ups I go clubbing in when I get wasted on Fridays and Saturdays. Maybe I have some excuse, these last two years, burying myself, sticking my head in some kind of dark hole after what happened, but it's dawned on me like the revelation of St. Paul that I'm a bit old for this kind of stuff, and that maybe I should – to used an overworked word – *reinvent* myself. Starting from tonight. These clothes were brought for creating a respectable image for what I have to do in Thailand, but they seem to work for this occasion too. Work very well, in fact. And I don't just feel 'respectable', I feel – womanly.

Fergus meanwhile is steering me to the dining room, where a table is reserved for us. I cannot actually believe what's going on! Nobody has treated me like this for – oh, I don't want to say. For too long. Much too long. *And whose fault is that, Lucy? You've spent the last few years – oh, shudd-up!! Let me enjoy myself.*

We sit down, study the menu. Oh gosh, oh golly gosh, I'd love the pasta starter, then a beautiful looking veggie quiche with garlic bread and maybe, oh come on, *definitely* potato wedges, but I'd better play safe and choose a melon, then something salady and light on calories. I don't want him to think I'm a pig, a greedy little piglet who gets curvy because she can't keep out of the trough. Sighing, I put in my modest order. Fergus frowns.

"No, Lucy." Eh? "*No.*"

Come again?

"That's not what you'd actually like. And if it's anything to you, I hate women who don't eat properly and think they've got to eat two lettuce leaves and drink minestrone soup, and pass on the puddings. Now, what would you really choose?

I look at him carefully, seriously. He's not kidding. He's looking back at me seriously, carefully. Yippeee! Yakkety-doo-dah-day!! I've met a man who doesn't want a stick figure, who likes girls who –

"Relish their food," says Fergus, chiming in with this delightful, mind-blowing thought and rolling that "R" in a most delightful way. "It puts a man right off," he continues, smiling a bit now, "if he's chomping through a heaped plateful and the woman he's eating with is picking at samphire and three cherry tomatoes."

"With her fake extension square nails on her skinny fingers," I add, and we both laugh. "In that case, as you insist, I'll have the pasta to start, and the vegetarian chick pea tart WITH potato wedges, and ricotta beans in butter. And some garlic bread on the side."

"Great choices," says Fergus, approvingly, "and I trust you'll join me in a lovely dessert? I don't want to be the only one noshing through a great slab of gateau."

Could this get any more perfect? Could a man possibly be any better? Could an ash cloud ever have come at a more divine moment? Oh, I could go and *hug* that volcano!

The wine arrives, and we toast each other, ash clouds, airport terminals, art, science and the whole universe. Even before I take a sip, I am utterly at ease. My skirt sits comfortably around me. No muffin top or fat ripples. My feet are cool and rested in the simple flat shoes. The lacy top covers me well, and skims the tops of my (toned) arms, whilst giving discreet and intriguing glimpses of my shadowy flesh. I like this new Lucy. I like her very much.

So, it seems, does the beautiful Fergus. We do not rush the meal, but take our time, and when the coffee comes, we go out onto the terrace, as it is a warmish night and the air is still.

"Ah," says Fergus. "Wouldn't I just love to have my paints here now? The light on your hair. Your profile. Yes. I could really get that." And then, suddenly, he stands up. "Would you excuse me a moment, Lucy?"

"Why sure, no problem, " I say, doubtfully, but before I can say more he's gone, whisking away on legs that I am sure are as magnificently honed as the rest of him. I am left to contemplate the starlight, though there's no moon tonight, the low and flattering lights of the hotel's balcony, and the humming of a busy transport hub around us. Then he's back, clutching a large flat, black leather case.

"My sketch pad and pencils," he explains. "Never travel without them. I get a lot of ideas all the time, and I need to get them down on paper."

"I see."

And I do kind of grasp what he's saying, though I cannot truthfully claim that I write down original scientific hypotheses or mind-blowingly difficult mathematical equations whilst out and about; but I suppose artists are different. Musicians and novelists, and probably poets too, I wouldn't wonder. It comes home to me again what a different universe I have somehow slid into, or been gently propelled towards. I think I am waking up, at last, from a five year slumber. Maybe Thailand was the start?

* * *

So he did draw me. Several times. Lots of small, quick, lightning speed sketches, thumbnail impressions, and all the while I sat perfectly still, perfectly content. Neither of us spoke. There was absolutely no need. Another new

99

one for Lucy. The ultimate gabbler, big mouth, chatterer, restless talker, compulsive filler of silences. It was totally peaceful, and made me resolve to do my Yoga more regularly, the only time in my busy week that I stop and listen to the sound of my own heart beating. Or remember that I have got a heart, and that it does in fact beat its own rhythm.

My goodness. This is getting untoward! Don't kid yourself, Lucy girl, that you can be like this for ever. Everyone needs times when they're loud, out there, enjoying a drink, pounding away to some hot music (though, equally, some folks never allow themselves to do stuff like that). Maybe what I haven't had lately is the balance. I could do with more evenings like tonight, that's for certain. Then it was over. He didn't push his luck with me; I knew, and him too, I guess, that any kind of physical vibes between us, echoing Ann's story so recently told, would have ruined that serene hour when he was so intently studying me, and making incredibly lovely drawings, far more lovely than I am, truly. But he put a quiet hand on my arm, and saw me back to the nest where my fellow chicks were already bedded down for another great dream-time, and his eyes widened a bit, and he looked troubled.

"You have to sleep – like that?"

"Yea," I said, casually. "But it's all right, really it is. It's amazing how soundly you can kip on a floor when you're tired."

"Ill take your word for it," he said, "but I'll see what I can do if there's going to be more delays, Lucy. Not just for you, but for your friends as well. They look rather, er, cramped."

I could think of nothing to reply to this, except that my inner voice was screeching most ungenerously, and in typically Lucy self-contradictory fashion, *Damn my 'friends', why don't you just let me share your hotel room? Who wants company?*

"I'll come over mid-morning. Will you be awake?"

Stamping hard on all mean spirited inner malevolence, and brushing those horrible little demons away once more, I put on my blandest, cheeriest voice.

"I shall. I always wake at six, whatever time I get to sleep."

"Incredible woman!" Another approving glance. "Much healthier than lying about. Well, see you tomorrow – or is it today?"

And then he was gone, and it was indeed, today, it being past midnight, and me feeling like Cinderella in borrowed clothes, which I shed in the wash room and where I pulled on my old sweaty sweatpants and the gym tee shirt; well, nobody around me is too fragrant, so to heck with it. And then I slept, hitting the carpet like a stone, with mad dreams of PF being my Fairy Godmother, and Samra and Ann as the Ugly Sisters… Fergus, of course, being the handsome Prince. Even in my sleep, I think I sniggered.

* * *

Now it actually is *today*, and yes, I am awake, and it is only six-fifteen, and I have spent a fidgety quarter of an hour trying not to move so that my soundly snoring, zuzzing, whistling and heavy breathing trio can get more of the one hundred and forty winks they seem to need. But I have to get up, I just have to. Fergus is coming in a few hours, and I want to get ready for that – oh, don't worry, nothing elaborate, just a new set of casual wear which I'll go over and buy from the sports shop I saw a few blocks away. I'm beginning to think of this terminal as a kind of metropolis, with our part of it like a high street district, with its shops and cafes and all. We're in an elite residential crescent; I've even named it: Axminster Close. How about that? The road we're off is called Voyager's Way, which has rather a ring to it, I thought, and those shopping outlets over by the cafe we use I'll name Endeavour Mall – 'cos what I'm embarking on is a new venture, if not an *adventure*, an attempt to start afresh, put right some things – oh, enough of that.

Then there's the downtown area opposite, where the *hoi polloi* are tumbled together, and crowded and cramped, to use Fergus's word, much more so than we, the Fortunate Four. Or should that be 'us', the Fortunate Four? Get off my shoulder, Miss Viner. I can do without memories of your flaming tedious English grammar lessons. Now what should I call these semi-slums? And if you think I'm being snobbish, take a look, just get a butcher's at that lot. Sweet packets, broken up and trampled crisps and biscuits, polystyrene cups, stains on the flooring, a few stray socks, never in pairs, abandoned here and there, a half eaten apple, ditto some repulsive variety of pasty, yuk, must have a trillion gadzillion salmonella bacteria crawling all over it by now, I wouldn't care to inspect that through a microscope, and for some unknown reason a solitary man's shoe. Rising out of this unappealing mess is a pong which I swear is growing riper by the minute. I'm proud of our barracks: we keep them clean and tidy, all of us. Ann is, I have to hand it to her, meticulous; a stray crumb on the carpet and she's on it like a human Dyson, and I'm no slouch 'cos I can't stand getting up to a dirty place. Another revelation for my friends back home, but there you go; I'm full of 'em. So I always clear up before hitting the hay. Well, I didn't last night, but there was no need. PF is fastidious, to the last detail of her appearance and what's around her, and even Sexy Samra, Stripper Xtraordinaire, is pretty neat. Could be all that flinging off of mini-skirts, g-strings, nipple tassels?

You'd need to keep a keen eye out for where they went, wouldn't you?

Tee hee. Bitchy, Lucy? No, only having a bit of fun. I feel well inclined to all my fellow women and some men, or, one in particular, this morning. Where's a baby I can snatch for a cuddle?

I'm up and walking now, with less than a handful of early risers browsing the closed shop windows and waiting for the coffee to brew and the airport to creep into sluggish movement – I wouldn't call it activity, as not much happens, courtesy of Mr., or Ms., Ash Cloud. It's as if the clock has decided to go more leisurely, forcing the hours and the days to wind down to a kind of stagnant slow-motion in which we are drifting around in a dream. I certainly feel as if I'm in some other reality, that's a fact. I mean, is Fergus just a figment of my imagination? Did last night actually happen? Can you live, or exist, on two different planes, in two different spane-time zones?

Just as I'm off on another of my daft rambling ruminations an older woman passes me; smart, expensive tracksuit, trainers, greying hair scraped back into a sort of knot, an expression of superb concentration on her leathery face. She walks fast, as if she's doing a circuit; possibly she is. There's nothing else to do. I offer a 'Hi', but she ignores me, swinging her arms energetically to get her heart rate up. Ah well. You don't win 'em all. On the other hand, ooh, what's this? A tall, hunky black guy also striding out winks at me and grins. Now if I hadn't met Fergus...

Behave, Lucy. One man is quite enough. Hah! Say it sufficiently often and you might persuade yourself. One man in the hand is worth two in the bush? Dunno about that. Two in the bush sounds more fun to me. Then it occurs that this is two men in two days, or less, who've given me the eye. Wonder heaps upon wonder.

"Hi there, early bird. Fancy a coffee?"

He indicates the cafeteria, where the shutters are just going up. Why not? Why not, Lucy? Come on, you've only just met Fergus, and this is just a friendly drink. We find a table – ooh, that was hard! – and take a steaming espresso each and a croissant. It's nice, it's easy, it's companionable. His name is Matende, and he's from Manchester. A lecturer in Engineering. We have these things in common, then: life in teaching, a love of science. How come I never meet people like this in my home city? This strange hiccup in our travels is sure turning out to be mind and soul-expanding. I can feel wings sprouting and spreading from somewhere in my shoulder blade region, and I'm not talking angels here.

"Well, Lucy," says the dishy Matende lazily, leaning back in his chair and wiping crumbs from his luscious mouth, "and what will you be doing in Thailand? A holiday, is it? And why on your tod?"

Oh dear. I'd hoped nobody would actually ask me that. I imagined that they would simply assume a package vacation, or some such; after all, what do most Brits go to Thailand for? I mean, there are other reasons, but I don't look as though I fit into those categories. So I lie.

"Yep. Much-needed break. Some spring sunshine, y'know? And I prefer going away on my own, then you can do your own thing."

He nods appreciatively. And where is he going, I ask – before we can go further into Thailand, as it were. He's going to China. Always wanted to see it; just separated from his long term partner, so now's the opportunity. Might look at colleges there. Fancies a change.

So we talk about China, and the Far East generally, and time passes until I realise with a start that I'd better go look for that snazzy sportswear or Fergus will have the dubious pleasure of seeing me in my jogging bottoms cum jimjams. And don't even begin to think that after last night he'd prefer me that way. But I've liked talking with Matende, and we part amicably, with a so-long, see you later sort of feeling. He's forty-one, I've learned, and he says it's a dilemma, and he doesn't know whether he's serious about leaving Manchester for good, whether the relationship really has bombed. By then, I've gotten involved in his soul-searching and I will *totally* meet him again for another coffee.

Besides, a sudden idea has come into my newly overactive head: I'm in a way 'with' Fergus, so shouldn't take this any further, though I have a hunch Matende might like to, but what about PF? She would go so well with him – blonde, and tall, and leggy, and he's so dark, and tall and – yes, leggy, and worked out and all that. I have a sense she's lonely underneath all the apparent aplomb – my, there's a good word for eight thirty in the morning – and that she hasn't found a relationship. Otherwise, why would she be flying off to Oz as a single?

The satisfaction of tying up these loose ends so cleverly makes me choose a particularly expensive but slick set of casual gear: well shaped pants that actually fit on the waist, no horrid drawstring type of thing, and slink round the backside, managing at the same time to make the old pins look longer and a bit thinner. I choose a matching jacket with zips and green edgings on the navy, just enough to add a zing of colour. A bust enhancing white sports tee and a sporty shrug in grey complete the collection. Finally, I invest in some trainers that don't look like battered fishing coracles and that also have a discreet flash of silver. Nor are they odorous. The credit card moans, screams and generally has hysterics as it is forced into the payment machine, but in it goes, there: down, down conscience and common sense. The deed is done. One smart, fit Lucy B. My own mother wouldn't recognise me these days.

(Although she would probably be pleased if she could see me in this lot, and particularly if she could have seen me last night... all those hints about *isn't that skirt just a wee bit short, Lucy? And wouldn't you like me to come and help you choose some nice dresses?* She means well.)

But before Fergus arrives at our outpost, I must make that all-important call. My cell phone – I'm becoming infected with Yankee-speak, thanks to PF – seems to be co-operating this morning, so I find a discreet corner and dial Thailand. After a seemingly endless number of rings, a human voice answers. Thank God, no answer phone; I cannot do this by leaving messages. A deep, deep breath to calm myself, and then he is put onto me. I can hear the explanations in the background, the announcing of my name.

"Hello, I say, suddenly awkward, tongue tied. I am scared. "Do you remember me?"

A pause that nearly kills me. A quavering sound from the other end, all those thousands of miles away, but audible. Audible enough for me to get the gist.

"Yes. Why you not come?"

The voice is accusing, as I knew it would be. They think I have let them down, not fulfilled my part of the bargain. I must convince him, right now, or I might as well go back home.

"I will come. I am coming. As soon as they will let us get onto the plane. I am stuck in the aiport in England. Do you understand?"

No response, only sounds of breathing.

"I need to know that you understand. I am not going to let you down."

Still he says nothing. I realise that his command of English is more limited than I'd been told. I must put it more simply. Pigeon English, then. I hate doing this, but I must get this through. I *must.*

"I no back out. I *come*. Very soon. Yes? Tell me that you know what I'm saying."

An eternity goes by. I am wilting on the spot, tension gnawing at my stomach, my heart. A long, heavy outbreath.

"Yes. I hear you. Okay."

Praise be. It is all right. He believes me – has forgiven me. In my relief, I clutch the vital packet inside my onboard bag, the one I must not lose, or all *is* lost, and I am lost along with it.

"Okay, then. I will see you very soon."

The call cuts off, though whether he or someone else has put the phone down on me or whether it's the connection I don't know. Weakly, I lean against the wall, sweat starting to stain my grotty old tee. I wish now I'd bought the green sweat band, for my hair is damp already and I need to get a shower before I put on my new stuff. It's nearly half past nine. Do I have time for another of those refreshing swims? That would mean getting over to the hotel and back, of course. But the –

"Lucy! Are you ill? What's up?"

Fergus. Damn the man, it's Fergus. Never imagined I'd say that, but this is just entirely wrong timing. He's looking at me closely, I'd say a pinch suspiciously. Why is he so early? He said mid-morning, which I'd take to be around half ten. Coffee break at school. But then, I guess if he's up at six like me, this is half way through his morning. Mustering some calm, I say, I'm fine, just a bit hot and over-set in my gym clobber, you know? Been walking quite quickly to get some exercise. And he seems to accept that, though insists that I have a coffee with him to get over my 'funny turrrn', which he says with those blurred Scottish R's that make my tummy do flips.

"Sorry I'm a bit on the premature side," he murmurs, and puts a warm, strong hand over my still slightly shaking one. "But I just couldn't wait to come over and see you."

Oh my. Oh jumping Jehosaphat, as my old gran used to say. (Though I can't say I know what she meant. Or who.) Just what is all this about? I mean, I like him, I like him a lot, he's a smashing guy, but I cannot in all truth say I was as eager as that; I could have waited till eleven, or mid-day, if needs be. At this precise moment, who should stroll by again but Matende, all six foot two inches of black, lean, muscular gorgeousness. He grins, widely, and raises an eyebrow. Ahah! The eyebrow says. So Lucy has a fella in tow!

And indeed it does seem to be the case, though I can't say I understand what is happening at all. Not at all. To hell with it! I smile at Matende, beckon him over, not sure why I'm doing this but I do it anyway. Safety in numbers? Trying to get Fergus jealous and even more keen? No, that doesn't seem to fit, doesn't feel right. Or do I not want to lose Matende? Oh dear. Oh my giddy aunt. Lucy, you are getting yourself well taffled up here – again. Then I recall my earlier brainwave. Time to introduce Fergus and Matende to our brave troubadours, who will by now surely be awake in our decent, clean little ghetto.

"Come on, guys. Let's go and meet the tribe," I say imperiously, savouring every nano-second of this new found power, and, meek as new born ducklings waddling after someone they take to be mother, they follow me.

Though it's a pity they're not in front of me, and then I could have compared their respective bums.

8: Thongs Ain't What They Used to Be *aka* Airing a Grievance on a G-string

"Hi, folks," I chirrup. "Meet two new friends of mine." And I wave my hand in the direction of the delectable men that for some strange and mad reason I seem to have acquired. "This is Fergus. And this is Matende. Guys, these good ladies are, respectively, Ann, Samra and Princess Faren."

Predictably, eyes bulge, so I explain, and Matende laughs, whilst Fergus, bless the boy, looks faintly disappointed.

"Sure," says Matende lazily. "I lived in the States for a while, and they call their kids Prince and Princess this and that over there. Duh –" Tactfully, he stops.

PF laughs. "Yeah, dumb habit. Too right!"

The beautiful Matende looks at her with approval. Aha! My cunning plan is working. PF looks especially amazing this morning; exhaustion made all of us sleep well, at last, and she has clearly visited the washrooms. The bluest-of-blue eyes shine with good health and amusement, her skin – well, to be honest, I think she's topped up her fake tan, but it's a good one, and gives her a kind of *sheen* – and the newly shampooed hair is softly tousled; she's even dug out some different gear from her case, a sarong skirt in jewel pattern and loose silk top and she looks – she looks a knockout. The faintest quiver of jealousy goes through me. Do I really want to give one of *my* men to her?

Before this uncharitable if not to say downright dog-in-the-manger thought can get going, Fergus takes control. Just as well, or I will fall into the mire of my own foul plotting and betrayal. Not to mention sheer stupidity. As if either of these stunning fellas is actually mine to withhold or give to anybody. *Slap on the wrist for you, my girl. Come down to earth.*

"Right," says Fergus, with a firm and distinctly Scottish sort of authority.

Immediately I imagine him striding some Highland estate, a heather-strewn moorland, the laird, the cold bracing mountain air blowing his hair all wild and riffling his tartan kilt, and him keeping everything in order and the ghillies doffing their tam o-shanters to him, and –

"Lucy," he says now. "Did you actually hear any of that? You looked miles away."

"Erm..."

I blush, furiously and furious. What a daft little shmuck I must look. PF, I see, is studying me rather intently, with that odd, slightly critical frown drawing her fine brows together and highlighting the iceberg eyes. Samra is grinning at Ann, who smiles back. This is not quite going as I had intended.

"Sorry, Fergus. Things on my mind."

"Ah yes. Thailand," he murmurs. "Your, um, vacation trip."

PF nods a little over emphatically. I allow them this, let them think what they like. No way do I need anyone to get inside my silly schoolgirl head just at this moment, with its lame fantasies. I visualise a whiteboard: a spirit cleaner. One swipe and poof! My visions are gone. Feet on terra firma. Better.

"So tell me, Fergus. I'm listening."

Fergus explains again. It appears that he has got us a suite – och aye, a *suite* – at one of the hotels, with two double rooms, a lounge, and a small kitchenette. How he has managed this he does not disclose and we do not ask, but it further seems that we do not have to pay. Now either he is considerably more successful than he modestly makes out, or he really IS a wealthy laird, and he really does have an estate, and his family is mega-rich. At once I see myself in some floaty afternoon tea dress, with a broad piece of plaid draped carefully over one shoulder, a diamond and emerald brooch pinning it in place, my discreetly beringed hand serving Earl Grey from a precious – probably eighteenth century – china pot to the assembled family, visiting lairds and minor royalty. *Whoops, Lucy, off you go again. Best to leave it there.*

So I let go of my hot air balloon, as it were, and sink back to real time and real space, which is as follows:

1. Coffee – with Matende in tow and us, the Gang of Four – and wicked little cakes in the hotel coffee shop;
2 Introduction to our suite, which is rather more luxurious than we expected, and has a balcony looking out on small but beautifully kept patio areas;
3 Session in the Health Club, each of us finding our own preferred activity, Matende coming as a guest, and boy does he look good in swimming shorts. Ann chooses to toddle sedately round the running circuit, in loose trousers and the kind of aertex shirt most of us leave behind at the end of Year Eleven. PF does weights and the rowing and step machines, Samra, in skimpy Leotard, does floor exercises that look physically improbable and further lengthen her already unbelievable legs. I swim with Matende, but Fergus, surprising us all, sits it out in the refreshment area.
4 Lunch served in our lounge, followed by coffee on balcony.
5 Siesta on lush, comfortable hotel beds.

It is five o'clock when we all come to, waking and rubbing our eyes like children on Christmas morning: will we wake up to ashes in the fireplace and empty pillowcases? This is not me, it can't be. Lucy does not sleep in the daytime; however tired, however little kip she's had the night before, she does not allow herself to stop. She keeps going, finds things to do, runs round the block, does more lesson plans, chases her own tail... And the thought homes in on me like a poison arrow. Yes, I've been chasing that darned tail of mine for a long time now, and never realized that I've been going round in circles. Well, these extraordinary few days have broken that mould all right. This afternoon, I snored through two hours of the most restful snooze I've had in years, fell into dreamland the minute my head made contact with that sinfully soft feather pillow.

I should explain that I am sharing a room with PF, Ann and Samra, now for some peculiar reason best buddies, having the other. I'm glad it's PF I'm bunking with, though; she's a quiet sleeper, easy in her movements, and if anything it's I who will disturb her in the morning.

I should also explain that the hotel has pledged to call us with any updates on the travel situation. The news today has been – nothing. Ash cloud happy where it is. Extremely contented with its billet. Not moving, no siree. No strong air currents detected for at least two more days. World economy totters, financiers rushing like lemmings for good old-fashioned gas ovens, travellers watching their credit card debt mounting – and that dog-gone cheeky mass of vapour just hangs out over our small island. It must like the view.

So we wait, and hang too. And I also quite like the view.

* * *

"Your story". PF points a languid finger in the direction of Samra. It is six o'clock, and we're all showered and awake, ready for some diversion. "We haven't forgotten."

112

"Yeah," says Samra peaceably. "I've a few tales I could tell, not just one story – in fact, it's two or three shorter yarns, if that's okay?"

"Sure. As long as they're true."

PF smiles, and we affirm our agreement, settle back on the expensive sofas and sip the exquisite coffee that Ann has made in the mini-kitchen. It sure beats the crap out of the school staff room, and my humdrum life in an English comp seems to be receding ever more rapidly. I could just take to this kind of treatment. *Have* taken to it. Am all-righty-right down there and into it. So I cosy up against a satin cushion and lick my mental lips (there's a nice metaphor for you, Miss Viner) at the sheer indulgence of it all, and in anticipation of the revelations of our hip-swivelling dancing queen.

"We-ell," she says, sitting forward and putting a crimsoned fingernail to her mouth. "I should begin by telling you a bit about what it means to be a dancer in a club. Pole dancing and lap dancing, you know?"

We nod. We do. I dare not look at Ann.

"Well," she says again, thoughtfully, "I guess everyone knows a bit about it, but it's only when you're up there and performing that you really get to see it is at is. I'll start by telling you about my first week in the first job I ever had. So lie back, close your eyes, and picture yourself as a raw girls from the sticks, from the backward *north*, what's more, and nineteen going on fourteen, in London, and you suddenly find yourself in a swanky club and you are the meat on the rack, you're the one being pushed onto the podium with a blaze of light in your eyes, and there's some metal poles that you're supposed to do something with and a haze of dim faces like masks from Phantom of the Opera or somesuch, all staring… And the music's pounding and grinding, and you feel butt naked, which you nearly are, which feels more naked than if you had no clothes on at all, and you've forgotten your moves, and you're sure that your heart beating so loud will drown out the music, and let me tell you girls, you *panic*."

We are all, as ordered, leaning back with our eyes squeezed tight shut; and yes, we can all see that lonely young figure, so exposed, so scared, and we are terrified *with* her, our collective short breaths fusing into the vivid picture she is painting. There's a dramatic pause. Does she make it? Is she booed off the stage? Does she –

"Yes," continues Samra relentlessly, "You just – panic, and stand there rotating your pelvis for want of anything better to do with this stupid body of yours, and like a mechanical doll you stroke your tits with sweaty hands, and then it sorts of kicks in what you have to do and you begin to focus, and you see another girl getting it on with her pole, and you teeter over to your own spot on your ridiculous killer heels, and you remember the routine, thank God, you remember your number that seemed so easy in the empty rehearsal room, and you twist and slide, and hoik yourself upside down and spread your legs, and then you do whatever little tricks make the act yours, and you hear some applause, and then you feel better and you get into it and you even start to enjoy yourself and the moves come easily, and you feel how *strong* your body is, your muscles, your arms, and it's like an athletic thing, not sexy at all from where you are and you must concentrate, focus, concentrate or you'll get it wrong and fall or look just clumsy and ugly, and they they will slow-clap you off and you won't be kept on the payroll, heaven knows there are plenty and plenty of girls out there dying to give this shit a go…"

Cautiously, I take a peep, look round at the faces: PF's blank, a blue gaze signifying nothing, as that old devil Macbeth would say (I hear Miss Viner quietly fainting) and Ann's, her mouth startlingly open but curving upwards in a strange little smile, almost as if she's about to laugh, though there is a blush at the neck of her sensible plain blouse... and mine? How am I responding to this introduction to a new art form, as Samra might have us believe? I can't see my own physog, but if I could I'd imagine it would be an expression of boredom. So far, she's not told us anything we couldn't have guessed for ourselves. Yeah, you're scared shitless at first, then you get into it 'cos you have to, and then you begin to enjoy it, and I've heard before that pole dancing in particular is more physically strenuous than it looks. Sporty, even.

Maybe I should try it to get some of the blubber off my waist and tum? If they could find a pole strong enough to take the weight, that is.

So, come on, then, Samra, give us something to bite on.

"So," she says, as if reading my thought, "so far so obvious. It's like anything new, you have to learn it all over again from the practice to the real thing. Rather like acting, I suppose"

PF nods at this, twice, pointedly. Oho! Has the stately, tan-enhanced one trodden the boards, then? Not no, not Hollywood, surely? If so, then it must have been in those Z rated, straight to DVD movies, 'cos I sure don't recognise her. Either her face or her name. But then, I can't associate PF with anything Z rated, so whether to ask? Not at this point, but I make a note to myself. Ann is now reuniting her upper jaw with the lower, and makes a funny sort of swallowing sound.

"Or like anything else that is a new venture," she says, rather huskily, "and that you think you know all about until you come to do it, and then it's quite a different matter, sure."

I stare at her for a moment and then decide that she could be talking about absolutely anything; she is, after all, flying long-haul to Africa, to work out there – and even with Mr. Right there waiting, it's a brave decision she's made, I guess?

"Go on," says PF "You're into the pole dancing now. What about the other things, the lap dances and the stripping?"

Samra shrugs.

"Much the same," she says, with disinterest. "It's all much of a muchness; once you've wiggled your pelvis in front of some bloke who's requested you, and who gawps at you with his glassy eyes and doesn't say a word or make a single movement, you've seen them all. And stripping – well, the first time you actually go the full Monty, it's a bit scary, but then it's just another routine – unless they ask you to do something a bit pervy, that is."

She senses the "*Like?*" in our thoughts, and answers it.

"Once I was asked to lie down on this couch thing after getting down to the buff, and toss myself off, at least, pretend to you know? And then the bastard club owner came on and asked if there was anyone man enough in the audience to finish me, and this guy came on stage but he couldn't get it up, and everyone shouted rubbish at him and I don't suppose he's got over it, and he kind of crawled away into the darkest corner of the room, and I – I just felt like –"

Her black-brown eyes are flashing anger, and I for one can well appreciate that. I let Samra explain.

"I didn't have control any more, you see. Up till then, you can take the stripping at your own pace, tease, flirt, hide a little, then reveal a bit, and get the punters gagging, but that was just humiliating for this daft guy and for me, and I couldn't do anything about it – it took me totally by surprise, so I walked off stage and never went back to that club."

"Oh, and the risks," murmurs Ann, who is now slightly crimson and puffy of face, and is looking distressed. "I

mean, sexually transmitted disease, AIDS, and that, and
– well – "

"We didn't actually have sex with them," says Samra
rather sharply. "OK, on that occasion it might have
happened, I suppose, though I think if it *had* looked like he
was going to – well – do the biz, I'd have got off that couch
and left the stage even faster than I did anyway."

Meanwhile, I am totally staggered; such words as
sexually transmitted and *AIDS* coming out of the pure
mouth of the Irish one. Maybe she's been around a bit
more than you might think?

"Still," says Samra, more quietly, "of course thing like
that do cross your mind – you don't live like vestal virgins
in that world – but don't worry, I was regularly checked,
and I'm fine."

"By the grace of God," breathes Ann, crossing herself
fervently, and I feel a strong temptation to bat her one.
Must she come over as the Catholic country girl all the
time? Then, to my further amazement, Samra mouths,

"Yes, thanks be to God." And she's not being sarcastic;
she means it.

"Would you say," drawls PF lazily, sitting upright and
putting her chin on her elegant hands, "would you say,
than, that that was the point where you decided to get out
of it for good?"

"No way." Samra laughs now. "No, that was early
on, and it taught me a valuable lesson: be absolutely and
one hundred per cent sure of what you're signing up for.
Apparently the girl who'd been in that job just before me
did that little routine and got extra money, and as she and
her boy friend were saving up for a house, she didn't mind
– and nor, it seems, did he. She left when she was four
months pregnant, but nobody told me about the extras I
was expected to do."

"Her *boy friend*?" I cannot help myself: I am for once in

my life utterly shocked. Thunderstruck. Astounded. "You mean to tell us that she had a boy friend who – didn't object?"

"Sure." Samra looks at me with some amusement. "Hookers often have boy friends. Strippers can be married women."

"Hookers, yes." I respond quickly, as I don't want to appear to naïve. "But night club work isn't like that, is it? I mean, I thought the men weren't supposed to touch you, even if you lap dance right in their face."

Samra nods.

"That's right. And that's what I signed up for. Sexy titillation, but no pawing the shop window display, as you might say. If anyone fingers the girls in a decent club, they're thrown out by very big strong bouncers. So you do feel safe. It's all about suggestion – giving them something to fantasise about in their lonely lives or, possibly, spicing up their sex lives with the missus. They pay to watch us writhe about, and we deliver the goods It's a trade-off. No harm done. Know what I mean?"

There's a rather long silence now, as we all, separately, contemplate these ideas. Then –

"I can't think that any true feminist would agree with you." It's PF, and her eyes have narrowed to cobalt slits.

"Would you call yourself a feminist then, with all your fake tan and your hair extensions and the painted toenails?"

Samra goes in for the kill, before I can say the same thing myself. And me? Where do I stand on that? Nowhere, that's where. Have sat on fence for about a decade. Given up thinking about it. Lost the plot after the age of around twenty-three. Lazy. Lazy, *lazy* Lucy.

"I didn't mean necessarily me," says PF calmly, "though I have to say I respect the rights of women to decide their own destiny and not to demean themselves by doing things solely to please men. Especially," she adds slowly and it seems to me deliberately, "if they take money to do it."

"Oh, so you think I demeaned myself, do you?" Samra flares up, and Ann visibly retreats into a shell of self-protection, sighing a strange little sigh.

"I don't know," PF counters. "I wasn't there, and I haven't seen your act. But you said yourself earlier that you'd had enough, and that's why you're going into this marriage in Pakistan. You gave the distinct impression that you'd got disillusioned with it all."

"Hm. Yes, I guess I did." Samra is unruffling her feathers. "But it wasn't so much the club work – it was just the whole western thing. So much freedom, you can do whatever you want – so how do you know what you really want? What you really, *really* want?"

The Spice Girls float soundlessly above us. Yes. What does any of us really, really, really want? It's hard to say. Maybe, out of the four of us, Samra finally knows? And Ann? I don't, that's certain. Oh, I know what I'm going to do in Thailand, but how that will work out, I can't say, and I have to admit that I'm nervous, afraid; and I sense that PF is searching still for some Holy (or unholy?) Grail...

"All right." Samra becomes mellower, and we relax. "That all got a tad serious. Now, let's lighten up. I'm gonna tell you about some of the funny things that happen in the job, and that, when you look back, you can have a giggle at and kind of be glad you were part of, and that it was a part of your life? We can't erase what we've done; it's there, cast in stone, and we have to be happy about it, or – or –"

"Or you'll never go forward. Never make good of the time you have on this mortal earth. Isn't that right, now?"

This, quietly and soberly from Ann, hushes us all, and we kind of curl up and suck our thumbs, and wait for

Samra to entertain us. We could use a few laughs, that's certain.

* * *

"I guess the funniest thing I saw, "Samra resumes, "was when one of the girls got a bit over-energetic twirling upside down, right way up, then crossed legged and sideways on that fricking pole, at a faster pace than we usually did it, and her thong – which was small enough to begin with – suddenly snapped. I mean, what we wear – wore – might have been teeny-weeny-tinier-than-the-teeniest-bikini style, but it was meant to cover the one area we couldn't show in the pole dancing acts. Between the legs," she adds kindly, apparently for Ann's benefit, who merely inclines her head, seemingly unbothered. "The girl bit where it all happens," she elaborates. "Funny, when you think about it. Such a little area of the female and what a lot of stuff goes on in there, and comes out of there – "

"Including babies," says Ann, flaring up with sudden energy. "Don't forget the most important thing that a woman's body can do. Babies," she says softly, "validate the woman's physical self, and are gifts from God. All of them," she affirms, "every blessed one. And, girls," she adds, "I mean that as a feminist statement. Believe it or not, sure."

Oh right, Ann. You're the Irish original Germaine Greer, and I'm crediting every word you say. And trust you to distract us from what looked like a promising tale. Must you be so bloody reverent all the time? Shut the fuck up, woman. It was just getting to the interesting part.

Samra glances at her, not unkindly, almost you'd say *meditatively*, and then PF gets things on back on track.

"So what happened when the thong – um – departed from its anchorage, then?" she says, and I silently thank her, and turn away from the terminally irritating Ann. Any benign thoughts I conjured up have abruptly vanished like snowflakes in July.

"You might well ask!" Samra grins, widely. "It flew off with some force; they're pretty taut, and when they go, boy they go! Like pebbles from a catapult. This girl just freezes then on her pole, starkers, and as she's mid-splits, we all get a good old eyeful – and you can see plenty, believe me, 'cos we all have Brazilians or total shave-offs, so we get the full package of information – she's what you might call generously formed in that department."

We are blessed, at this point, with slightly unwelcome images. It seems that she senses this, for Samra hurriedly carries on.

"Well, the audience is cheering and the punters are standing up, and some of them have their mobile phones ready to take pictures, which is strictly against the rules, and poor old Patti, she's just going red all over, and I do mean all over, and doesn't know what to do with herself – 'cos whatever she does now is going to look pretty silly. And the thong – of course, it lands in someone's drink, or most of it, and this guy leaps up waving the soggy bit of stuff around, and makes like to suck it to get the liquor off, and rubs his face with it, and by now everyone is laughing, and mobile phone cameras are clicking enough to cause a lightning storm, and none of us can, as they say, only in this case literally, get our act together... And the best thing, you know, was that the boss loved it 'cos the punters loved it, and there was this great atmosphere, and when Patti finally manages to get down from her pole and sashays across the room, one of the guys fell right off his chair and it brought the house down!"

We contemplate this scene in our different ways: PF is smiling but isn't rolling about, I am laughing gently, but Ann is the surprise: she's giggling, not just a bit, but really going for it, giggling, shaking, almost choking, and then she sort of collapses sideways. What the – ? I come to the sudden conclusion that no-one in this select gang of four is what she seems; we are all layers and layers of our selves, and at this precise moment, Ann is the most puzzling of all.

"Oh merciful Heavens," she splutters, "I can just see you now, you girls, it must have been great to have the monotony of it broken like that! A human moment, all too human, we're all too – too –" gasp, giggle – "*human!*" and off she goes again. The mood is infectious, natch, so here we all are, laughing our silly socks off, Samra no less. Talk about female bonding; who'd have thought it would have been Ann to get us to this point? And what, I wonder wickedly, does God think about that?

As we sober up, and I move to the kitchen to make some tea, Samra says, pensive now, "You know, you hit the nail on the head there, Ann."

"I did? With the human thing?"

"No. When you said 'the monotony of it'. That's just what I've been groping to understand I thought it was the sleaziness that got to me, I thought it was the confusing range of choices we have in the UK, and the lack of direction, but no, as far as the stripping and pole dancing were concerned, it was the sheer bloody boredom of having to to do that routine *tonight* and *the next night* and *all the nights after that.* That's why a lot of us give it up, I reckon."

There is a thoughtful silence. I stir the leaves in the pot briskly; we've been provided with high quality loose tea, none of yer actual flaky little bags, thank you very much, and a lovely china pot in which to make it. (I am taken back for an instant to my laird's-lady-of-the-manor vision.) Fergus – or whoever – has taste. We sip our tea; somewhere along the line, this evening has turned into something different. We are not four separate people any more; we are a small, elite club. Oh yes, we're still all very different, exactly how different might take years to fathom, but in another way we're the same, and I'm not just talking about being stranded because of an ash cloud. For the first time in ages, I don't want the presence of any *man*, not Fergus, not Matende, not anyone else I might conjure up. We are enough for one another; we are complete.

Then PF breaks the ice.

"I guess any job becomes monotonous after a while. But in most professions you move on; you get promotion, you change departments, you change career, even. I guess with night club stuff you can only see more of the same, stretching out forever in front of you."

"Spot on." Samra's head nods vigorously. "And even if that 'forever" is only about six or seven years ahead, when you'll be too old – they don't want to look at even the faintest wrinkle or hint of flab – even then, it seems like eternity."

"But you must have had some fun with the other girls?" I ask, hopefully. It seems a pretty depressing picture to me, and I don't want to think of it like this. Anyone as beautiful and glamorous as Samra deserves to have had some cool times before she locks herself away in her marriage? *Wow, Lucy. You've just had a truly kind and empathetic thought about Samra! What's happening here? Eh? You tell me.*

"Sure," Samra says, a mite wistful, I think. "Of course we had good times. I shall miss some of it, and that's the truth. Some nights in the club were great: good audience, nobody stepping out of line, polite punters, boss pleased, bonuses for us – and then a great girlie get together afterwards and some real laughs. Some nights were crap, though: men trying to grope you when they knew they shouldn't, then they'd curse at you when you moved away, lots who'd had too much to drink and shouted out disgusting stuff; but then we'd get our own back – make fun of the punters afterwards."

She pauses for a moment, then affects a different voice, a Brummie and then a London accent.

"'Did you see that fella with the great big wart on his nose? Wonder if he's got one to match on his willy?' ...'I thought that guy in the front was going to pop out of his pants at one stage – haven't seen anything as big as that since I went shopping for marrows at Waitrose'... 'What about the squint-eyed bloke two tables back? Anyone else dance for him? I couldn't tell which part of me he was looking at...' and all that stuff. We got our own back, I can tell you. On nights like that –" and she looks meaningfully at PF –"I can honestly say I think the guys demeaned themselves far more than we ever did. Far, far more."

Ann and I nod, sagely. PF frowns, but then grudgingly grunts acquiescence. Blimey O'Reilly, I think I've actually spelt that right. Miss V. would be proud of me. This trip, or at least this interruption to it, is turning out to be quite educational, what with learning about other people's lives and cultures, a hitch-hiker's guide to America, art, architecture, design, the politics of pole dancing, even... Not to mention long-forgotten forays into self-expression, English grammar and spelling.

And oh hell, oh burning buckets of blood, if that isn't a chemical impossibility, talking of art and stuff has reminded me – I've invited Fergus and Matende over later for drinks at our place. Jumping up, I announce this exciting fact to the rest of the gang, who take it serenely enough, though I am as usual fretting about what to wear, and then I resent myself for it: I meant what I said about not needing any male company, that it would be an intrusion. To heck with it, then; I shall not worry about what I'm going to put on, I shall just wear something comfortable, perhaps my new gym gear, and they'll have to take me – and all of us – as they find us.

I totally think that's the healthiest thought, man-wise or any other-wise, that I've had in a very, very long time. Quite possibly ever.

The evening is going well. Our drinks cabinet, well stocked, has done us proud. Of course, it helps that Ann is a teetotaller, so doesn't drain us of anything more than a couple of glasses of watered down orange juice. I'm about to think up some cattish remark about this – on the lines of *for God's sake lighten up and have some fun, girl* – when a remark by Fergus stops me in my tracks.

"Mm," murmurs the beautiful Scottish one. "That Ann, now, she's a painter's ideal."

Huh? And here I was thinking that *I* was that very thing. Ann? Plump, wild-haired, unadorned, slightly bushy eyebrowed *Ann?*

"Yes," he continues now, as we fix some more drinks in the mini-kitchen. "That wonderful, lucid skin – so white, so unspoiled, as if she's lived on fruit and clean air for her whole life. And the eyes! An incredible shade of green."

Oh, I'll give him the eyes. They are a good colour. Just a little squeezed up and – little. I have to concede she has good, thick, dark lashes though; a redhead's envy. But her body? Those rather obvious ripples of flesh, the undoubtedly heavy-ish thighs?

"And her physique," says Fergus, relentless in his justification of artistic, painterly perfection. "She must look absolutely great on a chaise longue, all languid and –"

Not naked! My mind screams out. I really do not want to hear this. Granted, I have not seen her even in her probably large undergarments, but the dreadful picture is forming as he speaks.

"– draped in something silken, to show off those Ruebensesque lines," he finishes, and I breathe out in relief. I still do not, however, appreciate the way he rolls his rrrrs again and says "great" with such north-of-the-border enthusiasm. He is saying all the things he said – only a day ago – about me. It is then that something clicks in my excuse for a brain: maybe this lovely Fergus is a bit of a gadfly? Maybe he fixes on one beautiful artist's dream until he sees the next? After all, painters must be constantly stimulated by beauty every hour of every day. Yes, I've heard that they make unreliable partners, lovers.

Something in me shrivels slightly; not jealousy, no, more a kind of shrinking back, a caution. And then something else hits me too: *I don't care that much.* It's as if I'm living on two levels here: in the one, I'm playing out a kind of fantasy, a drama which can only last as long as the ash cloud stays over our little theatre of the airport; on the other, there is Lucy, as ever, stolid, solid, scientist Lucy, mediocre school teacher, on her way to Thailand to carry out a mission in which she must not, cannot fail.

I smile at Fergus, indulgently, as one would tolerate a child, an eager adolescent with his coursework assignment, and we take our drinks back to the lounge.

On the way, I whisper in his ear. What does he think of the fabulous Princess Faren, in that case? But I think I already know the answer.

She's too – lanky, he says. Too blonde, too tanned, too – everything. And she has no tits. Artists like tits.

Well, Ann's home and dry on that one, then.

And then I look at Ann, who is engaged in quite animated conversation with Matende, and I really *look*, and suddenly I see her through Fergus's eyes. Her own eyes dance with spirit – and I don't mean the alcoholic kind – and her quite dainty mouth lifts upwards to reveal flawless teeth, and the pale, almost creamy skin with its faint rose on the cheeks, just where it should be, glows in the soft lighting of the lounge. The tangling hair has been ensnared tonight by a sort of snood – if that's the word – that holds it back into her neck, and shows a delicate line of jaw, right up to small, neat ears, usually hidden. The modest blouse she wears cannot totally conceal a glimpse of pearly throat, and those breasts are full and firm against the fabric.

Fergus is right, damn the man: in her own, rather chaotic, utterly natural way, she is gorgeous. Why have I not seen this before? I can only think that it's because she is so far from the magazine ideal of what women should be: skinny, blonde with long, straight hair, heavily made up, especially round the eyes, which look as if they've not slept for several months, and wearing shoes that look like instruments of medieval torture on the end of their bony legs. Clones of each other, the lot. Ann would not merit a second glance in a fashionable, cool bistro or bar. Which would be everyone's loss. More than a little stunned by the way my thoughts are taking me, I go quiet for a while, and watch the others.

The evening winds on. Matende has now taken a real shine to Samra, who is flirting with him in a rather half-hearted way. I can tell that it's about as genuine as her pole dancing: i.e., she might be enjoying the act, but there's nothing doing. Poor old Matt. I wonder if she's told him about her upcoming marriage? I mean, she's still a free woman technically, but she shouldn't lead him up the garden path. Or is it just supplying him with a fantasy to get off on, like she used to provide in the clubs? More importantly, do I feel jealous about this? Answer, no.

What is happening here? I felt oddly pleased that Fergus didn't think much of PF, for all her sophisticated glamour but I completely wasn't jealous of his professional adoration of Ann. I feel only sorry for Matende, but I don't blame Samra either. It's a free world, after all, and we're just bit parts in this present, odd little universe. Which, earlier or later, is going to end – at least, our orbit. Well, in about five billion years, anyway. Soon enough.

At this awe-inspiring thought, and remembering what lies ahead for me, I shiver, and pull my light shrug round my shoulders Fergus looks at me with concern.

"Air-con too high, Lucy?" he asks, and I nod, thankful for the get-out.

"Tell you what," he says. "It's nearly nine, and I don't suppose any of you have eaten? How about we go and have some dinner?"

And so we do, in an excellent restaurant in one of the hotels, which serves mostly French and Italian food, and even Ann joins us, which I thought she might not, and trucks cheerfully through a massive pasta dish and several side ones. I murmur to Fergus, wickedly, that this is how she gets in training as an artist's model, and he chuckles, and strokes my arm. This is pleasant, but – that's all. No real thrill there. Strange, that. But then, we're in public and – and –

Oh, I don't know what. Let the night roll.

Roll it does, then, with laughter and a lot of daft jokes about ash clouds and so on. Matt is amazing, with a sharp wit and a keen mind; good company, and we are all very taken by him, Fergus relaxing now that his attention is focused on Samra, and PF leaning back in her chair and looking tranquil and at ease. She noticed the stroking of my arm, and flashed her blue gaze at me quizzically. Without meaning to, I shrugged, and gave a small downward turn of my mouth. At which she smiled, and looked like a cat that had got the cream.

But I wasn't angry, merely pitied her. Don't think about Fergus, love, I mentally willed her to hear. You don't do a thing for him.

And then I wondered why I felt a bit angry *for* her. A bit annoyed with Fergus, of all things? Shouldn't I be glad that he doesn't like her? That she's too scraggy and tall and titless for him? Well, I reckon I should, but I'm not. I just feel somehow indignant that he can't see the loveliness in that long, elegant, form, that he he can't see the strong, carved cheekbones, the firm, lazily humorous mouth, the incredible eyes. It's not as if all women have to conform to one ideal, is it? Plump, angular, thin, curvy – we an all be pleasing just how we are.

"Right!" the man in question says now, interrupting all such wayward ponderings. "I propose a toast!" He raises his glass. "To the Volcanic Six!"

Everyone laughs, including me. I come back to myself, rejoin the moment. Glasses are lifted, and clinked.

"And here's to the Axminster Four," I say, "and all the memories of the happy hours we spent on that luxurious carpet!"

"You have to be kidding!" says PF, smiling broadly. "That carpet was more like punishment by concrete than any kind of luxury! My bones are still feeling it."

But she drinks to the toast amiably, along with the rest of us, and Fergus says, more seriously:

"You know, guy and gals, I'd love to stay in touch with you all. This has been – is being – quite an episode."

Strange that he should use that word; it is indeed, an *episode* and that is all it is. I am not so sure we should give contact details – you know the drill: emails, mobile numbers, Facebook addresses and profiles, all that stuff. Three months, two months down the line, a month even from now, when we're flung thousands of miles apart, will we remember? Will we care?

With a sudden jolt, I realise that only yesterday I was revelling in the fact that plain old Luce had managed to snare herself two great looking men, had been wined and dined, admired – and respected. Why am I out of the blue so indifferent to all of that? But it's a fact: I don't mind if

Matende gets it on with someone else and as for Fergus – I just don't know.

Coffee arrives, and we all sober up a bit. It's been a fabulous night, we all agree on that, and if we're still here tomorrow, we'll do it again. It's now that it strikes me: what Samra was saying about the tedium of repetition. Yes, it's been terrific but I wouldn't want it to go on exactly like this for ever. Rich people, celebrities who can live this lifestyle every day – I don't envy them. *Oh not another lunch at The Ivy... Not another evening at Stringfellow's...*

Fergus, with his uncanny instinct, knows my mind again; or perhaps he just reads my sobering face.

"Tomorrow is another day, Lucy," he says, quietly. "We'll do something quite different. How about I hire a car and we drive somewhere, get out of the airport. The others can message us if there's any change, though I don't imagine there will be for a day or two."

I am entirely grateful for this suggestion. Perhaps meeting five new people in a few days – and discovering a new Lucy into the bargain, or possibly rediscovering something of a long-buried old one? – has been just a little intense, if not overwhelming. A drive into nearby countryside would be –

"Wonderful!" I say. "Just the job."

Fergus smiles, his crinkly, Scotsman smile, and my misgivings vanish like butter in a heated pan.

"Good," he says, "I'll meet you at ten in the foyer."

We find a quiet moment now and he takes me in his arms. I have to stand on tiptoe a bit, or he'd never have managed the long, tender kiss he gives me. He kisses well. Not too much tongue bashing or going for the tonsils, but a nice range of lip play. His mouth is firm and dry, his skin just the right balance between smooth and a tiny bit stubbly.

So why am I analysing it? Why aren't I just into the

moment and snogging him back like crazy, forcing the pace? Why am I mentally giving him marks out of ten for technique? Eh? I try for ecstasy, run my hands up and down the back of his neck, tug a lock of that curling hair. It's all very nice, but nice is not quite what I want.

I wonder what it'd be like kissing Matende?

* * *

So now we have the big breakdown. No, I don't mean we're cracking up at last, I mean that girlie thing that we do, you know? Where you sit up half the night going over every little detail of what happened – who said what, what it might all mean, how you felt… sure, you've been there. We all have. Men, they just go home, switch on the TV in hopes of catching late footie replays, throw their clothes in a heap, and sack out.

But we women, we want to pick it all over, like the bones in a fish, carefully discarding the colourless bits and keeping the succulent pieces to chew over, as we are doing right now.

"Well," says Ann, surprising us by joining in with this gossipy stuff, and turning to Samra, "you seem to have caught the attention of one young Mister Matende, then? And you to be married soon, sure."

"Ah," I put in swiftly, oddly wanting to defend Samra, though I'm not sure why. Perhaps I suddenly like her better because she didn't seem to want him to chat her up? But then that would mean … and no, I'm not bothered. Am I?

"Ah," I say, "but the fair Samra wasn't really encouraging him, Ann. Didn't you notice that?"

Samra actually blushes. This is not something I ever thought I'd see in a stripper-cum-pole-dancer. There is a silence, broken by PF.

"Well?"

There is no mistaking that this is directed at Samra, and that it is not a question, but a command. In other words, *explain yourself.*

"Yes." As usual, I rush in. probably with both clodhopping feet, but Samra's will-she-won't-she behaviour tonight has got me both irritated and intrigued – if you can be both those things at once. "Yes, Samra, come on, tell us what you were about. Don't you feel tempted to just cut and run, get out of this marriage thing and go away with someone else? Wouldn't you rather have someone younger, really attractive – like Matende? Well wouldn't you?"

"Um," says our exotic dancer reluctantly, "I have to admit that I found him a tad fanciable, but I'm not interested in making out with anyone at this stage. I'm just preparing myself for my future life." She sees our faces. "Honestly. What I'm about to do is really serious. I've thought about it for a long time – years, in fact – and I'm cool with my decision"

"Yes," I say, before I can stop the old blabber mouth going into action, "I do half way believe you, but you're still unwed so why not make hay while the sun shines? Last Chance Saloon, know what I mean?"

Ann is looking at me askance. I can see she knows what I'm on about, and disapproves. Well, sucks to you, uptight lady. My heckles rise; and when they rise, boy they go up.

"Stop looking at me like that," I almost shout in Ann's face. "Just because you're a strait-laced religion freak doesn't mean you're always *right.*"

"Lucy, be careful what you say." PF intervenes, puts out a restraining hand, but I'm too far gone to listen.

"Can't a girl have one last bit of fun before she commits to something that I don't think any of the rest of us would willingly do? Life as a bride in a strict, third world country, where there's no getting out? Have you thought of it that way? Have you?"

Ann sighs; a curious, sad sound.

"As a matter of fact, I have. And it wouldn't justify an act of betrayal or stupidity, I don't know which is the greater."

"Oh for God's sake!"

Now I really explode, and get up to bang around in the kitchen with kettle, teapot, coffee and cups, rattling the spoons like things flying round in a tornado. It's the old, infamous redhead temper coming out, that's what it is; and maybe too if I'm truthful, a bit too much of the vino and a vague sense of depression that I didn't find Fergus's sweet kisses more sexy.

Carrying a heavy tray of supper stuff, I attempt dignity as I hold my head up high and put out cups, plates, pots of tea and coffee and small biscuits in a dead hush of my own creation. Tea is poured, and coffee is served, and nobody says anything for a while.

Then –

"I think," says Samra, the colour fading from her cheeks, "I think, Lucy, that you're trying to make me act out something you wouldn't mind yourself."

I gasp, and cling onto a chair back. The cheeky, cheeky bitch. The clever, smart-arsed know-it-all. Trouble is, she's right. This hits me like a blow in the stomach, and all the puffed up rage goes out of me. I sag down onto one of the deluxe sofas, all too aware that the other three are looking at me with what I think is some kind of *understanding*. Which I could do without.

"Don't be so silly," I say tartly. "I'm seeing Fergus, and he's smashing, and treats me so well. I'm really, really happy about that. Truly I am. Very happy. I haven't met such a great bloke in yonks."

And to my amazement, and consternation, I abruptly

burst into tears. No, more than tears – huge sobs and then a crescendo of howls like a tomcat in a night garden. WTF is the matter with me? I must want my head examined. In the silence that naturally follows, I restrain myself gradually to heavy sobs, then sniffles. It is PF who speaks first. Very quietly.

"Ah, Fergus. Yes, the unarguably remarkable Fergus. Every woman's dream, isn't he?"

Is she being sarcastic? I can't tell; she is looking at me with those penetrating eyes narrowed, as if weighing things up. Which she probably is.

"Mm, he is a dreamboat, that's for sure." This from Ann. Oh God, she's so outdated in her slang it make me want to scream. *Dreamboat* indeed!

"Fergus, I say, gradually recovering through sniffs and muted sobs, "is a very nice man. He's gentle, courteous, considerate, and doesn't push things."

"But maybe you want – or need – someone who does?"

It's PF again, blast her all-seeing psychic bloody intelligence. But you know what? I actually think this time she's wrong.

"I have done in the past," I say, firmly, sitting up straight and sipping the welcome tea. "But not any more. I want something else now. Something more grown up, less – trashy. You know what I mean?"

PF nods, the piercing gaze softens.

"I do," she says, "I do indeed. Well, Lucy then you'd best just get on with seeing him and let it go where and as it will. And Samra? What will you do?"

"Nothing." Samra too sits upright and takes a biscuit from the tray. "I'm going to stick to my resolution. I've had enough of what Lucy calls 'fun' to last me till the next millennium. The meal was fine, the company was great, but I don't want Matende hanging round me, and if he takes offence, well, so be it. I can't help that."

"Fair enough," I say, feeling a lot more well-disposed to her. "But I hope he doesn't think you're being racist."

Samra cracks into laughter.

"Oh Lucy, Lucy, haven't you noticed? I have brown skin Don't you think I've had enough racism thrown at me in my time? You just have to learn to take it, and to realise that not *all* rejection is because you're Asian or black."

"Mmm," I say. "Maybe. All the same, just be careful."

"I think," says PF, "that it's you who's going to have to be careful, Lucy."

Oh blimey. Back to me again. I thought we'd done with all that. Will this woman ever stop trying to sort me out? At least Samra doesn't try to give me advice, even if I'm doling it out to her.

"Look," I reply, "I'm taking on board what you said. I'll just go with the flow as far as Fergus is concerned. I like him very much and I guess I'm simply confused because I've never been out with anyone like him before"

"But you fancy Matende, don't you?" PF persists. I wish she'd shut up. You can go off people. Very quickly, it seems.

"In a superficial way. Who wouldn't?"

"Ah, you admit it." She is really getting my goat now.

"As I said, superficially, but it's nothing serious. Don't you find him just the tiniest bit attractive, my dear, posh Princess? Huh?"

And now she gives me a long, long, cool stare, and I feel my bravado wither on the vine. She can have this effect, and I can just see her making mincemeat of my most troublesome Science set, 9BG/K. Even that little pillock Stephen Foredock would crumple with her standing over him. Perhaps I could persuade her to come to England and –

"No, as a matter of fact, I don't." The voice is like the sea becalmed, and as steady as the Rock of Gibraltar, as the old song goes. (I know this one from my Nan; I'm not into things like that. Not that you imagined I was?) "I don't find Matende in the least attractive, wholly nice guy that he is, nor do I remotely fancy Fergus."

Oh. Ah. Okay. My two scrumptious men that I prided myself on acquiring have just been rubbished by the haughty Princess F. Well, I might point out to her that neither of them fancied her either, or took any real notice so could she be speaking out of the old sour grapes? Hm?

"And in case you're interested, Lucy," the mild tone continues, "I'm not piqued in the least. I go for a very different type. *Very, very different.*"

"Such as?" I can't help challenging her, and even Ann and Samra, who have been keeping their heads down during this little volley, perk up a mite and show a certain curiosity. PF has kept this side of herself utterly remote and distant during these three fraught days. In fact she has kept most of herself thuswise.

"Oh, you'll find out in due course." PF smiles, like that infuriating Cheshire Cat, and of course we are all left agog, wondering quite when Her Highness will deign to unwrap the layers of her personality and Reveal All. At the rate she's going, the ash cloud'll have to stay over us for another year.

Soon, we bunk down for the night in our blissful beds, Ann pouring oil on troubled waters as she flits through in her fleecy cotton pyjamas and sensible slippers – slippers! – brightly announcing that she had a "real cailigh tonight and enjoyed every bit of it". Such perky good humour is hard to resist, and we part in peace.

PF is right, of course, and so is Samra. I must leave the latter to go her own path, batty though I think she is, and I must calm down about Fergus and Matt and just enjoy what it is, or is not. After all, compared with Thailand, it really isn't so important – in fact, not important at all. This strange and unlooked for – episode, as Fergus calls it – will fade quickly, and we will forget each other, or begin to, the moment the plane leaves the ground. But if nothing else, meeting Fergus has reacquainted me with that other part of myself, one that has been too long ruthlessly ignored. I suppose you might call it the sensitive side.

But as I drift off into the sinking sensation of sleep, when thoughts become absurdly scrambled and which state I love, I idly speculate as to the type of man – "very, very different" – that PF might go for. A Harvard professor, all cool casual gear, long hair in a neat pony, gold rimmed specs, spouting political insights? A rich banker in New York, with a snazzy apartment, villas here, there and everywhere, possibly a yacht? A latter day hippie with giant Easy Rider bike, genuine perma-tan and headband, who is actually an avant garde rock musician known and loved only by the *cognoscenti*? Oooh, Lucy, there's a big word for this time of night – or at any time for that matter. And I think I even spelled it right.

Go to sleep now, girl, before your brain implodes like a Chemistry experiment gone wrong.

The last vision I have is of PF directing her iciest blue glare at Stephen Foredock in the Science lab, and him on his knees, sobbing remorse and pledging never to use That Language again, or wave an inflated condom around near a Bunsen burner.

Accordingly, I giggle myself to dreamland.

The morning comes, as mornings tend to, I've found (there's a brilliant piece of scientific deduction for you), and brings the reliable Fergus, looking good in casual, day-in-the-country gear. Is there anything this man would not look cool in?

"Not that we'll be able to go very far, Lucy," he warns. "I listened to the early news and it looks very much as though we're in for a change of wind direction that'll blow the cloud away, and then after perhaps another day, flights will start to go out. We should be reasonably close to the airport to pick up information."

There's a pause here. I think they call it a hiatus. I seem to remember Miss Viner using that word quite a lot, back in the distant fog of time. Never imagined I'd find a use for it, but there you go. So this – hiatus thing goes on for a bit. Is he waiting for me to say something? If he's thinking that I'd imagined we might take off and stay the night somewhere else, he's barking up the wrong proverbial tree. So I say nothing.

"Darn it!" says Fergus almost inaudibly and, swinging the car keys, escorts me out to the hire car – which is snazzy. Very snazzy indeed.

I wonder not for the first time just how much money this man has and who he actually is? I also recognise that I do not wholeheartedly share his unmistakable regret at the thought of this strange interlude ending. I have managed to get through to Thailand again from the phone in our room, and though I know they – he, in particular – now understand the reason for my delay, I can sense a kind of wariness, a growing feeling of being left in the lurch.

Well, I might feel the same way if I was at the other end, I suppose. So I'm wanting now to get on with it, to go ahead with what I have to do; to shake off this delightful state of illusion and re-enter the real and probably quite grim world. You simply can't stay in five star hotels for ever; it isn't *living*. You'd miss the messiness of cosy, everyday life – the collection of unwashed mugs from last night's natter with the girls, papers and books in a pile on the dining table, the slightly chaotic kitchen with its muddle of plants and unmatching plates and bowls and cookery books and funny little ornaments, the old cat on its hairy blanket in the basket chair in the corner – the clutter of a natural lifestyle, not out of a brochure. Know what I mean? Yeah, go and hug that cat.

I'm also musing on the peculiar conversation with PF this morning, when we were both just awake (PF has started getting up not long after me for some reason, though maybe she's too polite to tell me that my early rising disturbs her? No, don't think so) and having a leisurely coffee in the lounge, Ann having taken herself off to the running track again in her baggy sweat pants and the same PT shirt, the stunning Samra snoring quite loudly from the bedroom.

"I hope her hubby-to-be is either deaf or has a good supply of ear muffles," I said, rather nastily, and PF suppressed a guffaw.

We looked at each other then, the *contretemps* of last night forgotten, and without thinking, and right off the cuff, I said,

"PF, you're incredibly calm and level and all that, but I get the impression that you're sitting on something – I don't know quite what. Oh, I'm sorry, that was clumsy of me. If you don't want –"

"No, it's okay, Lucy." PF refilled her cup and took it up in her long hands with the long fingers and immaculately painted nails. (How does she manage it in these conditions? Mine break, chip the varnish and generally get tatty within a day of doing them. I suppose she might have those acrylic false ones, but even so. The only time I tried those they snagged my science lab gloves and some of them dissolved in a solution I was working with. Science teacher + glamour does not equate.) "So are you saying that you think I'm unhappy? Seriously, tell me."

Now she'd caught me on the hop. I was not sure what I meant, which means that, as per usual, Little Lucy should have kept her mouth well and truly shut. Not for the first time in my life, I found myself hoist on my own petard, hamstrung by my own curiosity, like the cat. (Which got killed. My gran used to prophesy darkly that I would end up like that. Beginning to believe her.) However, PF was actually looking at me in quite a friendly way, so perhaps I hadn't done too much damage. More carefully, I thought about it for a short while, and then, slowly, I explained.

"Not – unhappy exactly. Just that you come across as kind of – biding your time? You look as if you're watching and waiting, if that doesn't sound too daffy."

I was surprised again as PF blessed me with the most radiant, slow-burning but beautiful smile.

"Very perceptive, Lucy," she murmured. "Though what I'm waiting for, and who or what I'm watching, will have to remain a secret. For the time being."

"Fine." I know all about keeping things to yourself, and I didn't blame her in the least. Still, she'd got me itching to find out now. So – "But will you tell me – us? – before we all go our separate ways?"

PF pursed her lips, considered, head on one side, still studying me like a lynx after its prey. This, I can tell you, was unnerving.

"Yes," she said at last. "I don't see why not."

And with that I had to be content. I could get no more

out of her. She clammed up again into that watchful stillness, but she thanked me for caring, and remarked that I had strong and accurate intuitions when my impetuous tongue didn't get in the way of careful observation and reflection... blah-de-blah-de-blah. I regarded all this as a bit of a back handed compliment, if you ask me, but then we quite peaceably got showered and dressed, and went our separate ways – though PF didn't say where.

Before Fergus arrived I was in for another slight shock, even if I could have partly seen this coming. Ann came back just as Samra finally roused herself (she's the latest sleeper of all of us, probably due to all that late night work; she'll have to shape up when she's a good Muslim wife, won't she? Breakfast for Hubby, all that stuff. God preserve me from marriage) and the two of them shared a kind of brunch in the kitchenette – Ann having managed to procure the ingredients for what she called a "terrific old fry-up". I noted that Samra noshed through the sausages but left the bacon, or didn't take any, and I wondered, until I realized that Ann, more considerate than stupid blockhead Lucy would have been, had got beef bangers, the fair Samra being Muslim and all that. I only hoped they were *halal*. Anyway, there they were, Samra and Ann, that is, emptied and greasy plates in front of them, chomping mountains of toast and swilling it all down with a huge pot of tea, and I honestly couldn't help overhearing some of what they were saying.

(Well, you can't avoid it when you creep as close as possible to a doorway without being detected, whilst appearing to be doing your makeup and needing the door frame to lean on, can you?)

"It seems to me," mused Ann, then, "that Islam and Christianity have quite a lot in common – though some big differences too. The biggest worry I'd have is the treatment of women."

142

"In Pakistan, you mean?"

"Well, yes. Without being offensive, I hear that they're a bit – traditional. Are you sure you can take this, after all the freedoms you've been used to here?"

I could almost see Samra shrugging – as if to slough off Ann's words, though to be fair, our Irish friend was speaking quietly, mildly, and and it came across as genuine concern.

Reluctantly – "I've not had a problem when I've visited in the summers. You just – change your habits a bit, dress a little differently, is all."

"But a holiday," persisted Ann, "is not the same as living somewhere for good – and especially not as a wife. Are you absolutely sure that –"

I could feel Samra's irritation, and I sympathised, but Ann – in my opinion – had valid reasons to say what she did.

"Look," Samra, impatient. "We'll be living in a big city, not out in the sticks somewhere, and city life in Pakistan isn't bad, especially if it's Karachi or Islamabad. Don't forget I was brought up in a Muslim family in England – and my dad was quite firm about the rules. They make sense, you know, when you think about them. They really do."

"Well." This was Ann, "I just hope you're right, and you do know what you're in for. Are you absolutely, completely sure you're ready for it? You're still very young, isn't that so?"

A silence. And then Samra said, very low, so that I had almost to rest my ear on the crack in the door frame to hear, "If I'm to be entirely truthful, I will have to work at it. Faisal is a good, good man, and together we'll face up to the difficulties. I'm lucky. His family likes me, and are happy for him – and that's a good start."

"Ah, yes." Ann's voice gave away that she was smiling. "Families. The blessing and curse of our lives! But it's really going to test you out, my dear. You must be ready for that."

Goodness. Apart from anything else, Ann saying Samra is "very young", when she is herself only – what? Twenty-eight at most? – and then calling her 'dear'. It made her sound like a maiden aunt or something. But there was a long sigh from Samra, and the sounds of more tea being poured, toast being crunched.

"It is – going to be the test of a lifetime. But my destiny is to marry Faisal, and the difference in cultures, the way of life – I guess I'll just have to do a lot of learning quite fast, and have a heap of patience."

"You will, sure." Ann spoke very softly now, tender, and I could feel her arm going round Samra's shoulders. "I will put you in my prayers every night, so I will. Every single night."

Before I could begin to heave, I moved hastily into the bedroom, busied myself in there tidying up. If Ann had said that to me, I'd have been mad as hell. *Who asked you to pray for me? I'd have said. Who needs all that patronising crap?* And yet, Samra from what I could hear didn't seem to be objecting – regardless of the fact that an infidel woman was praying for her. This was getting odder by the day, the hour. And then that admission that Samra's known she was going to marry this man since – when? – childhood. So an arranged, if not a forced marriage after all? Maybe her own family are flying out later, when the arrangements have been made? She must have relations over there, for sure – all those summer visits. I shook myself with annoyance; why was I getting so wound up about Samra's stuff? It's her problem, after all.

Besides which, all this talk of cultural differences cross-culture clashes, the problems of adapting, was starting to get to me. I couldn't help wondering if… if… thinking of my own situation… And there I stopped myself right

144

away, and turned my face and my attention to my day out with Fergus.

* * *

I am mulling over these strange events as the car glides swiftly and smoothly away from the airport and its ugly network of approach roads, its nest of hotels, it runways and loading areas and wire fences and all the junk of modern travel, and quite quickly we are in lanes, with trees arching overhead and fields to either side. I marvel, and Fergus chuckles.

"Heathrow isn't so far away from open country," he reminds me. "Airports seem ginormous when you're in them, but in fact they're quite economical in land space. Now, I happen to be familiar with this area. How about a walk, and then some lunch at a nice wee pub I know?"

"Sounds good to me," I respond, and mean it. This is my chance to get to see Fergus in more normal surroundings, in a more normal way; it feels like a daytime date, which it is. He's very relaxed, and takes my hand quite spontaneously as we park the car and find a convenient walkers' path through pretty farmland and a bit of woodland. It's sunny today and there's a light wind which makes it perfect for walking, though if you weren't on the move it might be chilly.

"Funny," I remark, looking upwards. "There's this cloud of ash up there and yet the sun's shining through. I expected it to look all grey and grainy – like a partial eclipse or a badly developed photo."

Fergus laughs. "I know what you mean. But it isn't like that. The ash is very fine, and its danger is that it could fly into plane engines at high altitudes and kind of clump together to clog them up – and that wouldn't be at all clever."

I did know all this but I don't want to say so. It's just that knowing something scientifically doesn't mean that you're any the less likely sometimes to visualise things in quite a primitive way.

"Umm," I say, reflectively. "I'm kind of disappointed. I almost expected an enormous, hovering mass of a great burnt-out fire – you know something dramatic. I mean, it's caused all this disruption, and there's nothing to *see*."

Fergus laughs at me again, but gently, and equally gently draws me to him.

"Ah Lucy, Lucy," he says, and his eyes become serious. "What am I going to do without you?"

"Erm – survive, I guess," I say, rather ungraciously, and firmly detach myself. "Just as you did before you met me."

There's a bit of a silence as we walk on, and then Fergus stops. I turn round to look and he's staring at me as if seeing me for the first time.

"You're a puzzle, Lucy," he says finally. "You're a lovely woman in every way. And yet there's this hard edge to you that I don't understand."

Immediately I feel a real lowdown, ungrateful moron. Just what is wrong with me? Only two or three days ago I met this fabulous bloke, this every-sane-woman's- dream, Fergus, and was on cloud nine, and since then my emotions have been up and down and sideways and all over the place. I am not even remotely likely to be pregnant and it's far too soon for me to be menopausal. I am not in the dreaded PMT period, so I can't blame that get-out of "my hormones".

"Look, I'm sorry, Fergus. It's just... it's just... I have to... have..."

"You have a lot on your mind," he finishes for me, and for the second time in less than twenty-four hours I start to cry. And all at once I wish I was back in our hotel room, with the other three in our little gang-of-four, with other women, and that I could snuggle into that deep, lush sofa and eat chocolates and drink Ann's good tea and watch rubbish television. Out here, with a man I don't actually know at all when it comes down to it, in the open fields and paths, under that wide expense of sky, it's all too much in the harsh light of day – which quite apart from anything else must be making my freckles stand out like mud splashes on putty. At this totally disconnected thought I splutter a half choke of laughter and tears.

"Here, Lucy," says Fergus moderately. "Come and sit on this log with me. Here's a tissue. Cry as much as you want. Talk if you want, or not if you don't want. I'll listen – or not, as you choose. Take your time."

The empathy comes through, and washes over me I might not know this man, or much about him, that is, but I think that, odd though it sounds, he does know me – or enough to appreciate what I need right now. Which is to sit on a log, with the sun on my wetted face, the wind drying it, and breathe deeply for several minutes, as if letting out all the tension, all the fear, the worry and the apprehension. And the sorrow. Yes, the sorrow.

At this, my eyes water faster and it runs down my cheeks, and I cry for her as I have never been able to, all this time. It is a good feeling, and Fergus just sits beside me, not touching, not even looking at me; just there. A bird sings in the hedgerow, and I pull myself out of the misery to listen to its beautiful music.

And then, I find myself telling Fergus, this lovely, kind, patient man that I truly do not deserve, all that is on my mind and all that lies ahead of me, my fears about what I am undertaking, the terrible uncertainties, and he only listens and nods or shakes his head occasionally, and then he holds me again, but as a friend, a true buddy, and I know that I have found a friend indeed; perhaps nothing more, but I am thankful.

"And you will keep in touch?" he says at last, when I am done. "You brave, brave wee soul, Lucy,. I couldn't do what you are about to do, and I am in awe of you for that. No –" as I protest that nobody on this earth should ever be aweful of short, pudgy, freckled, bog-standard Lucy (other than Stephen Foredock when he disrupts my lessons) – "I mean it. You're quite wonderful, in every respect, and I would like think you will at least come to see me in Glasgow when we're back in this country after all our exploits. Is that a deal? Say you will, Lucy."

I look into his eyes, the generous face; how can I refuse? And in any case, I don't want to. I like this man. I might never do anything more than like him, who can tell? And I have far too much on my plate right now to consider such questions in any case, no emotional energy to spare. But liking is a great deal, and so I say yes, I will most definitely come and see you in Scotland, and he smiles, a bright, happy smile, and then I swear him to secrecy.

"I might tell the other three about my trip to Thailand," I say, "and I might not. I suspect we all have things that we haven't told each other – even Ann – so we'll see how it goes. But for the moment – don't say a word."

"Very wise. My lips are, as they say, sealed." Fergus gestures approvingly. "And now, lassie, ma braw wee lassie, how about that lunch?"

* * *

"And how did your day go with the adorable Ferugus?" Samra asks teasingly. For once I do not mind; I feel more relaxed than for – ages, longer than I can remember.

"I would say it went rather well," says PF before I can get a word in edgeways, "judging by Lucy's expression and the glowing complexion."

Am I mistaken, or is there a tinge of envy here? Certainly

it does not come over with particular goodwill.

"It was fine," I say lightly. "We agreed to stay in touch as friends."

"Is that all?" Samra wants to provoke, I can see, but I don't rise to it. I am feeling much too spaced for that. I note, however, that PF has visibly softened. So she said she didn't find Fergus remotely attractive? In denial then, as they say on daytime TV? Or possibly just envious of Samra and me reeling in two very good looking guys, whilst she's seeing no action at all? Bitchy-bitch Lucy, at it again. Oh heck, it's all too tiring to try and work out. At this precise nano-second, a revelation flashes across my mind: *But PF is not looking for any action.* Now where did that come from?

We're sitting down for our ritual pot of tea around six when PF abruptly reminds us that we each have a second story to tell, and that we are still honour bound to keep to the pact and judge the best at the end.

"In that case we'd better get on with it," I say, briskly. "Fergus thinks the cloud might shift in another day or so, and then, soon after, they'll start to get the planes off the ground."

"Thank the good Lord," breathes Ann, piously, clasping her hands in front of her prominent tits. If I hadn't begun to see her more as a person, I'd have thrown a sugar lump at her, but I let it pass.

"Why?" demands Samra. "Are we so horrible, then?"

"Ah now, you know that isn't the thing at all," says Ann serenely. "I am just anxious to get on my way and join him in his valuable work."

Of course. I think we've all forgotten that this dowdy, if strangely lovely young woman has a man waiting for her someplace in Africa, and that this must be quite a torment for her. I start to picture their night of reunion: tight zips are struggled with, a skirt is forced over wide, wriggling hips, the large undergarments fly off and up into the air in abandon, the plump thighs…

No, shut that out. I really don't need nightmares.

Instead I say,

"Okay, PF. It's your turn, 'cos you told the first one. You'll have to recap on that for Sarma, won't you?"

"Guess you're right they-er," drawls PF in an exaggerated accent.

Now Samara shocks us rigid by saying, placidly, "It's okay, PF. Ann filled me in on this one."

And for once, PF just sits there with her mouth open; for once, she looks slightly less than dignified; for once, she cannot think of anything to say. I don't blame her; I have to admit I am equally stuck for words, for the second time in this strange situation; I cannot quite get my head round Ann relating the flasher-iin-the-woods story, as it were, in its entire unwholesome detail, but Samra firmly asserts that yes, she got the lot, and found it interesting –

"Especially," she finally murmurs, "as we get a few like that in the trade – or should I say got. I'm out of it now."

"And God be praised for that," says Ann, rather too loudly, at which I frown, PF looks stony, and Samra bends her head, whether in embarrassment or some kind of submission is not clear.

"So," says PF, evidently wanting to move on from this moment. We all do. "Well, my turn again. Are you sitting comfortably?" – this last with an playful, sideslung smile. No, she's not taking the piss, just having a bit of fun, which I could do with, so no hard feelings there. We nod solemnly, like nursery kids. I could swear that Ann's thumb actually has found its way to her mouth.

"Then I'll begin."

"There was a child born who was neither boy nor girl. And yet, both."

PF begins thus, quite flatly; we all adjust our heads to get round this phenomenon – which of course we've heard of, but didn't expect to come up like here, like now. Ann says, quietly,

"Ah yes. A hermaphrodite. Poor soul."

Shoving aside my amazement that she should (a) know about such a thing, (b) use the correct word for it and (c) mention it aloud in company, I follow her lead.

"Mm. It's true. Such things do happen – although nowadays we call such individuals Intersex, which is probably more accurate. It can be when the ovum divides and then each part is fertilised, with the fusion of two zygotes early in the development, or an ovum can be fertilised by two sperm, carrying different sex genes, or even when two ova fuse with one male zygote and one female; and there can be a mutation in the SRY gene. All these things are quite rare and – "

"Thank you for that priceless information," says PF drily. "I'm sure we'll all be joining your Chemistry class in September – or shouldn't that be Human Biology?"

Her eyes quiz me, and I'm wondering if she's questioning my knowledge and expertise, though I've given a pretty accurate account, so I don't think so. Just her usual sarcasm, directed, as usual at me; and I can't be bothered, at this point, to go into why. She's probably pissed off that I've hijacked her story, though I didn't mean to. It's the scientist in me. Through and through like a name in a piece of seaside rock.

I reply tartly that I might have done Chemistry 'major', as they call it in the States, but I also took courses in Biology and for that matter Zoology and Botany. Ask me anything about the Dianthus Barbatus (Sweet William to you) or mammals of the subfamily Erinaceinae (order of Erinaceomorpha) or whatever and I'm your woman. PF humphs, and the laser beams recede.

"Well," she says at length, "Ann's right to say *poor soul*. It's a tortured existence, which doesn't get any better as the person grows up, in fact worse. And you can forget all those sexy images of lady-boys and tales of abandoned shenanigans with guys who swing both ways – the reality is tough."

"I'm sure it is." Samra joins in and puts a hand out to PF. "Please go on. We really want to hear this story."

Again, unfairly, PF's gaze sweeps round to me and, wanting to lie low for the moment, I simply murmur assent. There's a bottle of red opened; PF is sipping hers in a leisurely way, whilst I gulp it down and fill up again. For some reason, I could get totally hammered tonight.

"Good. Well, this was a child I knew – or rather, I knew when they were adolescent. We were in the same high school, so I got to know quite a bit about him. Yes, *him*. That was the gender identity chosen by the parents – who were understandably shocked and distraught when he was first born, but they got on with it, dressed him like a boy and treated him like one. For a while, all was well."

Another longish pause. Ann sits with her chin on her hands, leaning on a suitcase (for some reason she's been packing and repacking – checking on whether she's got some fancy knickers for that man of hers? No, probably not). She looks plaintive, and a little older now that her face is serious. We wait for PF to resume. She lowers her eyelids and takes up the tale in a dreamlike voice.

"In the early years, the lack of a definite gender didn't

matter. The child was given one of those names that could be either male or female: Leigh. When children are small, they tend to accept each other, and Leigh passed for a boy for quite a number of years. After all, he could pee up a wall with his pals, and as he was tall for his age, he could climb trees and was a natural leader. Leigh did not know that he should not have had a split between his legs, an extra opening that he could put his fingers up, and as he didn't show anyone this, nobody cottoned on. Until he was gone eleven."

Thoughts and images churn around in my mind. I am trying to visualise someone with both male and female – equipment. Much as I am familiar with the technicalities, as it were, I still find it difficult to grasp – if you'll pardon the expression – the notion of a real, living, breathing Intersex. After all, you don't come across them in all their exposed glory in the supermarket or on the bus, do you? I confess that in my 'hood we were firmly either male or female, and if someone turned out to be gay, well he was still a man, he didn't have any ladies' bits, he just liked other men; and the same in reverse for girls. But yes: the notorious lady boys of Thailand the Far East. A bit of a joke amongst Westerners, though I don't think it's at all funny. Not at all.

PF has her eyes open now, and smiles at my expression.

"I an see you're wondering," she says. ""As you know, hermaphrodites do, indeed, have more or less the full sex organs of both man and woman; sometimes less, sometimes more obvious and developed. The problem comes at puberty; which sex will they assume? Which public toilet will they use? Will they want to have babies? Can they? The breasts swell, at odds with the descending of the testicles and the erections that happen nightly. You can imagine the mental confusion."

"Yes. Oh dear Lord, I can."

I am at once aware of Ann, whom I had forgotten temporarily as I sat hunched into myself, lost in reflection. Her face is a picture: the pretty mouth is screwed up in some kind of sympathy, and in her eyes is an expression I cannot quite fathom. Pain? Shock? Outrage? Horror? None of these, and yet –

"As if that time of life isn't bewildering enough, sure," she says, very very softly and it seems to me sadly.

"Exactly." PF nods. "So, the parents and Leigh herself together eventually decided, after a great deal of talking and counselling and research, and a good amount of time to make absolutely sure that Leigh was taking the right path, that it would be best if she became a woman, but it meant huge doses of hormones and a lot more emotional stress. It took until she was nineteen for her body to even begin to properly sort itself out."

Yet another harrowing pause.

"And even longer for her mind."

I cannot help it. I blurt out, "But the surgery? I mean, the willy has to – "

I notice Ann wince. Looking down at her shoes, plain black flatties, she is blushing, I swear it. Is it the concept, or the language I'm using? But I'm darned if I'm going to walk on egg shells for her benefit The wine is doing its work. I blunder on.

"And the knackers. They shrivel with hormonal treatment, I think? But there must be more surgery there too?"

Now I can't see Ann's face at all; the dark wool of her hair escapes from its pins and bobbles, and shrouds her head as it drops onto her folded arms.

PF laughs, but silently, and opens the second bottle of red. When her noiseless mirth has subsided, she further enlightens us.

"Yes, girls, surgery. The surgeon's knife. This was the

last stage, or stages, rather, of the physical side of things and Leigh, poor Leigh, she suffered agony and scarring and weeks of hiding away from the world – months, years even, all for the sake of becoming a woman. Sometimes I think she must have asked herself If it was worth it, whether it wouldn't have been better to stay as she was – both."

"But then," I say, mercilessly, "she'd indeed have been one of those lady-boys. Very adaptable, when you think of it – I mean, when things are a bit slack in one direction, you can always turn to the other."

PF doesn't look my way, but I can feel a kind of chill in the air, and not just from her. Groan. Me and my goddam big bloody *gob*. She pours herself more of the red, and slides a long fingernail round the rim of her glass. The painful squeaking grates on all of us, I think, and I hope she's not going to continue until the blasted thing shatters.

I have to justify myself. "I do know a bit about all this," I say. "As it happens – "

And there I stop. I'm too aware of the bitterness in my voice. Time to change tack.

"And anyway, PF, how come *you* know so much about him – her?"

"I told you," says PF, patiently. "I kind of grew up with her – well, him for a while. We ended up at the same college for a while, that was when she'd had all her procedures and was back in the world. I'd taken a break myself, and went to college later than others, so we had that much in common. We became close."

And Lucy's brain logs the snippet of information: PF had a few years out. Why? What happened during that time? Right. Filed away. Carry on.

"But the emotional side...?" This from Samra, who is studying PF closely, her eyes darkening to almost midnight black. "That must have gone on affecting her?"

"To an extent, yes. But once she'd made the final transition, it was easier. She also found it helped to move to a new area, where nobody had known her as a boy. Her parents were incredibly supportive – she was lucky, there, I guess."

Here PF drops her head and studies her nails. Then, with a deep exhalation, she adds,

"Not all troubled young people are so fortunate."

There is something else that gets stored in that weird filing cabinet I call a mind; something clicks. *PF has needed support at one stage of her life – and didn't find it. Hm. Anther one to mull over. Later.*

"Pass the wine," I say, companionably, and she looks up and rewards me with a lopsided smile. I pour a large portion, and drink it a little fast; I'm not sure quite where we go from here. It is Samra who takes us forward.

"So can she have normal sex?"

PF regards her for a moment through narrowed eyes. I am glad I'm not on the receiving end of that.

"And what, exactly, is 'normal sex'?"

"Well, you know, a man penetrating a woman."

Samra shifts around, discomfited, and I sympathise; I've had to come out with dopey statements like that in those futile PHSE lessons at school, and the kids always guffaw or groan and roll their eyes, or, at worst, offer me their own, personal interpretations of 'normal sex' which I could well do without. Normal sex? It's a minefield.

"Ah yes, she can have that kind of sex. And other kinds too," says PF, with a faintly wicked grin.

This silences us, until Ann chimes in.

"And the poor wee thing – can she have babies?"

Oh God. Babies again. Will this female ever get off this subject?

"No. Not ever. No babies."

Ann gasps at this, and her cheeks redden. The bright

eyes swim with sudden feeling.

"No children? Ever? But I thought you said she'd have had a womb and all?"

"Not fully formed," rejoins PF, gravely. "Remember I did say that the organs were more, or less developed in different people. For Leigh – not ever."

"How terrible."

Ann and Samra simultaneously sigh, and even I take this seriously; we are quiet for a time, visualising this pretty young woman, as we assume she now is, with her wounded and butchered body, no longer male, not fully female, though desirable and desiring.

"What happened to her? Where is she now?" I ask, to get us out of this pit of despair. PF's stories are so fucking *dismal*.

The golden one sits up, flips back her hair extensions takes out a pocket mirror and ruffles the tousled tresses.

"She's doing well, getting on with life. Finished college, got a job – in advertising as it happens. You know?"

"Do you still see her?"

"Did she get married?"

Two questions, from Samra and Ann, ride over each other, and PF laughs.

"Steady on there girls. Give me room. Yes, she did get married, but it didn't work out – though not because of what had happened to her. Just a regular divorce – found they had different needs and interests, the usual reasons. She still dates guys. And yes, I see her from time to time, when I'm in her part of the woods. As I said, we became very close." She is silent for a brief moment.

"Mmm." Ann hums a little tune. Then: "Why did you tell us this story, PF?"

PF kind of corrugates her forehead, thinks.

"I guess I thought it might be interesting to hear a totally different woman's story, one you might not have heard before so up close and personal." She pauses. "Situations like this … us being stuck here – like we are prisoners in an open jail – you get to thinking and talking about stuff that you wouldn't in the normal run of events."

"Right." We are all agreed on that, then.

"And," continues PF, "it might be interesting to think about what such a decision means in feminist terms? She's chosen to be a woman – and a very girly one at that – skyscraper heels, sexy dresses, jewellery and false eyelashes. The works."

Once more, pictures float before our eyes; unhappily, I can only see a sort of Boy George-cum-Edna-Everidge-cum-Mae-West-meets-Dolly-Parton sort of figure, and it's not a welcome one. I am sure the real thing is much more pleasing.

The second bottle of red is almost gone; I can feel its mellow liquid through the glass and pour out a last helping. PF quietly opens a third, so I have some more. Ann swigs her water. We are all grateful for this break; I am surprised by the serious turn of the narrative, though in the same instant not surprised. Why did I expect something lewd, raucous, explicit? Have I not got the measure of this woman by now? This was straightforward, and moving, if a bit sombre on several tumblers of the old vino. My own bawdy little tale, that I had thought I would tell for my second story, seems sordid and ridiculous now.

"Aren't you going to ask any more questions?" Says PF, holding out her glass as I rather shakily pour. "You can ask away. It's not too often you get to meet something of an expert on hermaphrodism."

A sudden, drunken though flashes across my mind.

"Are you a psychologist?" I demand. "A psychiatrist?"

"Now why would you say that?" The braids fling themselves around again as PF laughs, rather shrilly, in my view. "I'm a simple girl, me."

That I very much doubt, I think, but I do not say so, and I can see the incredulity in Ann's honest , open face too.

Shockingly, Samra puts in her oar, and stirs up the waters.

"So – how exactly do they do it? These hermaphrodites?"

"You actually want to know? I'd have thought," says PF, slowly, "that in your – profession – you'd be up to speed on things like that. You must have seen all kinds of punters and met all sorts of variations."

I watch Ann's jaw drop. I think, *she is just a fairly naïve young woman from Eire.* I feel a sudden flush of annoyance, an irritation with PF as well as Samra. Can't they see that Ann is uncomfortable? Come to that, oddly, so am I. This is going just one step too far. Okay, it is fun to speculate on, as the old limerick has it, who-did-what-and-to-whom, but I'd rather do this in private, or with people I know a good deal better and have known for a hell of a lot longer.

It also dawns on me that lil' Lucy has changed in more ways than one. Time was when I'd have laughed my socks off at such a discussion, probably getting drunker and ruder by the minute; but now, all I want to do is – is what? What I'd truly like to do is go to bed and have another kip. Failing that, go and have a civilised conversation with Fergus. So there's a revelation.

"We actually do not want to know," I say now, firmly. "At least, I don't. Nor does Ann, I reckon."

Ann wags her head from side to side.

"Sorry, PF. No offence to you, and all, but it's not my sort of thing. I mean, I feel sorry for the poor thing, and the good Lord have mercy on her, and I hope she goes on happy in her life, but –"

PF shrugs.

"Suits me. You're not missing much." She points meaningfully at the now half drained third bottle. Samra has also been partaking, which is mildly surprising. "We might need some more of this."

"Well," I say in some relief, "then it's my turn."

I am glad of the diversion, and wend my way out of the hotel to the wine shop – cheaper than ordering it through room service by a mile. Large gaps are appearing on the shelves already; it can't all be us, can it? Two more of the red beauties find their way into my hands, and as the harassed assistant puts them tenderly into tissue paper, and then a carrier, I am aware of the increasing heat in the terminal. What some classic writer once called, as I remember it, the 'common press of humanity'. (Gee, where did that spring from? I can't have *read* this? Probably old Miss Viner having a go at our stuffy, adolescent sweat-filled classroom. Sarky hag.) At any rate, it shouldn't take long for this lot to reach room temperature.

Back at the old corral, I find that PF has gone out. I guess she felt rather more emotional than she'd admit, telling this story about her friend, but she keeps so much hidden or at least in check that it's hard to tell. Apparently she has gone to the gym. More toning of those beautiful limbs and the firm, high muscles. Bah. Whilst I have probably put on three kilos in an afternoon, with all the calories in that wine.

As this thought strikes me, I suggest a large pot of tea – and the good old basic stuff, not anything fancy. Builder's tea would suit me fine right now. Obligingly, Ann gets it together and we sit drinking the delicious, dark gold fluid as if it is nectar. Why do I drink so much wine? I contemplate this conundrum. Why, when I find a hunking great pot of char just as good, if not better? There's summat to chew on, as my old grandmother used to say.

There are biscuits, too – luxury ones, with dark plain chocolate and ginger. Oh to hell with the kilos; here, give me that plate.

Suddenly, Samra sits up straight in the armchair, looks at us keenly.

"Do you think," she says, "that when PF was telling that story she was talking about – *herself*?"

"*What?*" A chorus from Ann and me.

"Well, how come she knows so much in detail – and calls herself an 'expert' on the subject? I mean, she would have given quite a lot of more intimate detail if we'd let her. Not that I want to say we should have," she says hastily. "But all the same…"

"Hm. She is very tall," I muse. "And she said Leigh was tall. She could well have worked in advertising – with those looks and a good brain to boot. Maybe this is her secret. Maybe that's why she keeps things so tight to her chest."

"Precisely." Samra purses her lips. Then, "My God. That means she was once a man – or half a man. Or whatever."

Samra and I mull over the image of the Fair One with a todger, at which I burst out laughing at the absurdity. Samra joins me and we fall around a bit until Ann, with a smile, quietens us.

"Hush, girls," she says. "Not kind to gossip about the poor woman when she's not here. And I don't for one minute think you're right."

"Oh?" I say, a bit huffed. "And why is that?"

"Well, now," says Ann, carefully, "let's just say that I think PF has some problem she's working on, but that it's not that. Not what she told us about. No, I think she's still going through something in her life, and this – Leigh – by all accounts has worked out her way, and is contented with it."

She pauses, looks at us.

"And I don't think PF is at all contented, right now."

Woh. Is this woman psychic? It hits me like a brick that she's bang on. I kind of knew it, but she's put it into words.

It's not that PF is deeply, traumatically unhappy – she's too assured and self-contained for that; but there's this feeling of – of – what I can only, in my befuddled state, call a cooling of the heart. And if Ann can spot that in PF, what does she see in me? Huh? None of this as as simple as it once seemed.

* * *

It's nighty-night time again. This is becoming a familiar routine, and it feels, I think to all of us, that we've been here most of our lives. Travelling is bizarre. It does that to you – kind of suspends time and makes you get used to new situations very quickly. I guess it's survival; we are an adaptive species. The human brain – *Oh shutup, Lucy, you're not a teacher here and now.*

Anyway, I'm sleepy. I want to get up earlier tomorrow, get back to the real me. Huh. What's the real me? Do I want to know? Do I care? The wine is still trawling round my circuits, that I can tell. I snuggle into the cosy bed and start to drift off. PF is likewise settling down, and turns off her bedside lamp. Deep, deep quietness. All is still, all is well.

"PF?"

A question buzzes like an impatient visitor. I have to ask it. Now.

"What, Lucy? My God, you'd drive a man mad."

"Too true! Have done on more than one occasion."

A snort, possibly of laughter, from the other bed.

"But I need to ask you this. Didn't want to raise it in the group, you know?"

"Wh-why not?" says the Princess, on a yawn. (I bet she looks elegant when she yawns, too. Not like ordinary mortals, who just look as if they're catching haddock.)

"Don't know exactly. Partly because of – well, Ann."

"Sure. I can appreciate that. Okay, ask away."

"Um." I hesitate, not sure how to put this. "Um, did your friend, did Leigh ever talk to you about the sexual side of her life? Before *and* after?"

"Oh *Lucy!*" PF is exasperated now. "At this time of night? It's a heavy topic. Can't it wait?"

"Okay," I say, reasonably. "I suppose it can. But – you will tell me?"

"And why," says PF, audibly turning over in the darkness to face me, "and why should I just tell you, in confidence, and not the rest of the gang?"

I clam up. I can't answer that – not without sounding like a right little sycophant, a teacher's pet, someone seriously into brown nosing...

"Dunno. As I said, maybe embarrassment?"

But I do not say that I feel, despite all the digs and the unspoken clashes we've had, that there is a kind of bond between us that I do not have with the other two, however much I've grown to know and quite respect them, despite minor irritations. I dare not say this – it would sound too feeble, and if PF laughed in my face, well, I don't know. It would spoil something for me, though I cannot pinpoint what.

"Then if you're embarrassed by talking about it with others, you shouldn't be talking about it at all. *Goodnight, Lucy.*"

Phew. That was a real put-down; but not as bad as one I might have got.

Clearly there's nothing more to be milked from this situation; the udder is dry, the well used up. Goodnight, Lucy. Night, gang. Goodnight hermaphrodites everywhere.

Oh – and in case you're going to lose sleep unless I tell you, an example of the Erinaceinae mammal is your humble hedgehog.

163

Apparently it is now my turn to tell a second story. We've all woken quite early, and after a hearty breakfast – as eaten by the condemned man (and woman, one assumes) – PF has rounded on me.

"Well, I've done my second tale," she said, leaning back in her chair, very relaxed it seems to me, "and if we're to follow the rota, as it were – you're up next, Lucy."

Bloody hell's teeth. The woman is right, so I'm going to have to sit here and try to think up something better than my first yarn, but not as crude as the one I had planned on following it up with. My mind is horribly blank. Truth is, after those few carefree years (of the Claude era) travelling with a bunch of mates, life has become much less interesting: school, home, preparation and marking, school, home, etc., and the weekends uneventful until – well until *it* happened and everything changed and I went into robotic mode. But *ca suffit*, as they say across the Channel. (I might have learned that from Claude. I learned more French that night than in five years at school – not that they were the sort of phrases you'd have found in your school text books, natch.)

Mind you, it's not that I haven't more stuff to tell; I've lived, for God's sake, and I'm thirty-two. It's just that... What I have to undertake in Thailand is coming up big in my thoughts today, and I should really try to make contact soon, or they'll think – well, I know what they might be thinking, even if they've seen and read the news. Anything I can drum up to tell the gang here about seems grubby, to be honest, tame, faced with – with something of such humongous significance. Something that I've never had to do in my life before, and I honestly don't know how I'm going to handle it.

I am in grave danger if blurting it all out and blubbing all over the place, as I did with Fergus. Which I most decidedly do not want to do.

I am saved from a fate which I am rapidly feeling is worse than many things, if not actually death, by a knock at our door With suspicious eagerness, I dart over and open it, expecting sweet, dear Fergus, of whom I am, really and truly, very fond, or the beautiful Matende/Matt, perhaps, come to drape his gorgeous self amongst our harem?

But no, it is a stranger; a very well dressed one, who very formally hands over a sealed envelope. Gives a slight, equally formal bow, and disappears. Wow. Kooks-ville or what?

"And what in the world was that, now?" asks Ann, who has come to stand behind me.

"No idea," I say, and turn over the envelope, which is addressed to The Occupants of Suite 2071. "But it's for all of us. Mm."

"In which case," says PF, quite brusquely, "open it and let us all see it, Lucy."

Achtung, oh fair one. I shoot an equally keen glance at her, and, wonder of wonders, she blushes slightly. I never thought she could. Or would.

With deliberate slowness, I withdraw the single sheet of paper, upon which are the following words:

"Dear travellers, We should like to inform you that the latest world weather reports suggest that a brisk prevailing wind from the south west will move in over the next forty-eight hours, strengthening sufficiently to move the thinning ash cloud comfortably out to the North Sea and the polar regions, and that a high pressure system will consequently settle over the British Isles. We anticipate, therefore, that flights from this airport will start to resume by the early morning of the 28tth. We trust..." and then there is more blah and bumf about hoping we have not been too much inconvenienced by circumstances beyond the airport's and the various airlines' control, and so on, and so on.

My heart – or is it my stomach? – gives a tremendous lurch. Suddenly, I am on that plane to Thailand, gripping my seat, that vital packet safely stowed where I cannot, must not lose it. Suddenly, England is behind me and this room, and these motley companions, and dear Fergus and magnificent Matende and the hotel, and – and –

"Thank the good Lord!" Ann intones, and I can't blame her. She's wanting to go and join that hubby of hers, with her white knitting and all.

To my surprise though, Samra and PF both look solemn, deep in contemplation, as I suppose I do, come to think of it. I'd have imagined Samra would've been cheerful – she hasn't got a husband yet, but she's going to one she assures us she loves. Or at least is happy about marrying. As for PF – what could be gloom inducing about a nice long vacation trip to Oz to see a fav aunt?

It dawns one me that they must also wonder about me; might start to ask questions. And I suddenly know for sure that –

"I can't tell another story right now," I announce, flatly, forestalling argument. "Sorry, but I just can't. If I do, it'll be something that'll send you all down, and I would guess we all need a bit of cheering up. Am I right, or am I right?"

"You're right, Lucy," says PF, rather more gently than I've come to expect from her. "Okay. It's okay."

A glum silence follows. Are we going to stay this way all day? It's only eleven in the morning, and the only alternatives are going to the gym – again – or the telly which has about 59 channels and all of them crap. Big choice. And in any case, with the news that we'll all be out of here within two days, we'd best get on with this lark, this telling of stories. We don't have to; we could let it drop. But for whatever reason, I don't think we want to.

Samra lets out a huge, plaintive breath. "I'll tell you another tale," she says, with a musing smile. "You'll like this one. It's a folk tale from Pakistan, and I think you might just begin to guess why I'm choosing it."

"Oooh, lovely," squeals Ann, and claps her hands plumply. Some of the wild curls escape from their elastic band and bounce merrily round her ears and onto her full white neck. Again, I see her through Fergus's eyes, a painter's eyes, and again, I wonder whether her husband revels in such sights. Yes, he most surely does...

"I love a good folk yarn," continues the Irish one. The green, slanting eyes dance and light up the room. Indeed, he is a lucky man.

"Don't we all," murmurs PF.

The ice blue of those strange, deep set eyes warms like an ocean under sunlight. A grin stretches her wide, firm mouth, and I forgive her the sharpness, the mean looks. I forgive her everything she has ever done. Such a face, such a mouth, such eyes could melt stone... Hey, what the heck? I'm not that way inclined believe me. Not at all. Have had offers in my time, you might want to know. Uh-huh, so you didn't . But it's true. I have had approaches, and I am completely straight. It's just that – well, I suppose with someone as stunning as PF, she could entrance anyone, male, female and anywhere in between. You know? And even if I was that way disposed, what chance would I have with such a beaut? I mean, she could have her pick. The top of the crop. Right? Why would she go for a dumpy little ginger?

Shush, Lucy girl, Shut up and listen to Samra. Who is sitting almost lotus fashion, cross legged anyway, on a cushion on the floor, her back absolutely upright and her rather well shaped head poised gracefully on her slender neck. She's pinned up her black, silky hair today, and in profile she looks like one of those classical paintings of Indian girls when the sub-continent was all one, and girls like Samra would probably have lived in a big family house in the Hindu Kush and been confined to the Zenana. See I'm not jut an ugly freckle-face. I know a thing or two. Oh the Zenana. It's where the women had to live, and even if they were married their husbands couldn't openly live and sleep alongside them; they had to creep up the stairs and visit in the night and then go away again, as if nothing had happened, and abracadabra, soon the young married girls would pop out a baby or two. Sounds freaky to us, but when you think about it, it's quite romantic; you don't have the fucker under your feet all day nagging and moaning at you and throwing his sweaty socks around and generally getting in the way, so when he visits it's special, and you don't even have to wake up to his face on your pillow in the morning. Hmmm. Wonder if Scottish castles afford such accommodating bedroom arrangements…

But Samra is speaking now, a low rather monotonous, drowsy tone that has us all quickly in thrall, listening as if our lives depended on it. And in a spooky sort of way I suppose they do; we have to last out these remaining hours and stay sane or else – or else what, Lucy? Well, I guess the 'else' is that each of us stands to lose a great deal, though quite what I'm not in a position to know. I only know about myself. Oh stop, it , stop it girl. Listen to the story. I *am* sitting comfortably, so let Samra begin.

* * *

"This is the story of two lovers, Heer and Ranjha. The name 'Heer', by the way, means like a diamond, and Ranjha has come to mean a devoted sweetheart, a romantic man."

168

"Like a – a Romeo?" I cannot help butting in.

"Yes. Indeed, yes. In fact, this is the tale of star-crossed lovers, similar to Romeo and Juliet. So now," says Samra, pulling a rueful face, "I've spoiled it a bit 'cos you can tell it's going to end sadly."

"Never mind," says Ann, seeing me flush with annoyance at myself. I shouldn't have interrupted – as so often. "Not to worry, Samra. We'll be fascinated to see how the two of them meet their fate."

Ann shows more understanding than I've ever given her credit for, and I vow to stay quiet for the rest of the tale, which Samra picks up again.

"Heer was, of course, very beautiful – as lovely as the moon, they said, her eyes sparkling like gems, her teeth as white as the petals of jasmine flowers, lips as red as rubies. You know the sort of stuff. She came from a wealthy Jatt family who lived in or near the city of Jhang, in the Punjab – surely one of the most beautiful regions of the subcontinent. Dheedo Ranjha, though, came from a more lowly tribe, the Ranjha clan; some say he was the youngest of four, some say eight brothers but whichever, he was the favourite, and whilst the others had to toil in the fields, he led a life of ease playing his flute – which he played extraordinarily well. But then his father died, and his brothers got their own back, and ill treated him out of spite, and would not let him have any of the fields to earn his living. He quarrelled with them, and left home, wandering the countryside, finding food and work where he could, and eventually, he reached Heer's village in the Jhang area. Now, one version of this tale says that he saw Heer one day, walking in her garden – and at once he fell in love with her."

"Ah," sighs Ann, "the poor dear boy. The poor wee thing. Love at first sight – it's a big mistake, you understand."

PF's mouth twitches a little at this; I think she's trying

not to laugh. I feel a bubble of mirth rising up in my throat, but we contain ourselves and Samra carries on.

"Anyway, Heer is not aware of him, and he sees her again in the garden, so he pleads with Heer's father to give him a job herding cattle. One day, he manages to get quite near to the girl, and he takes out his flute and starts to play. Heer is immediately entranced by the music, so pure and lovely it is. Sooner or later, she notices Ranjha and how handsome he is, with his curling dark hair and his fine face. She knows that her father would not let her marry a cowherd, so they can only meet in secret – which they do by going into the forest where they can be hidden. There they sit, Ranjha playing his enchanting music, Heer leaning against his knee; much against the rules of her society, of course, though nothing untoward takes place. They continue to meet in this way – for years, as some versions of the story have it. You might like to know that many Bollywood movies have been made of this piece of folklore, because of course it was all India at that time."

PF is curious. "Is this based on a real couple?" she asks, quietly. I remember PF's stern instruction right at the beginning, that our stories should be true. But I think she's perhaps forgotten that, and is merely intrigued. I hope so, for Samra's tale is good.

"They say so, yes. Around the 15th century, but not written up until around the 18th century – it was made into an epic poem, and it is still read and enjoyed by generations of Indians and Pakistanis, though more Pakistanis now as it took place in our part of the continent. As I said, it's been filmed many times with Bollywood stars."

We sigh, in unison, and think of the all-singing, all-dancing Indian movies, with their energy, colour and drama. This story would fit well.

"And another version," Samra goes on, "which I like

better, has it that Heer was with her girl friends one day and went to the ferry, where the boatman had a boat with luxurious couches and they would drift along the water for their leisure. On this occasion, to her annoyance, Heer saw a youth lying on the couch that was reserved for her, and she was angry, and about to beat him. He awoke, for he had been asleep, and of course it was Ranjha. The boatman gets it in the neck from Heer, by the way, but he explains that the magical flute playing had bewitched him, and he could not refuse Ranjha a place to sleep in the boat. When Heer sees Ranjha's lovely face, all her anger melts away, and she is utterly charmed by him. She sits on his lap – *outrageous* behaviour for a young girl at that time, or even now in Pakistan, if it comes to it – and they declare their love for each other, make promises of eternal fidelity, with many embraces and soft strokings of their loving faces, and thus they spend the long, drowsy afternoon in the barge, with the sweetness of flowers all around them on the river banks perfuming the air, the bright sunlight on the water fading to gold and rose in the late sultry heat of an Indian sunset..."

Samra stops there, to give us chance to picture this – the lovers entwined, however innocently, floating along the calm, pearly waters in the hot, still air, murmuring their endearments; I in particular am imaging a Ranjha with that wonderful olive-dusky skin, his deep brown, thickly lashed eyes shining with adoration, his toned torso hardly concealed by the lightest of tunics, his refined, musician's hands with their smooth brown fingers...

"Of course," Samra resumes, jolting me out of my vision, which might be just as well or I'll be changing my flight to Islamabad, or wherever, "they cannot risk being seen in the boat again, so in this tale, too, they start to meet in the forest, and they go on like this for a long time."

"They must have been very tempted to – to misbehave,"

says Ann, tentatively. "All that time alone in the woods."

"Probably," Samra says, and laughs. "But according to legend, they didn't. Or not much – though there is some mention of 'four lips meeting' – like your Romeo and Juliet again, isn't it? – so I guess they kissed at least. Who knows? Reminds me of your earlier story of a pure passion, Ann. All that longing, that closeness of bodies, and they remain chaste."

Ann laughs too, but a little self-consciously. "Well, maybe, but we weren't hidden in a forest and our friendship would not have been forbidden had we taken it further. And there was no sitting on laps or lips getting together, you understand."

"Still," says Samra, "there are some similarities. The yearning, the temptation resisted? Anyway, of course one day they are caught out, by none other than Heer's jealous uncle, Kaido, and her parents. Heer is disgraced, as even meeting a man like this was – well, *haram*, and to cover up the shame, they force Heer to marry another man, of their choice."

"And she does?" I break my pledge. "She actually goes through with it?"

"As I said, she is forced," says Samra, calmly. "Such things happened a lot and even today there are such cases, though thankfully much rarer. But getting back to Ranjha, he, naturally, is broken-hearted, and leaves Jhang to wander the country again. After a while he meets a Jogi – that's a kind of monk, if you like, one who lives a simple life of meditation."

"An ascetic," murmurs PF, and we all bow to her superior knowledge. Well, kind of.

"After a while, Ranjha becomes a Jogi himself; he pierces his ears and renounces the material world. He travels the Punjab, and after a while finds the place where Heer now lives, with her much-detested husband. She has to live in her in-laws' house, where she languishes, refusing food and nice clothes. She lies awake thinking of Ranjha every night and pining for him."

"Ah," sighs Ann once more, putting a white hand to her generous bosom, and I think we're all with her on this one. There is nothing more to say.

"However," continues Samra, "Heer has refused to sign the *nikkah* – that is, the papers giving her agreement to the marriage, so her father signs them for her. Now some versions of the story have it that Heer protested that she was already married to Ranjha, that she had signed the *nikkah* in the presence of Allah, with his brides as witnesses, though not in front of a wedding party, but that this had been done with Ranjha, so she could not be married to the new 'husband'."

"Confusing," says PF. "Is she married to either of them, both, or neither?"

"It isn't very clear," admits Samra, "but some accounts say that she did not let her 'husband' touch her, but went into a kind of decline."

"As she would, the sad girl," says Ann. "As you would yourself, isn't it so?"

"Mm," Samra says, "perhaps. But as for Ranjha, he has been granted the full status of a Jogi, so he can roam the country with a begging bowl and go around asking for alms. Most people would give something to such a holy figure, perhaps as a kind of good-luck charm if nothing else: hedging your bets, if you like. He goes to Heer's in-laws, which is where he finds out that Heer is in their house – they do not know who he is, of course. What to do? Well, as it happens, Heer's sister-in-law Sehti has a secret lover, whom her parents don't approve of, and she takes pity on Heer. Sehti considers that her brother's forcing Heer into marriage is un-Islamic, thus she sees a chance to right her brother's wrong doing."

"And get what she wants as well?" PF has second-guessed, though I at least am up with her.

"Indeed she does! Sehti cunningly bites Heer's foot when they are walking in the garden, and pretends that a snake has bitten Heer. The in-laws call in fakirs to give Heer special potions, but they are not effective – obviously! Sehti tells them that there is a flute-player nearby who can cast spells through his music, so Ranjha is brought into the household and lodged in a hut. That night, Sehti's lover Murad brings two camels, and he and Ranjha escape with their respective brides."

"But they are discovered?" says Ann. "Oh, I have a terrible feeling they're not going to get away."

"You're right. They *are* found, and Ranjha gets a vicious beating. He seeks justice from the Raja – like the king of the province – and the inlaws are brought to court. But after hearing both sides, the Raja hands Heer back to her 'husband's' family!"

"*Shit.*" Again, I cannot hold my tongue. "Would you ever?"

"Ah," smiles Samra, "but Ranjha and Heer get their own back! They invoke curses on the city of the Raja – Allah does not stand for injustice, you see – and the place catches fire. There is a terrible inferno, so the astrologers tell the king to let Heer go with Ranjha, her rightful husband. They go back to Heer's village, and this time her parents agree to the marriage, probably because the Raja has relented and let them be together. So a marriage is prepared, and a great feast. All seems well; everyone is happy. Heer and Ranjha are filled with joy. But ..."

Oh-oh. Here comes the Romeo and Juliet bit. I can feel it in my bones.

"But the jealous uncle, Kaido – remember *that* snake in the grass? – poisons some of the wedding food that Heer is about to eat. She takes it and dies, collapsing in front

174

of Ranjha and the guests. He rushes to her, but when he realises what has happened he cries out that he does not want to live without her, and also takes some of the poisoned food. He dies by her side."

"And I often wondered where Shakespeare got his idea from," I mutter. "Now I know."

"Mm," says PF. "There are other, similar stories, you know, in European literature. And as this was written up in the 18th century or later, Shakespeare couldn't have been aware of it – or not of the poem, at least."

Oh, clever Dick, I think, feeling quite ill-tempered. So you not only know everything there is to now about old Chalfour, or whatever his name was, but now you're the expert on our world famous playwright. Great.

"However," says our intellectual, more reasonably, "you may be right, Lucy. He might have been aware of this folk tale – or versions of it. After all, it was the age of exploration, and merchants travelled far and wide and brought back all kinds of strange stories… "

Hah. Try to get round me, why don't you? Still, I feel a tad better. She has an odd way of going for the jugular, really kicking your head in, and then soothing you with silver tongue. Foxy creature.

"So that's the end of the story, then?" Ann, seeing and feeling the slight tension, smooths over the moment. "I mean, they're both dead, poor young things, but what about Sehti and Murad? And were lessons learned by the families?"

Samra shrugs. "Not really recorded. It's Heer's and Ranjha's story, and the dramatic climax of them both being poisoned and dying in each other's arms is what readers and cinema audiences want to hear and see – the more melodramatic the better! There is a mausoleum to them in Heer's home town, or village, and lovers come from far and wide, and other people too, and pay to see it. They've become immortal, in their way – like Shakespeare's lovers, I suppose. When we did Romeo and Juliet at school I was reminded of the story of Heer and Ranjha, but I was too shy to tell our English teacher about it. I wish now that I had."

Samra – *shy?* The mind boggles. A pole dancer cum stripper doesn't strike me as the kind of girl who is backward in coming forward, if you'll excuse the expression…

There's a pause as we all digest this rather tragic tale. I reflect, though, that even if it's sad, it's not gloomy like PF's contributions. It's actually very romantic, and is quite beautiful in its own way. I even think of looking up the poem when I get back to England and reading it. Come on, Lucy, you never will. Well, possibly not, but it's a thought. If I get back to England, that is; if all goes to plan, and I can return, job done, success. *Hell's teeth.* Need to get my mind off this. So, I take the plunge.

"Okay, Samra – nice story. Very nice. But at the very beginning you said that we'd probably begin to realise why you'd chosen this to tell. I'm assuming it has some connection with your own situation, then?"

PF sits forward, the intense eyes fixed thoughtfully on Samra; Ann holds her breath.

Samra doesn't say anything for a while, and we wait it out. I'm not sorry I asked, though. Something tells me that she probably needs to talk about – whatever it is.

"I'll make some more tea," says Ann, and paddles her way to the kitchen.

I follow, and in unwonted harmony we set out the tea cups, warm the pot, pour the milk into the pretty jug, and clink around with teaspoons and the teapot. Biscuits are put on a fresh plate and the big tray is carried by the sturdy Ann into the sitting room. It is almost mid-day, and we ought to think of something else to do for the afternoon.

Eventually, Samra resumes, sipping tea in between bits of explanation.

"Yes," she begins. "There are some parts of the legend that relate to me. Mainly the bit about marrying a man of one's own choice and not being forced into a marriage that your parents think you should have."

We absorb this in silence, not sure how to ask what we would like to. I hadn't got the impression that Samra's parents were the repressive type; but then, maybe I'm wrong. Maybe that's why she escaped to London? And took up her own life?

As if reading my thoughts, Samra nods.

"Yep. My dad in particular had this man he wanted me to become engaged to when I was seventeen – the son of a business friend of his. Pakistani, that goes without saying, and Muslim. Not that I have anything against either of those things – I'm Muslim myself. The problem was that when I met this guy – we were allowed to meet each other, I wasn't dragged off by the hair! – I just didn't like him. Quite the opposite. Everything about him turned me off. He was superior, arrogant, didn't take much notice of me, seemed to make the assumption that all he had to do was turn up at our house and the matter was settled. He wasn't bad looking, but not that great either; I just – didn't fancy him in any way at all. And of course, I had formed a great attachment to Faisal when I met him in Pakistan years earlier, and on the occasions I'd seen him since. There was something there from the very start, even though he was a lot older than me."

Ann frowns. "And how old were you at the time? When you first met him? And how old was he?"

Samra looks uncomfortable, as if she knows that her responses will not go down too well.

"Erm, I was twelve, coming up to thirteen. He was then thirty."

A gasp from all of us. That's some age gap, especially if one is only thirteen. I mean, couldn't it just have been a teenage crush? *Thirteen??*

But the mind-reading one puts our doubts into the shade – makes them disappear like the early heat haze on a July morning.

"You might think that's just schoolgirl stuff, but I met him every summer until I was eighteen, and managed to see him secretly quite a lot – I had a cousin who'd cover for me – and every time I was just more convinced that he was – and is – the only man I would ever want to marry. He's forty now, but it doesn't bother me a bit. Pakistani men tend to remain good looking (and he is, by the way) well into older age. I mean, look at Imran Khan!"

We all look at the still *phwoarr-worthy* Imran in our heads, and simultaneously we agree.

"He has something about him, besides being handsome, and that is kindness, a gentleness, a courtesy – he never put a foot wrong, never behaved disrespectfully, and we had such great discussions – oh, about all sorts of things! I couldn't wait for the summers."

"But –" I don't quite know how to put this – "you went off to be a pole dancer! Why didn't you just tell your parents about him and go off to Pakistan to get married?"

"Have you forgotten Heer and Ranjha?" says Samra. "Like Heer's, my father and mother would never have allowed me to marry Faisal, and certainly until I was eighteen even under the laws of this country I couldn't have married without their consent."

"I see the similarities," says PF slowly, "the meetings in secret, the years of waiting, the lack of approval from your family. But why were they so against it? The age gap?"

Samra shakes her head.

"They've never met him. Don't know him at all. Never heard of him. It's nothing to do with age."

We are all completely baffled at this point. Then I remember the story.

"So it's a class thing – or caste, or whatever you call it."

"Caste is only in India," says Samra. "But no, it isn't to do with class – though you're getting warmer."

"He's married already!" Ann bursts out with sudden inspiration. "Muslims can marry more than one wife, and your parents wouldn't let you do that – they're more modern."

Again, Samra rejects the suggestion.

"He's never been married. He too fell in love, even though I was so young. He has waited for me."

We find this romantic, and even perhaps a little improbable; but then, this is a different culture. I can't picture a thirty year old man in England keeping himself for a thirteen year old girl to grow up. But then, maybe that doesn't say much for England?

"And does he know," says PF, picking her words, "about the – er – job you had in London?"

"He advised me to see something of the western world, the way of life, especially in London," Samra replies, a little defensively, I think. "He wanted me to be sure that I didn't prefer the freer life, that I wouldn't meet a young man of my own age and forget about him."

"But *pole dancing*?"

"He's liberal in ideas, and lived in the States for a while in his early twenties. He knows what goes on."

"But did he know you were a pole dancer, even a stripper?"

We are really pushing her now; she blushes, and the dark eyes flash.

"No," she says, at last. "And there's no need for him to. I never did anything immoral, and he's had girl friends – especially in America."

"He has?" PF and I speak together, and Ann's mouth

opens as if to catch air.

"Well yes, you wouldn't expect him to live like a monk for ten years, would you? What we bring to each other now is our selves, just as we are. How we have lived before is not relevant. We have waited, and we are sure that we are going to marry. Nothing else is of importance. This we have agreed."

"Well," says Ann, straightening her skirt and sitting up very straight. "That's not how I had imagined a Muslim marriage to be."

There is just a tinge of disapproval in her voice that I am sure must annoy if not offend Samra, and for once I feel like sticking up for our exotic friend. However, before I can say a word, she flattens us completely with her next bombshell.

"And who said it was a totally Muslim marriage?" Pause. "Let me enlighten you. Faisal is a *Christian*."

* * *

Several pots of tea later we are still mulling over the implications of this shattering statement. Ann for some unbeknown reason has become almost tearful, then hugged Samra, and called her 'sister' – I suppose on the idea that Samra is marrying a man of the Christian faith – and Samra did not seem to mind this. We have each one of us explored the difficulties such a marriage would – will – create. We are aware that a woman in Muslim countries is meant to follow the religion of her husband. But – and it's a big but – a woman (or man) born Muslim cannot change her (or his) faith. No problem if the husband is a Muslim and the woman a Christian; woman has to take on the Islamic faith. BIG problem if, as in this case, the man is Christian and the woman Muslim.

Very dangerous situation; we shudder, collectively,

at the thought of what could happen to Samra if their respective religions come to light, especially in these troubled times and in a country where Islamic rule is predominant. The only other option, as we understand it, is for Faisal to convert to Islam – at this point, Ann sobs again. I guess one lamb escaping from the fold is too much for her to contemplate – no, that's downright nasty, Lucy. *Shuddup* – however, it appears that quite reasonably this he is not prepared to do, and Samra does not want him to. Now, more questions spring to mind.

Viz:

Would their marriage even be legal? Could they conceal Samra's Muslim background? Can she pretend to be a Christian? Perhaps in a big and fairly sophisticated city, like Karachi, it might be possible to get something arranged? But Samra does not want to discuss all this right now; enough, she says, and trots off to get dressed in something nice and go for a walkabout. We three are left to mull over what she's told us so far, and we don't make much headway, I have to say.

All in all, we conclude that Samra is (a) very brave (b) very loyal and devoted and (c) totally insane. We all go with (b), Ann in particular goes for (a) but I suspect that PF as well as me goes for (c).

And I thought my dilemma was a big one.

I must be the magic of Samra's story. For indeed, it was magic – as if we were all transported back to childhood, to our mother's knee. Or in my case my father's, as it was he who told us wonderful stories, some made up for us specially, some old well known ones but told with a twist of his own. Happy, happy days. Who'd have thought that – well, who'd have guessed that what happened would come to pass? In this life, you have to grasp the moment, that's all. Something I haven't been doing for a while, and something I've found myself doing these past few crazy but incredible days.

After lunch, we all sacked out for a couple of hours – another thing that Lucy *does not do*. Daytime sleeping. For wimps and the very old. And now – me.

I, for one, slept for a couple of hours like a babe lulled to sleep with a bedtime story, and I guess the others did too. Everyone gets up again, fresh faced and chirpy, at around four o-clock, and we make afternoon tea, with scones ordered from room service for once – hey, we'll be out of here in a day or two, let's splash the cash – and they're just right, risen well, but not doughy, and with butter dolloped on like makeup on a drag queen's face. Who cares about dieting? There's strawberry jam, blackcurrant preserve, and, oh joy and gladness, somebody has added a complimentary carrot cake. With fresh whipped cream in a jug. *Who ever really, really cares about dieting?* Fergus likes me as I am. I have a suspicion Matt does too, and at least one of them admires the curvaceous Ann. Let the skinny ones rattle their bones around; I'm content with mine to be covered in a fair bit of flesh. This afternoon,

I am suddenly sure that everything in Thailand will go fine, and that I'll return safe and sound, and that –

"Lucy!" A voice interrupts my happy contemplation. "What have you planned for this evening?"

"Um, " I say, turning to PF, who is smiling at me for once, with no judgement in the blue gaze. "Well, a bit of this, and a bit of that. You know? Why?"

"Just that I fancied a swim" says the Princess. "Wondered if you wanted to join me. Or are you seeing Fergus?"

I eye her suspiciously. But no, there isn't a flicker of sarcasm, or of anything untoward Just genuine enquiry.

"Probably," I say, lightly, immediately aware that he has not said anything about tonight. And that I am only mildly bothered by that – if at all. "But it'll more likely be later. I think he does have things of his own to do. Like work!"

PF is pleased, I think.

"So – a swim?"

"Yeah. That would be great. When were you thinking of?"

"Oh – say an hour and a half? We've just eaten a lot of starch."

"Right. See you at the pool. I'm going to wander for a bit," I say, and then I add, since the Sareed One has gone to shower, "Wasn't that story of hers amazing? And the connections to her? It made me see Samra in quite a different light."

"Rightly so," returns PF with a touch of her old tartness. "Lucy, I don't mean to be too harsh, but I think you judge people very quickly and don't allow yourself time to strip off the layers – if you know what I mean."

I do know what she means, and I also know why I've become this way. I don't want to go into it so I merely grunt, and then mutter about getting ready to go to the airport shopping mall. This is not just an excuse. I need time to think. I want to think about Samra, for one; she's quite a girl, and if I've come to see that later rather than sooner, well at least I'm really trying to look at her now, in depth. And I want to think more about Fergus. About all of them, all of us, when it comes down to it. Ann I've somehow assimilated as a decent woman, not my cup of tea, but worthy, if that's not too damning a word, good and nice in her own way, if a bit caught up in the religion stuff. Last of all, I want time to think about PF herself. She is the Big Puzzle and I don't have the faintest idea where is the key to unlock even the first door to getting to know her. Never mind unpeeling God knows how many of those layers wrapped round each other beneath that shiny steel exterior. Why does she keep herself so aloof, as a rule – and from me in particular?

I can't be that bad. Can I?

Huuuuhhh.

Time to go walkabout.

* * *

Ah, the old familiar airport lounge; the hallowed bit of carpet against that wall where – what seems like a lifetime ago – we huddled together like rabbits in a burrow and snatched sleep when we could, ate airport crap and joined the queues for the toilets and washing facilities. I notice that there are far fewer people now; some families still sit in disconsolate heaps, jaded, exhausted but hanging in; a straggle of lone travellers have set up camps with sleeping bags, and bored-out-of-their-skulls kids play wearily with toys that have clearly been bought to keep them out of the grown-ups' hair, or play hide and seek in a listless way and run aimlessly round the rows of bench seats. I feel terribly sorry for these folks – and even more grateful to Fergus and his wizardry for getting us into that hotel.

I'm wondering where all the rest have gone, and how many have perhaps given up, or lived near enough to go home and wait for news, or who have decided to swim to their destination, this being (a) quicker and (b) possibly safer. Amidst these silly thoughts, a welcome figure hoves into view.

"Hi, Matt," I say, truly glad to see him. And then I observe that he is not looking his usual cheery self; in fact, he seems quite downcast, though he greets me with a smile and a slightly crushing embrace. My, those pecs!.

"Lucy! My, you look great. Time for a coffee?"

"Sure," I say. "I'm going for a swim with PF at half six, so I'm not going to eat anything. We had a fantastic afternoon tea in our room."

"Lucky you," says Matende, rather miserably, and I realise I've been tactless. Poor Matt, condemned to sleeping on the carpet still? Or is he? It occurs to me that I don't know much about this man any more than I do about Fergus. Less.

"Look," I say, wanting to make amends. "If you're stuck for somewhere to go, please, please feel free to come to our hotel apartment – any time, any day. You could have had tea with us, for instance – there was plenty of it."

"Thanks, Lucy." Matt smiles again, this time more genuinely. "You're very kind."

"Where are you staying at night?" I have to ask this. Not that I'm offering him our hotel rooms – can't do that without asking the others – but I'm concerned.

"Oh, it's not so bad." Matt sounds resigned. "I rang a family member who lives not far away, and I've stayed there a couple of nights. Problem is, it's a shared house with about a dozen people, and I can't really stay around all day. It's okay to crash there, but I get out as soon as I've got myself together in the mornings. Anyhow, it'll only be for another day or two at most, so I'll be fine. In any case – "

185

"Yes? In any case?" I prompt, after an awkward silence. Matende sighs. "Let's get that coffee and I'll tell you."

Two cups of coffee later and I'm listening to Matt's story. He has startled me by saying that this "ash cloud thing" has been good for him; it's made him come to terms with what's happening in his life, and he's had time to think things through. It turns out that he might cancel his flight – "Yeah, I know I'll lose the money, but what the hell? Time to do the right thing" – and not travel.

"Matt." I feel my way cautiously. "Hadn't you better tell me the rest? Strikes me you need to talk about this to someone, and it might as well be me."

He looks at me gratefully, reaches out and puts a hand over mine.

"There's no-one I'd rather tell, Lucy. So, here goes."

Another sigh, but a bit easier than the last one. I don't imagine that Matende is going to burst into tears, as I did with Fergus, but there's a feeling that he's relaxing, letting the tension go. I know all about that one, so I simply put my other hand on top of his, and wait.

"Well," he says at last, "you have to know that I'm *supposed to be* married."

"Supposed to be? What does that mean?"

"It means," he says, turning his head so that he cannot look into my eyes, "that I did get married – three years since, or just about – and that I ran away from it four months ago. Yes, I know, that's a bastard thing to do, and I am not at all proud of myself, but I just couldn't go on with it. I felt totally, like, trapped, you know? Stifled. Suffocating."

Tentatively, I ask, "But was this a family arranged marriage? Or did you love your wife? What is she like? Why did you feel so badly about it?"

"A string of questions there!" Matende laughs, but in a nice way, squeezes my hand. "No, it wasn't a family

186

thing – my folk are totally western and we don't go in for traditional weddings. I met my wife at a party, and fell for her. She's beautiful, and elegant, and intelligent. We were married eight months later. And I'm the biggest clown this side of the North Pole."

"Well," I remark, pedantically, "that means you're the biggest clown in the world, since anything beyond the North Pole stretches to the ends of the globe in all directions."

Matt puts his head back and howls, thumps the table and almost sends our coffee cups skidding onto the floor. A couple near us raise their eyebrows and make movements to go. Humourless pratts.

"Lucy, you don't change a bit! Okay, so I'm the fool of the world. Won't argue with that. Yes, I did love her – still do, that's the oddest thing. It isn't her that's the problem, it's marriage itself. And it's not that I want to play the field or be Jack the lad – oh, I know I flirted with you, and with Samra a bit, you're both cracking looking women, but – no offence – I guess I was just distracting myself from getting down to some hard thinking and decision making."

"I notice you say 'was'," I remark. "Sounds like there's been a sea change."

"Exactly. I've had twenty four hours on my own, staying at the house in a bloody uncomfortable bed – not that I wasn't grateful for a place for the night, but – well, then a day wandering round this soulless dump. I didn't come to see you because I needed to get my head round what was going on in my life."

"And you came to a conclusion?"

Matt heaves another long breath, and when he does speak, it sounds sad, but as if he has decided.

"Yes. I'm going to go back to the marriage. Abi will have me back – she wants us to have another go and she's not hostile or angry. That's the kind of fantastic woman she is. We – I – want to work through it, make a few changes, both of us – and I have to change more. Besides, there's – "

"There's – ?"

"There's our daughter to think of. She has to come first in all of this."

Bombshell number whatever it is or what? So the gorgeous Matende is not only a married man, but also a father. Well, as my granddad used to say when I was little, I'll go to the end of our street. Funny thing was, he never did – or not when he said that, at any rate. As a kid, that used to puzzle me a lot. I must have laughed at the memory, for Matende is looking at me a little askance.

"Oh, sorry, I wasn't laughing at what you said. Just a silly thing from the past. So you have a little girl, Matt," I rush on. "How old is she?"

"A year and a half. Want to see a photo?"

Before I can answer, he brings out a snapshot of the cutest little thing, all curly hair and big, big eyes – and skin a good deal lighter than his. I look at him, questioning.

"Mm-huh. My wife is English. Your actual White Aryan." And he pulls out another snap, and I gasp. She is an absolute knockout. Model and film star looks, but with the sweetest expression and character in that lovely face. Why he ever cast an eye in my direction will be something I will wonder at for the rest of my days.

"Oh, Matt – you mustn't lose her. And your smashing little girl."

"I know that now, Lucy." He speaks very softy, humbly almost. "And you know what? Meeting you, and then the other girls, put a lot of things into perspective"

"Hah! You mean, we were all ugly old bags compared with your wife, is that it?"

"No, no, NO Lucy. It made me realise that although there are very attractive women out there that I could probably have if I really wanted – and I don't mean to be like, totally up myself when I say that, just that the world is full of terrific people wanting to make it with someone else – but my heart wasn't in it. My heart, in fact, bugger the thing, the treacherous blood pumping organ, is given to one woman. and I guess it always will be. Well, two women as it happens" – he sees my face – "my wife and my enchanting daughter.."

"That's truly great," I say, warmly, and mean it. For Matende has not only sorted his own head out by saying these things, he's helped to sort mine. He's a brilliant guy, I'm privileged to have met him and had that little dalliance, or whatever you might call it, but he's not for me, nor me for him. I feel only – relief. For myself, for him.

Comfortably, we sip the remains of our coffee, and there's no need for talking. Then it occurs to me: Matt is leaving, and we might never see him again, so –

"Look," I say, impulsive as ever, but this time with reason, "you have to come over this evening, after PF and I have had our swim, and we'll order some food and we can say our goodbyes to you. I'm sure the others will be glad to know what's happening. That is, unless you're planning on going back to Manchester tonight?"

"No, not quite that soon. One or two things to sort out first." Matende puts up his hands in protest.. "Probably tomorrow some time. So I'd be delighted to come and see you all – and please, do me a favour and tell the rest what I've told you, the bare bones of it anyhow. I can't face saying all that again."

"Of course I will." I press my hand firmly on Matt's arm – his wonderful, smooth dark arm – and I feel just the faintest, faintest regret, which whisks away almost before I'm aware of it. He is one lovely fella. "Say eight thirty, then? Chez nous?"

"Done deal!"

Matt stands up, and quite suddenly gives me a bear hug

and a kiss on the mouth. Yes, the *mouth*. It is a lovely kiss, full of warmth and friendship, and even though I know he's spoken for, and is not mine in the remotest way, I can tell you that there is more fire in the boiler than when I kissed Fergus. Oh dear. Oh my giddy aunt, as an elderly and probably giddy aunt of mine used to say. Though why the aunt had to be giddy I couldn't tell you. But now Matt is saying something again. I shake myself out of stupid thoughts and listen up.

"And Lucy – you must come and see us in Manchester some time. You've helped me more than you know."

Dazed, I can only agree. I don't reckon I've done much at all, but then, sometimes you don't know, do you? Time for a good, challenging swim.

* * *

We are sitting round, very relaxed and comfortable. The nearest takeaway has done us proud, and bugger the hotel's room service – a good old hot Indian curry is just what we needed, though Samra laughs and says such food is not really at all like the subcontinent's cooking; she trucks through it just the same, I note. There's naan breads, popadoms, chutneys, raita, and a small mountain of aromatic rice. YUM. Strangely, although I've been eating for England these last two days, I don't feel an ounce fatter and my nice skirt (the one I wore for my first dinner with Fergus) fits just as well as ever. Now there's a thought.

Matt has come over as promised, though to be honest I wondered if he would, and brought some beers, which go better with Indian than wine, and we've also stocked up on juices and spring water. Still no word from Fergus, however. I'm so mellow that I don't even stress about this, just accept that maybe he wants a day or so to himself, or has a lot of work on. I'm quietly sure that he won't leave, when flights start taking off, without seeing me. I might not want to take anything further, but I'd be sorry to lose touch. In fact, darn it, as just hits me like a lightning strike from a clear sky, I don't want to say goodbye for ever to any of these folk sitting with me right now.

Even Ann.

Honest.

The only thing we lack is music; the radio alarm clocks in our bedrooms don't really do the job. Oh for a boom box. But then, Matende suddenly stands up, and we all look at him in surprise. Is he leaving already? Is it something we said? But no.

"Tell you what," he says, with a slightly wicked grin, "I hear from Lucy that you've been having a little competition – giving your stories, am I right?"

Without waiting, he carries on. (I think that was something called a rhetorical question. Miss Viner would know.) "Well, I'm wondering if I'm allowed to take part. Oh, not exactly a story, but a few little things to entertain you."

We're up for this, and we variously indicate our agreement, as much as our over-stretched bellies will allow us to. (And there's ice cream in the fridge. Help.)

"Yeah, that'd be fine," says PF, lazily. "What have you in mind?"

"I'd like to give you some idea of how we amuse ourselves – and each other – in Kenya. Oh," he adds, hastily, "I live in Manchester, but I wasn't born in the UK. I have family in Africa, and I do visit when I can."

"Ah, Africa," breathes Ann, mistily. "Beautiful, amazing place. How old were you when you left, Matende?"

Matt smiles at her in appreciation.

"Yes, Kenya in particular is very, very beautiful; and I was about seven, nearly eight, so I do remember my early childhood there."

191

I am doing a lot of re-arrangement of my thoughts. So Matt wasn't UK born; somehow I'd assumed he was. Not that it matters in the least, but it's a new dimension on him. Was he planning – after China – to flee back to the place where he was happy and free as a child in escaping from his marriage? Did he hope to find answers there? And as for Ann – now she seems to know Africa, has been before. Mysteriouser and mysteriouser, as they say. The plot indeed thickens. But I'm not fretting over it; just let it all roll tonight, lie back and let others do the talking. This is a first for me, or at least a rare thing, to want to be background, not to chatter and put in my sixpennysworth. I put it down to the curry. All that rice has a sedating effect.

"Okay." Matt sits down again, but he's in command, he's holding the floor. Well, not literally – isn't English a funny language? – but you know what I mean. "In Kenya, like countries all over the world, we have our own folk lore. Our stories are often about animals that you find in the wild, naturally, as it's so much part of our lives, or was in the past. Even stories about characters are put in the form of creatures – for instance, tricksters can be portrayed by the hare and the tortoise. Evil characters might be in the form of ogres, which are described in blood curdling ways... And our folk lore is passed down orally from one generation to the next. It's become an art form in itself, and each of our ethnic groups will have different sayings and tales. These are still very important, so much that they are part of secondary school and university syllabuses, where students have to 'collect' folk tales from their parents or grandparents – it's part of their heritage."

"That is so good," says PF, clapping her hands softly. "I really like that."

"Indeed." Ann joins in, her eyes dreamy and wide. "We have something a bit like that in Ireland, but it's dying out.

To be part of education, that's brilliant, sure."

"How many – er – ethnic groups do you have in Kenya?" Samra speaks up for the first time, and her face is bright with interest. "And which group are you from?"

Matt laughs. "I think you should say 'they' have, I'm not really part of Kenya any more. I'm a British citizen, have been since I was eighteen. But my family was originally from the Kikuyu. Oh, and you might like to know that they have a lovely proverb. It goes something like –"

He pauses. We hang on his words. Again, that teasing smile.

" – *women and the sky cannot be understood.*"

This creases us up, and we fall onto each other laughing. It is so clever of Matt to choose this; after all, he's the only man amongst four quite strong, independent (yes, even Ann, I'm slowly realising) and feisty women. Matt joins in and after a while we sober up. This won't last, of course, as more cans are opened, and even the Irish one is getting tiddly on sparkling water.

"That brings me onto what I wanted to present," says Matt, a little formally now. "I really wanted to try out some riddles and proverbs on you. As I said, each of our forty groups have their own favourite riddles, or proverbs, perhaps made up by ancestors a long time back, and some of them are quite hard to solve."

He looks at us questioningly. Do we want to hear some? Yes. Yes, we do.

"Right, then. Here goes. But before I tell you the riddles, I should explain that they are not in question form, like an English riddle that goes something like, 'my first is in X, my second in Y, what am I?' and so on. Our riddles are statements, and they deal in images. You have to really try to picture what the words are saying."

"Mm," says PF thoughtfully. "I get it."

"Sounds fun," affirms Samra, and Ann just smiles

again, as do I. Never in the whole of human history – at least since I've been on the planet – has little Lucy been so meek and silent. Some cat must have got my tongue, as that old gran of mine used to say darkly when I wouldn't answer a leading question such as "Did you spill that jug of gravy on my best carpet?" (Well, you wouldn't, would you, to misquote a certain Ms. Rice Davies.)

Back to Matende.

"First one, then, ladies," he says. "Here's the statement – an easy one for starters.

My lamp illuminates the whole world."

We think for a few seconds, and then Samra and Ann shout respectively that it is the the sun/the moon. I don't say anything, but my vote is with the moon.

"It's the moon," says Matt, and I feel oddly pleased.

"Right, second riddle. A bit harder, this one. *I always hear it, but I cannot see it.*"

This one takes us all longer; Ann looks baffled, and Samra is blank. My mind is going through several more scientific possibilities. Electricity? No, you don't really hear that. Sound waves? It would answer the riddle, but I doubt that hundreds of years ago the tribal Africans knew about them, any more than we would have done here. Could it be –

"The wind." PF offers this in a sort of murmur, as if she's not certain.

"Exactly! Well done," says Matt.

"Mind you," says PF, "you don't see the wind as such, but you can see eddies and flurries, and trees bending and so on – you kind of see the effects of it."

"True." Matt accedes to this, out of goodness of heart, 'cos you actually don't see the wind itself, do you? But we know what PF means, and we beg for another puzzler.

"*I have travelled all my life with one who never tells me to rest.*"

Now we are stumped, well and truly. Who or what on earth keeps you company all your days and won't let you rest? We don't get it. A few pathetic stabs at the answer, and Matt laughs.

"I'd better give you another clue. How about *one who follows me at my heels?*"

Well, it won't be a dog, that's for sure, and I can't think of anything else that would stick to you like that. There's a long hush as we all chew our nails. I reach for a beer, and then, like a flash, an image of my day out with Fergus comes to mind, that bright sunny day when we walked down country lanes with the sun not quite overhead and I remember thinking that –

"My shadow!" I yell, startling the others and setting Ann off in hiccups.

"Attagirl, Lucy," Matende approves, and I get a little round of applause. "Okay, seeing as you're all so clever, I'm going to give you some really hard ones now."

We groan in mock dismay, but we are loving it. We're like a bunch of kids with a new and cool teacher. Maybe this is how we should teach children, or adults for that matter? Jokes, puzzles, riddles – really getting them to use their minds, their imaginations, both sides of the brain? Must try it some time. I make a mental note to store up the more difficult ones to land on Stephen Foredock next time I have to be in the presence of that obnoxious little –

"I am an elephant with one ear."

Oh Lordy. Now we are in the mire. After a while, we admit defeat, at which Matt triumphantly tells us that the answer is *a cup*, and gets two cushions thrown at him and a lot more groaning. I can see what he means about the visual aspect, but I mean… And then it cheers me up to think of telling S. Foredock that he can't leave the science lab at lunch time until he's solved *that* riddle. Along with a couple more of his undesirable buddies.

"You want some more? Or do you give in completely? Are you fed up with them?" Matende asks, and we assure him that we do want him to go on, and that it is a fascinating insight into another culture's way of thinking – and communicating.

The next two are stinkers, viz:

"I have a house without a door or window."

Which turns out to be *an egg*. We mull this over, and I guess eggs might be a big feature of diet in Kenya; normal sized ones, bigger ones – lots of nutrients – and that children are used to picking them up or collecting them, as kids used to be here until we went all sanitized and stopped them touching anything that hasn't been purified, washed, wrapped in plastic and sprayed with God knows how many anti-infestation/anti-bacterial agents, so that people would rather buy a plastic tray with fifteen tasteless blackberries in it than go out onto a railway siding and pick the sweetest wild berries they'd ever eat. I have to say that Matt's riddles are giving a lot of food for thought, pardon the pun.

More mental torture follows with:

"It can neither be caught nor held."

Ann is nearest with this one, suggesting that it could be 'air', and when Matt guides her a little – "That's a bit too close to the other one about the wind, think around it" – she finally comes up with 'fire'. The answer turns out to be *smoke*, but we all agree that she was pretty much on the ball. I cannot hold back at this, and protest that you can indeed catch smoke if you fill a bag with it or, indeed, a sealed room, at which I get a lot of 'Oh *Lucy's*' and good natured chaffing. Matende winks at me, and I feel okay with it all. Very okay. More okay than I've been for centuries, it feels.

Last one coming up.

"I have something that stays between two swords but never gets cut."

196

Seeing our utter bewilderment, Matt relents and gives us a further hint.

"It's something you have in your body," he says, and after some while of more nail biting and downing of good ale, Samra gets it.

"My tongue," she says, and of course the image falls into place, though I do personally wonder why only two swords when we have thirty two in our mouths in a full set. Perhaps in the old days, as everywhere in the world, before dentists, the elders of the tribe would only have a few tushies left? I rebuke myself. This is silly, and misses the whole point of these puzzles, which is just to try and see the overall picture. Oh bog off, my overly scientific, finicky mind...

Matt, plainly delighted with our responses, leans back in the big armchair and downs a can of beer. He further explains to us that in Kenya, competitions are held in the form of riddling sessions, and that proverbs and sayings are still an important part of daily speech; they reveal key features of a culture, and show young people in particular how to behave, what is moral, and what is not.

"It sounds wonderful," says Ann, with great sincerity. From this I guess that she does not know Africa well, even if she has been there, or not in the depth that someone like Matt will do. But I have to agree with her; I only hope that modern life, western influences and the rest will not spoil this amazing tradition.

As if reading my thoughts, Matt goes on to say that despite all, the Kenyans are keen to uphold the customs and that he doesn't think they will die out.

"It is part of the country's identity," he says, quietly, "and it needs that."

We sit contemplating this for a few moments, and then Ann perks up.

"I have a wee riddle for youse all," she says, with what

is surely an exaggeration of her brogue; I have noticed that after her first contact with PF and me, back in the far-gone Axminster days, her accent has gradually become far less broad and colleen-ish. It *must* be the sparkling water tonight. "Would youse like to hear it?"

We would. She laughs.

"Well, then, there's this child who goes into the sea with his mother and the water is deep, but he doesn't get wet. No, not at all. Not wet at all. How is this possible?"

"Ah!" exclaims Matende. "We have a similar one. But I'll not spoil it – let the others have a go first."

Of course, we go right round the houses and back, and then up the street, and around the block, and ask if the boy was in a wet suit (no), in some kind of box or glass case (NO!), if he had some kind of costume on or magical, wet-proof skin (don't be daft) and other stupid ideas, until gradually, putting the remnants of our brains together, we work out that (a) he must have been contained in something and (b) Ann is obsessed with babies, so this could only have been –

"His mother's stomach!"

"Yes," beams Ann, "that's right. The woman was pregnant with her wee boy, and of course he had to go into the water with her, but he never got a drop of it on him."

More laughter and good feeling. Matende confirms that the African story is just about the same, and that it might be one that has travelled the world, which is another nice feeling, that people can share their humour and their amusement. We are all extremely mellow by now, what with the spicy rich food gurgling its leisurely way through our digestive systems, the rather tepid beer sluicing it down and the warmth of the room and the company. I am relaxing totally into all this, wallowing in it, swimming in it, head right under the water, as it were, when our room phone rings. PF answers with mock solemnity and then hands the receiver to me. It is Fergus.

"Lucy." The voice is low, and serious. "I need to see you. Talk to you."

My head sort of reels. It's nearly eleven. I'm mildly pissed. I like where I am. I like it a lot. I love all my room mates. I love Matende. Oh heck.

"What, now?"

"Just for a short while. I'm sorry to drop this on you."

There's that in his tone which makes me sit up. He's never sounded like this before. Something is wrong.

"Okay."

"Meet me in the foyer lounge in five?"

"Yes – but ten?" I need to splash water on my face, cool down.

"I'll be waiting." Pause. "And – thanks, Lucy."

We've had lunch, though a later one than we'd intended. It was all the fault of that perishing TV; more news kept coming, and of course we were riveted to the screen. First the weather forecast again – wind def picking up, getting stronger by the minute, though still, I note, at the rather pathetic speed of 11 mph... not exactly a hurricane and not guaranteed to make several tons of ash particles hurry themselves in departing. The weather man got all excited, however, and was making sweeping movements with his hands to show us "*where* the cloud will go" – as if we care, frankly, just as long as it does get up and go – and rather as if he could shove it out of the way himself. We wish. By now, the suspense was getting to us a bit, so we all went off and tidied ourselves up, showered, put nice clothes on, that sort of female biz.

Then, finally, we watched some more telly – the hotel channel again, with a few more flights booked for maybe mid-day tomorrow. Still not ours, but the countdown has started.

Lunch: well, we insisted on paying for this directly ourselves. I mean, we've had a great freebie, and can't swing it any more, though I do know dear old F. wouldn't mind a bit, so we get room service to bring us more health food and with a great effort Ann and I resisted ordering gateaux. (We more or less have to gag each other.) A lush salad arrived, with everything you could want, and some smoked salmon, a veggie quiche with asparagus and clearly made with cream, yum, and wonderful fresh baked half rye bread, and to finish, a kind of fruit compote that had us all oohing and aahing. They'd also given us just two dark chocolate truffles each, and after that lot, not feeling stuffed but as they used to say in the days of good manners, *replete* (there goes my grannie again), we had a little chill out time, reading papers and magazines, and turning the TV firmly OFF since there wasn't going to be anything much for a good few hours now.

More of Ann's amazing tea at four thirty – boy, am I going to miss that too – and just a biscuit, my fav. Ginger Thins. This hotel sure knows how to look after a girl. I reflect not for the first time that this level of luxury could be mine if – well, just *if*. But, like I said before, it would surely get boring. Wouldn't it?

So, without warning, PF shakes her newspaper, folds it neatly, sits up, and says,

"Come on, Lucy. I think you're due for the second story now."

To distract myself, I look at the clock. Blimey. It's six already. Another day in Utopia has slipped by. Ticking like my own biological clock, not that it bothers me greatly. Not in view of what I'm going to be doing in the next two weeks – and after that, and after that…

"Erm, well," I say, into the silence that has fallen. (Why does silence fall? Why shouldn't it go straight up? Or sideways? Why does it go in any direction or move at all? Same thing we say about night falling, darkness falling. Ridiculous. Bloody absurd. *More distractions, Lucy. Get on with it. You know you have to.*)

I'm stuck. Can't think how or what to tell. So I fall back on relaying Fergus' news from yesterday – that urgent request to meet me, which I almost didn't agree to. (Selfish Lucy. But no, I was enjoying myself, I had all the company I needed or wanted, and doesn't that say something about how I see Fergus?)

"Before anything else," I say, stalling madly but also thinking that the gang should know about this, "I should tell you about Fergus. You remember I nipped out to see him last night?"

General nodding of heads, and Samra mouths "A quickie? You were very very quick, Lucy." At which I actually chuckle. For starters, I'm feeling generous about her, and for second she couldn't be further off the mark.

"No," I say, keeping myself serious, for this is serious stuff. "No, as it happens, Fergus wanted to tell me that his father has suffered a heart attack and is in intensive care in a hospital in Glasgow. Obviously he's taken the earliest express train up there this morning."

"Oh Lucy, I'm so sorry." Samra has the grace to go a bit red, and bites her lip, but I brush aside her apology. Murmurs of sympathy from the other two encourage me to go on.

"We agreed just to stay in touch. Nothing more. I guess he's too worried about his dad at this moment to get into anything else. And I'm not at all sure I want him to, in case you don't believe me."

"Actually, I do." This from PF, who leans forward and puts a hand over mine. "And please, please give Fergus our best when you contact him next, and our wishes for his father's recovery."

Ann assents vigorously to this, as does Samra.

"Will do," I say in response. "Oh, and in case you're interested, turns out our lad is very well off, if not to say stinking rich. His father is that laird I though Fergus might be, and he helps run the family estate and the businesses, though he also works as a free lance designer."

"Aha!" says PF, rather triumphantly. "So that's why he was able to get us this great accommodation out of the blue? A reserved suite for the business friends that most hotels keep, huh? Well, our grateful thanks a million for that. Make sure you tell him that too."

More appreciative murmurs and a jibe from Samra

about my being laird's lady of the whatever if I play my cards right, to which I offer her a good natured finger. I have no intention of revealing my fantasies about just such a thing only a day or two ago.

So that's that over, then; it's filled about ten minutes . Now that bloody hiatus thing creeps round us again, or me, anyway. Now I have to talk. They're expecting it. Demanding it. Slavering for it. But where do I start? There's so much to tell. Mind goes blank. As it does. A long, long pause.

Ann helps me.

"Lucy, why don't you go by what you said to me? Begin at the beginning," she says, ever so softly and gently.

And now – now I can't escape this any longer. Everyone is just staring at me – as well they might, I suppose, 'cos I guess I look a real old sight, the abrupt tears streaking mascara all down my face and a nose that feels as though it has swelled into an overblown, squished tomato, with all its appeal.

Right. Here goes, then.

Somewhere along the line I think we all knew that we'd be 'fessing up', as the Americans call it, an expression I loathe, probably in common with fussy old Miss Viner, for once, but it comes in handy now. It looks as if I'm going to be the first one to do so, but to be honest, I've held in the worry, the tension, the doubts and the fears for so long that I can't hang onto them any longer, or I'll explode into a zillion fragments of emotional meltdown. And that wouldn't half make a mess of this lovely hotel apartment.

I take the traditional Deep Breath. And another. A third. Silently, Ann passes me a moist tissue, and I wipe away as much of the damage as I can. The world, or my small corner of it, waits. I look at their faces.

Samra is serious, concerned, her dark eyes kind of pooling into blackness, and her mouth hangs slightly open. Well, I suppose she never thought to witness Cool Hand Lucy go to pieces like this. On reflection, I think I've probably come over as a bit of a hard nut – though not to PF, who is studying me carefully, and nodding gently, as if she has been expecting it. Ann, dear sweet innocent Irish thing that she is, just looks at me all motherly and soft. I could wish that Fergus was here; he knows my story, or most of it, and somehow that would make it easier. But I'm on my own – again. On my lonesome. Whatever else I felt, or feel, about Fergus, or did not, do not feel, it sure was good to have someone around for that short time. But he isn't around now, and I have to get on with this.

"Okay," I begin cautiously. "Okay, so you must have worked out by now that I'm not going to Thailand for a holiday." Several nods of agreement, PF's the most definite. That is one bright cookie. "So let me begin at the beginning, which is about six years back."

Now I have their interest; I can feel a quantum shift in attention. There is a leaning forward, almost en masse, a narrowing of eyes, a parting of lips. In times past I'd have killed for an audience like this; now, I wish this wasn't happening, that I was home, back in England, safe and sound, with mission accomplished and all well. But I'm not, and it isn't. I have so much to go through, so much that is even yet uncertain.

"Six years ago, then. My older sister Mickey – short for Michaela, by the way – and yes, I haven't ever mentioned her, and if you'll be patient, my dears, you'll see why."

I have to focus hard on something neutral here, or I'll not get far without ruining what miniscule amount of mascara I have left on my soggy, wilting lashes.

"So, Mickey. Two years ahead of me, very different, we were completely different characters. We didn't even look alike. I'm like my dad – he was a dark ginger – and she – well, she got her colouring from my beautiful mum;

the long, shiny brown hair, the lovely hazel eyes and the perfect face. Oh, and yes, tall and slim."

I spot PF grinning slightly. "Yeah, PF, that probably does account for my complex about being a ginger freckly midget and all that. I admit it. I was always jealous of her – so so jealous. She was bright, too – oh, I did okay, but she had… she had *flair*. Know what I mean? She was more into languages and that side of things, and she always wanted to work her way round the world using her Italian and Spanish and Russian and Serbo-Croat. Yeah, some people do actually learn that. She just seemed to soak up any language. Anyway, it goes without saying that the fellas clustered round her like the proverbial bees to a honeypot, but – and this was the weird thing – she didn't really take any of them seriously. She'd have relationships, a few flings if you like, but then she'd pull back, and get into some new career move, and poor old Tom, or Dick, or Harry, would be shed like an old pair of smelly shoes."

Ann's nose wrinkles, and PF mutters something to the effect of "and especially Dick, I imagine", at which Samra snorts with laughter. Yes, well. They won't be laughing in a minute.

"And there was poor little Lucy, all flaming hair and itchy skin, with a sister who got a golden tan in the first half hour in the sun, trailing along behind with not much going for her except a degree in Chemistry, a job in the local comp., a one bed flat and the odd loser boyfriend. You think I'm exaggerating, PF –" for the blonde, leggy one has opened her mouth to protest – "well, I'm not. I really am not. Oh, I was content enough in my own small rut, I never aimed for the bright lights or the high life, I wasn't cut out for that, and I did *admire* Mickey. You couldn't help it, because, on top of all her other virtues, she was nice. Yes, she actually was nice – and kinder and more generous to me than I probably deserved."

Here I have to stop; I have to focus on that impersonal object, the window blind, in order to be able to carry on.

It is Ann who speaks quietly.

"It sounds as though you feel guilty, Lucy. And what you're telling us is all 'was' and 'were'. Are we to take it that things changed? That it's not the same now?"

That old window blind sure comes in handy at this point. Stare at it, Lucy, keep staring until the plain cream and the straight slats are all you see and all that is in the forefront of your mind; the back story will tell itself, it is burning away like a bush fire and won't be stopped. Another long, slow intake of oxygen, and I'm ready to go on.

"Yes, Ann, everything is very different now, and I tell you, if I could relive those years of our growing up, but then, you can't, can you, go back I mean; things are just as they are because of how they were. If that makes any kind of sense."

Three heads incline simultaneously; I've struck a chord, I think. It will be interesting to see how that relates to their stories, when they tell them – well, PF and Ann, that is; we know quite a bit about Samra already. But first, I have to plough through my own.

"So. That's the background to what I'm going to say. Mickey and me. Sisters. We did love each other, there was affection, it wasn't all bad, but my own feelings of being massively a lesser mortal got in the way far too often, that's all I can say."

Here I must stop for just a second. Swallow hard. Carry on.

"Anyway, six years ago, Mickey went to the Far East, and spent time in several countries there. She learned Malay, or the main dialect, at any rate; and she took a job as a kind of personal aide to some high flying diplomat. We all thought she'd end up married to someone like that

– she mixed with a lot of Embassy people, and with her looks and abilities, well… My mum was planning her own rigout at the posh wedding she was sure Mickey would be having. Mickey just used to laugh at Mum's fantasies, and go along with it to keep her happy. But in the end, she did something way off the mark as far as Mum was concerned – as far as any of us were concerned, come to that. You could say that we were well and truly gobsmacked."

I allow a deliberately long pause now, so that the others can digest this and form some pictures of their own. Also because I do not relish what I have to say next. Not in the least. It still sends shivers of repulsion right through me. I sigh, and Ann passes another tissue, but I am not tearful again – not yet. I will be.

"We got an email from – from Bangkok. Yep, Thailand, the very place our Lucy is headed. Clue, girls, a clue."

And now Ann leans further forward, breathlessly, that pretty kitten-mouth in its characteristic round open O.

"She was in trouble, then? Ah, sure, Thailand is a dangerous place for a young girl alone. Oh, Lucy, I'm sorry. That might have been very tactless of me, since you're going there yourself. But your sister can't still be in any bother, can she? All this is six years ago, you said it yourself."

"No," I say, very quietly, sitting very still. "Mickey is no longer in trouble. But I have to sort something out. The legacy of what her email told us, all those years back."

I notice PF's face sharpen. As I said, a smart gal. She's starting to catch on. Samra just looks puzzled, but worried.

"Well, the email." I keep my voice as light as I can, to kind of skim over the next part.

"She told us that she had met a Thai fella whilst travelling with her diplomat boss, and that she loved him and wanted to marry him. We were all a bit surprised, but okay, if he was a nice guy, why not? But he wasn't a nice guy, as it turned out. For a start, he was – well, this sounds horrid and snobbish, and really I'm not a bit like that, but he wasn't in Mickey's social world, and there've been too many true stories of Princesses and the like who've married boatmen and peasants and had the scales ripped from their eyes. This man was a taxi driver, she said, but very intelligent, and couldn't get a good education, blah, blah. Well again, we went along with that; we knew how hard it is for people in the third world to get up the ladder, and if he was kind and loved Mickey... So we sent our best wishes, and asked when and where the wedding was going to be."

It's Ann's turn to look anxious. She's leaning forward, hands clasped on her knees, brow all furrowed and worried.

"I have a nasty feeling," she whispers, "that there never was a wedding. That..."

Her voice trails off, and she bites her lip.

"Spot on, Ann," I say, levelly. "There couldn't be, because it turns out he was married already, *and* had a couple of kids into the bargain. Of course, when that email came, Mum just told Mickey to get herself right back home. We'd pay the fare and all that. But Mickey refused. She loved – Ngyan – there, I've said his hateful name, and I never want to say it again, so I'll call him N, if you don't mind." Three heads move from side to side in unison.

"Fast forward." I continue, resolutely. "Fast forward to a few months later, and after a long time of not hearing anything – Mum and Dad were off their heads with anxiety by now – we got a letter, by ordinary, snail mail, enclosing photos of Mickey and this – N bloke – and she is very obviously pregnant. Turned out they were living together, and the baby was due later that year. She didn't say what his family thought of it all. What did come across, though, was the fact that N was a bit of a shifty piece of work. Yes, Ann, I said shifty, but you could add shitty to that if you wanted. She sounded a lot less carefree than she had in her emails, and of course by now she'd given up her language work, though she was teaching at one of these EFL outfits, for piss poor pay. Still, Thailand was cheap, she said, and they were managing fine."

Ann frowns. "How was this – N shifty, exactly?"

"Well," I concede, "we weren't ever really quite sure, but it gradually came to light that he did other things on the side as well as being a taxi driver. Maybe drugs, but also to do with the sex trade. And all that – lady boy stuff we talked about a while back. Sorry, Ann," I say hastily, before I can launch into a graphic explanation of under-age prostitution, and the whole seedy underworld that goes on in a lot of places, not just the Far East. But to my astonishment, Ann simply smiles, and says, serenely,

"Ah, I wasn't born yesterday, you know. I am acquainted as it happens with what you're hinting at."

Acquainted with? The saintly one? Despite my present anguish and heartache, I feel a lightening of spirit. What tale exactly will this one be telling, I wonder?

"Well, then," I say, hastily, "I needn't go into detail – and in any case, we never did know for sure, just that N seemed to get money from some dubious sources, and a lot of unsavoury characters used to call at their apartment at all hours of day and night. Mickey got increasingly freaked by this, and tried to leave, but N always talked her round."

I grimace at this point, feeling all the disgust of six years and more, and see it echoed on PF's face. Hastily, I continue.

"He obviously knew he was onto a good thing with her; she could earn money through teaching and her flat was a damn sight nicer than anything he'd have been able to get by himself, bearing in mind he had er, other responsibilities. God knows what his charm was: he wasn't particularly good looking, or not from the photos she sent. But he had some kind of hold over her, and she was, I guess, having his baby. Which turned out to be a boy."

"Ahhh!" A long, exhalation of relief and delight from Ann. "A son! And your nephew, and grandson to your parents. So it was all right, then, in the end? At least, the child was born healthy and all?"

"Oh yes, the child was – and is – fine. A lovely little boy, called Joseph. Mickey got her way and gave him a western name. I don't think – N – particularly cared."

"And now? Where are they all now?"

Ann blunders on, and I catch PF giving her a warning glance, putting a hand on her arm, but there's not stopping the flow.

"So that's why you're going to Thailand!" she beams. "To see your sister and your nephew! But – haven't you seen them before?"

"Of course I have." I speak rather impatiently. "Mum and Dad and I flew out early the next year, as soon as we could; wild horses wouldn't have kept Mum away! It wasn't too bad, then. N was half way civil to us and quite nice to Mickey; the apartment was clean and tidy, and there weren't any weird people around. Joseph was just adorable, and Mickey seemed happier – now, of course, I think it might have been because we were there, Mum and Dad for a fortnight, and I stayed for a month. I guess it was all one big act."

A shuddering breath now from Ann makes me realise that she, too, is beginning to cotton on, and Samra is biting her nails in apprehension. I think they know the sort of things that will come next.

And these I run through quickly, without pause, deadpan, without feeling. N's downward spiral into wife beater, drug addict – if not dealer – and sex maniac. Everything that moved in a skirt he had to have it; to be fair to the man, he himself didn't do underage, it was all consenting adults, but there are plenty of them around, and he didn't spare himself.

"Mickey tried to leave, again, but he kicked up an almighty fuss, and said she could go, but without His Son. You know, the patriarchal line all of a sudden – and a sound awareness of what he could get out of her. A lot of what he raked in, it turned out, went on his own drug habit.

"So she stayed on, miserable except for the joy that Joseph brought her. It was lucky, really, that N didn't want to screw her much any more, or she'd have got pregnant again, or some horrible transmitted disease, as he surely wasn't one to bother about things like that, and to her knowledge fathered a couple more kids in the next three years. Probably there were more."

So, we come to two years ago, and here I slow down again, not for the benefit of my audience, but so that I can pace myself up to the really terrible bits, that are still so raw.

"Two years back, to the month," I say, keeping my eyes firmly on the cream slats and watching the light filter through and the dust motes idly whirling round, "that was the last time we heard from Mickey. She used to email regularly, phone if she could and there were the odd letters and cards. N didn't seem to mind, or even notice, and in any case she was so browbeaten by this time that her messages to us were just about the child, and general things; it was enough for us to know that she was still there, and at least partly all right."

Another long breath; I need some kind of energy to go on with this sad and sorry tale.

"N left her alone a lot, which was all to the good, and

she had one or two women friends – Thai girls who also had kids. N tolerated that; probably he screwed one or more of them on occasions, but Mickey was past caring. Then – nothing. We had no emails, no cards, no calls. We tried ringing her mobile, the house phone, *his* phone even, but we never got a reply. After about a month, Dad went over there, just him this time, determined to find Mickey and Joseph, and go to our Embassy, and get them back here."

My voice trembles now, and I feel a lump the size of the Rock of Gibraltar in my throat; I'm not sure I can talk past it. I have to. *Go, Lucy, go.*

"Turns out," I say, laconically, throatily, "turns out that he'd battered her once too often, and that she'd been taken to hospital by one of the neighbours as she was screaming so much that they broke the door in. N just ran, and went into hiding."

The faces of Ann and Samra are pictures of pure horror, as I glance briefly from the window to where they are sitting. Samra has both hands over her mouth, and Ann is clutching hers tightly together as if she is going to wring them.

"And the *child*?" PF asks sharply, as well she might.

I look away again, and I speak fast, very very fast, all in a rush.

"Joseph was in his bed, with the sheets pulled up over his eyes, shaking and crying. The neighbours took him in, and the next day they went to the hospital with him, to see his mum. But it was too late. Mickey had … had died in the early hours of the morning, dead from the massive head and body wounds. So Joseph never saw her again, and by the time Dad got to Thailand all that he had to do was identify her and organise the funeral."

Samra gasps now.

"In Thailand? Couldn't he have brought her home? Oh

–" she realises. "I don't mean to criticise your dad. It just seems so awful – "

"It was so awful," I say, grimly. "Mum and I flew out, and I need hardly tell you that it was the saddest day of our entire lives. After the funeral, and I won't dwell on that, we had the grim business of the court case – yes, they found N and with neighbours as witness, and one or two of Mickey's friends, who were brave enough to come forward, he was identified and charged. He didn't deny it, so it was fast-tracked, and we had at least the satisfaction of seeing him convicted."

Quietly, Ann asks: "And condemned?"

I can only nod at this point. "Thailand has a harsh justice system. I apologise, Ann, if it offends your beliefs as a Christian, forgiveness and all that, but we weren't in the least sorry. I never thought I'd feel that way, but –"

"It's all right, Lucy," says Ann, "I understand. I think we all do."

"Yes," murmurs Samra, "Pakistan is pretty strict on murder as well, if it's proven. I know we don't hold with it in England, But sometimes I think… in cases like this …"

Here she trails off, and PF takes over.

"Well, maybe. In the States, as you know, quite a few States still have the death penalty. I'm not in favour of it, you know, but I can appreciate why you would feel that way, Lucy. I really can. I probably would myself – though heaven save me from having to make such a judgement call."

We are all stuck for a moment, me most of all, though this is not the end of my story, and PF realises this.

"So – if you can tell us," she says, very gently and calmly, "what has happened to the child? Your nephew?"

Somehow I pull myself from the depths; it is good to have got the worst part over, and I turn to my audience.

"Well, Joseph was taken immediately on Mickey's death

213

by N's family, before N was found and before the case came to court – and apparently we couldn't do anything about it. His father was still alive then, you see, and he went to N's parents. We couldn't put a case of our own. At least, not at that point."

"Not at that point," murmurs PF, who has put the last piece of the jigsaw into place, I think. "So now is a different time, and you're going –"

And I say quickly, flatly, without emotion or any kind of expression, just to confirm what PF by now knows, that –

"Yes, I'm going out to Thailand to fetch Joseph, to bring him to England. I'm legally adopting my sister's child."

Now there is really a silence. Like I've never heard before, like an emptiness, as if I've hollowed out a space, that hangs between us, and nobody can think of quite the right thing to say. Eventually –

"Bloody Norah, Lucy. That's amazing."

This is Samra, and although I know she was born and brought up in the North East, it still sounds funny from her. I smile very faintly in spite of myself, a watery sort of half grin, and she utters a soft "*pheeww*", as if she too has been holding her breath for a long time. Ann is openly moved, tearful.

"Oh, you poor wee colleen," she says, and leans forward to take my hands in hers. "What you're doing is just fantastic, and I know the Lord will bless you and look after you and the little one." For once, I do not want to pull away; the warmth of her grasp, even of her words, is welcome, so very very welcome.

"Well," says PF finally, "I'm like broken up by your story, Lucy – I mean, your sister and all – but you are doing a really great thing here, a fine thing. And I think it will bring you happiness and – and – "

She stops, and it is clear that she hesitates to say what was coming next, so I make it easy on her.

"You were going to say that it will change my life, and that might be for the good, huh? Well, PF, I agree. You're absolutely right – spot on. I needed to get out of the rut of grief, and guilt, and sorrow I've been living in these past years, and yes, it will be good to have someone else's needs to have to meet, and to have to care for Joseph. It's just that – "

""The hardest part is yet to come," PF finishes for me. "The stuff you're going to have to do when you get to Thailand?"

"Yep." Three deep sighs echo my feeling, and then, out of nowhere, comes a huge belly laugh, and it is noisy and joyful, and it fills that awful blank space; and even more miraculously, it is coming from – ME.

I am conscious of three pairs of eyes looking at me anxiously; I can read the thoughts. *Has she flipped? Should we do something?*

"Hey," I say, my stomach still heaving. "Hey, girls, it isn't so bad. In fact, it's all good. You know? These last four days have been great. I've been able to get all of it off my chest before I even get on the plane, I've met some wonderful people to share this time with, present company not excepted of course, and you've given me strength and courage, you actually, truly have. So let's laugh instead of crying, let's tell a few more stories, let's have some jokes. It's going to be OK. Very, very much okay."

Suddenly, unexpectedly, PF comes over to me and hugs me; holds me very tight. Says nothing. Doesn't need to. Another silence, but a happier one, and the place is buzzing with goodwill. Mmm, yes it is. Don't believe it? You'd better. I never knew that goodwill was so tangible, but I could slice it and serve it up right now. With cream on top. I feel like dancing, light as air, as if a great eff-off stone has been lifted from my back; but better not say that aloud. I'm still not sure that Ann, for all her unforeseen knowledge of some of the darker sides of life, is quite up to the language.

It is Samra who speaks, slowly, questioningly.

"Would you say, then, Lucy, that Thailand is a bad place? Is that why you want to get little Joseph away?"

"No, no, Samra, that's not it – not in the least. I'm not saying that N was a bad lot 'cos he was a Thai. There's good and bad in every race, in every country; Mickey was just unlucky in getting tangled up with him. No, if N had really loved his son, if Mickey had died for some other reason, and if Joseph was being properly loved and looked after I wouldn't dream of doing this. But he's not. I went over a year ago, and it was pretty obvious that N's family were getting sick of having to support Joseph – after all, they're not well off, and good old N had sired a couple of other kids, as I said, and the parents had to pay something for them too when all the nasty stuff got in the papers. They didn't argue at all when I offered them money to adopt – and I don't altogether blame them. Joseph is very much Mickey's child; he might be half Thai and born there, but he's Mickey all over again. So I started the long process of international adoption, and the fact that the family went along with the idea it made it much easier. There are still some of the formalities to go through, but I feel much more hopeful now. He's going to be mine, and he'll be coming home – in every sense of the word."

"Amen to that," murmurs Ann, and again, for once, I am not irritated, in fact, I could almost hear myself echoing the feeling. Jeepers. Strange things certainly are happening on this trip.

We have another welcome tea break; all is peaceful, like the flat, calm waters after a storm, and we bask in it; I reckon we feel we've had enough emotional drama for the time being. I know I have. Tea, coffee and little cakes are drummed up, and I gradually pull myself together. I am in a good place, both literally and metaphorically. These three have journeyed with me, and I know that I for one do not want to let them go into the blue yonder and never hear about them again.

After a good while, Samra cannot restrain herself; this is something she has wanted to ask, that is clear, and when she starts to speak, I know what she's going to say. I'm right. We are that much in tune with one another.

"So that package in your bag you keep checking on," she says, "and the phone calls you sneak off to make?"

"Uh-huh," I say, smiling rather mischievously, as I contemplate Samra-as-spy, secret agent; I thought I'd been so careful, so unobtrusive, discreet. "Not drugs, Samra, and the calls weren't to my drug lord in Thailand."

She blushes, and looks at the floor.

"Lucy, I feel so ashamed. I totally misjudged you, and I want you to know I'm genuinely sorry."

"Sure," I say, breezily. "A mistake anyone could make. Don't even think about it."

"Well," says PF thoughtfully, "I reckon there's quite a lot of mistakes we've all been making. A lot of misjudgements too, not just yours, Samra."

She's right, of course, and suddenly I feel very keen to hear the real stories of the other two. As of one mind, our eyes – PF's, that is, Ann's and mine – swivel in the direction of the Saree-d One (only I mustn't call her that now, must I?) and she looks up in alarm.

"*Me?*" she says, quavering.

MMM-humph. Yes, Samra, you.

"But I've told you my second story, and then I let you into my secret – about getting married to a Christian in Pakistan. There's no more to tell."

"Oh, I think there are things you haven't completely come clean on, Samra," says PF, rather forcibly I feel. "Come on, now."

"Such as?" Samra is very much on the defensive, and I can't say I blame her. There are some things which she might want to keep to herself, and I don't totally feel happy that PF should be prying. Still, I am curious myself. We'll get to hear some more. Oh, *goody*.

To my amazement, Ann puts her head above the firing

line in support of PF, only she's a bit more tactful about it, and it comes across as affectionate, different from the definitely accusing tone from PF. For the hundredth time I wonder just why PF is so abrasive with others. Maybe her real story – and she'll have to give it now, she can't get off the hook – will reveal why? I sure do hope so. (I am beginning to recover, back to the narky old Lucy. Well, excellent. It will see me through.)

"Samra," Ann says, moving closer so that she can put an arm round the rather stiff shoulders, "I think PF is right, you know? I mean, we learned how you met Faisal, how you waited so faithfully for each other and all, and then you shocked us by telling that you're marrying against your own faith and that it will be hard to find someone who will allow such a thing. We all felt for you, we did, so. But what I'm asking myself is, why aren't you going over with your mum and dad? Your sisters and brothers, if you have any? Other relatives?"

Samra brushes off the arm, stands up so suddenly that we all jump. The dark eyes narrow, and flash.

"Why the hell do you think?" she virtually spits at Ann. "How can I tell my family I'm marrying a non Muslim? Do you think they'd let me travel if they knew that?"

Oh-oh. So Samra hasn't let on to her parents – or anyone else. My mind begins to function again, to work this out.

"That suggests, then," I say, slowly, thinking as I go, "that in effect, you're running away. It's the opposite of what usually happens – I mean, generally girls might run away from an arranged marriage in, say, Pakistan, to the west, and here's you, running from the UK to a non-arranged marriage in somewhere that isn't even really your country. It's kind of funny, Samra, if you don't mind my saying so. I mean –"

I break off, not wanting to say more and hurt Samra's feelings. Heck, this situation must be difficult beyond belief for her, and so I add hurriedly, as she paces the room restlessly,

"What I meant to say is, I really sympathise, and if there's anything we can do to help, well, I'm sure we all would be glad to."

Oh, that sounds pathetic again. But what else can anyone say? To my surprise, Samra visibly relaxes and sits down; she is even faintly smiling.

"Yes," she says ruefully, "I guess it is a comic turn of events. I told my parents I was going on holiday with some friends – in England, that is. They don't know I'm travelling overseas, and most certainly not to Pakistan – otherwise the family there would be alerted, and then it would all be over."

Really? Do families have that much control, we wonder? But yes, apparently they can have, and Samra wouldn't get far off the plane before they'd intercept her plans. Oh God, this is certainly risky, to put it mildly, and I don't think we three would want to be in her shoes – however glamorous and sexy they might be. The whole thing has eerie echoes of her folk tale. Except that I am sure nobody would poison her at the wedding feast! Just drag her back to UK, I expect, and try to get her hitched to someone else, quick.

"So," questions PF, "where are you meeting Faisal? Is he waiting to meet you in?"

Samra nods. "Yes. He looks old enough to be an older brother, or an uncle, even. Islamabad airport is always incredibly hectic and swarming with people. Nobody will take much notice, and in any case, I think he's bringing his sister with him so it will look like I'm being met in by a couple. Believe me, that isn't the real problem."

"And what is?" I ask, though fully aware of the answer. She flushes, bites her lip.

"As I think I said, finding a sympathetic imam to

marry us. There are some who will do this, but only very forward thinking ones, and I'd have to swear to keep to my Islamic faith. Not," she adds, quickly, with another flash of the eyes, "that I have any problem with that, and Faisal doesn't either. We truly respect each other and our separate beliefs."

"In that case," PF muses, "I hate to say this, Samra, but why didn't you bring Faisal to the UK, where I imagine there are more liberal priests – imams, I mean."

Samra laughs. "Not necessarily. England is actually a small place where its Muslim population is concerned; people have relatives, connections, all over the country. Word would get round, believe it or not. And anyway, Faisal really couldn't have come here; he'd have to have come on a visit visa, as he wouldn't want to claim refugee status and has no reason to, and that wouldn't have given us much time. Also, there's his work, his vitally important work."

"Which is?" Our eager voices together.

"He's a doctor. In a hospital funded by Christian churches. In quite a poor area outside Karachi."

Inevitably, Ann's face lights up.

"God bless you both," she says. "Oh may the lord bring you great happiness in your marriage and in your Faisal's work, which is most surely to the glory of Him."

"And to Allah," rejoins Samra a little wickedly. "Don't forget that."

"I won't," protests Ann, "but you know, it's all one and the same God. We just go about worshipping in different ways."

I am now – despite my restored *bonhomie* (thanks, Claude) – just a mite sick of all this, so I get onto another topic that I think Ann will like and might get us off the religious stuff. Not that I sneer at it, no, these few days have taught me not to, but – scientist to the core, *moi*.

Everything explainable; cause and effect. No miracles. Am I persuading you? I'm not sure any more that I'm convincing myself. Oh-oh. Hastily, I ask Samra a further question.

"So what about your kids? Will they be brought up Christian or Muslim? Isn't that one of the stumbling blocks to a mixed faith marriage, especially this way round?"

"It would be," says Samra, unruffled, "if I was going to have any."

"But –" Ann – "you are going to have children, to be sure?"

"If I could, I probably would." Samra now stuns us once more. "I had some tests done in UK because I had a feeling that things – down below – weren't quite as they should be. And don't ask for details, 'cos I'm not giving you any. Well, it turns out that I probably can't have kids."

Oohhhh. Now we are embarrassed, and in Ann's case, most obviously downcast. Samra laughs again.

"Oh, we're a tad disappointed, but it's not a tragedy. Faisal's sister and brother have little ones, and I'm gonna be helping at the hospital along with him, and there'll be lots of children being treated. I'll get to be a big auntie to loads of them. To be honest, I think I might prefer it that way. I'm not sure I'm cut out for domesticity."

I study her closely; the dark eyes are tranquil, the brow clear. You know something? I think she's actually telling the truth here. And you know something else? There's a parallel, isn't there, between her situation and Ann's. Both going out to be with their men, both doing some valuable work where it's very much needed. Well, I have to say – hats off to them both. I'm not at all sure I could commit to such a future. I'll be only too happy when Joseph and I are back in England, in my little house, and I can get on with the wonderful job of bringing him up. A child of my own, even if I wouldn't have wanted it this way. And I realise, in this instant, that I am so looking forward to it, after all the years of stress and worry, and that it is going to be good. More than good. It's going to be, as Ann says, *fantastic*.

* * *

Some time – and many more cups of tea and coffee later – I get round to thinking that, right, we've heard all of Samra's story now, and I've told them the low-down on mine. I've also had texts from Fergus and Matende, the latter telling me how glad he is that he turned round and went back home, and that he's seen his daughter. He promises to update me, which I very much hope he will, and sends his love to the 'gang'. Fergus is a little more terse; father very poorly, in intensive care, but they're hoping. He doesn't put "and praying", but I have a weird feeling that they might be. Something about him is, despite his artistic talent, his travelling on international business, very conventional – even orthodox. I'm thinking Scottish Presbyterian here? Anyway, again there's regards (yes, more restrained, our Fergus) to the 'girrrls' and pledges to keep me posted.

So, that stuff all wrapped up, what exactly is PF's end story? She surely isn't going to duck out of it, when she was the one who thought up the idea of the Airport Tales? Mind you, it was only our two entertainment pieces we were supposed to be judging, not our true life stories, but ... two of us have come clean. And really, we know Ann's, even though she hasn't spelled it out, don't we? Screwing up some remnants of courage from within, I spit it out.

"Come on, then, PF. We want to know."

Languidly, unflustered: "Want to know what, Lucy?"

An impish glint from the sapphire orbs. I glare at her.

She knows very well, the cow. Evil bovine. You are not going to get away with this, I mentally will her, and she laughs.

"All right, Lucy. You have the most expressive face, you know that? But I think I might need a stronger drink than coffee to tell my tale."

Oh. Ah. Right. It's going to be that dramatic, is it? Or difficult for her? I'm sorry now for badgering her, but perhaps she needs a push? We call up trusty old Room Service and get a really nice red, full bodied, mellow, and some light eats with it. And of course more sparkling water for Ann. Finally, wiping her fingers and licking the delicious sauce from them, PF settles herself and begins.

"You remember," she says, taking her time, not hurrying, sipping her wine reflectively, "you remember the story I told you about a young woman called Leigh who was – "

"A hermadphrodite," I finish for her. "Yes, I don't think Ann and I will easily forget that one, PF."

"Okay, then. Well, I have a feeling that one or more of you might have imagined that Leigh was me, that the story was what you might call autobiographical?" She pauses, and looks at us unnervingly keenly, each of us in turn.

Ooops. I certainly don't want to be the one who lets her know that we discussed her account, and more or less decided it couldn't be her. Now I'm wondering if –

But before the question has fully formed in my mind, PF calmly dispels it.

"Leigh is not, was not me." Another pause. "We did become close friends, as I said, and I do hear from her every now and then, but we were also different. Her problem was not mine, nor mine hers."

So what was – or is – your problem, PF? I can feel three minds in sync here, all impatient for the revelation. She smiles, lazily, keeping us dangling. God, she should work

224

for the FBI or some such; she'd drive suspects barmy and they'd confess everything, just to get her to actually tell them something so that everyone could go home and watch TV.

"No," she continues, and takes a generous gulp of the red stuff. We're going to need another bottle or two, at this rate. "No, we didn't have the same dilemma. I was born a girl, with all the right bits and pieces, nothing there that shouldn't be. And yet... and yet, I suffered confusions right from being oh, I don't know, maybe seven or eight. I kept them all to myself, though, and it was only when I met Leigh and started listening to her problems and talking with her that I began to realise that I could perhaps do something about my own mess."

"Which was?" Samra interjects, leaning forward, her eyes very dark and focussed. I think she might be onto the truth of the matter, though I'm a bit left behind, and Ann is frowning in what looks like puzzlement.

PF regards us long and hard. It is as if she is doubtful about trusting us with this last step; then she seems to decide that yes, it will be okay, and, flatly,

"I knew – had known for years, really – that I wanted to be a man."

A *what? A man?* But she's an utterly gorgeous, drop-dead-pull-blokes-from-the-North-Pole-to-Antarctica-and-everywhere-in-between, blonde, leggy, beautiful *woman*. And then I start thinking: or is she? She doesn't have much in the way of boobs, though there are some; her hands and her limbs are very long, and her feet – well, they're not dainty, though I put this down to her height. She is all of five eleven. Then there's the reaction of Fergus and Matende; neither of them found her attractive in the least. Did they kind of sniff her out? Pheromones, and all that? I look round at the other two. Ann is nodding, sagely, not looking too surprised; Samra is leaning back with her hands folded over her stomach, a kind of satisfaction on her face. It hits me now, with sudden fierce force, that this is why PF has been so guarded, why she can be so spikey; hers is the biggest secret of all, and, by the way, the most extremely personal. So...

"So," say PF, with a slightly self-conscious shrug of the wide, strong shoulder – and why didn't I notice that before? – "you see, I'm going to Australia to stay with a sympathetic aunt and her husband, and I have to live as a man, with a new identity, and prove to the medics that my intention to have a sex change is valid – that I am completely serious and okay with it, and that I can cope. That kinda stuff." She shrugs again, as if to dismiss the idea, but we all know that it is not a light matter; this is literally life changing, changing one's whole self. My problems, if they are such, fade into the middle distance, and I can only begin to think about the hell that PF will go through. Probably has gone through all these years.

"Well, now," says Ann, very very quietly, "I'd imagine that you've not had an easy time, y'know, especially when you were a wee teenager, isn't that so?"

"I don't think I was ever a 'wee' anything!" PF snorts with amusement, and the tension lessens. "I was always really tall and lanky, and I was a tomboy too – oh, I know a lot of girls are and they don't want to be men, and they grow up as well adjusted young women, but I wasn't like that. I didn't just want to play boys' games, play with the boys, I wanted to *be* them. And you're right – being a teenager was pure hell. Like, I was supposed to date with guys, and at some stage fuck them, and I didn't want to do that at all. I wasn't even attracted to girls, though, that was the thing; I just felt all out of place, all wrong in my skin, so I couldn't reach out to anybody and went along with the dating stuff and I even – you might not believe this – enjoyed sex with men when it came along; after all,

I had the female bits to give pleasure. It was just in my head that it didn't fit. Do you follow me?"

Once more, Ann startles us.

"Indeed, yes, I do," she murmurs. "You mean that your emotions weren't being engaged, that you were sort of… frozen. Am I right there?"

PF nods, and I at least have a sudden riotous thought that maybe Ann is wanting to change her gender? But no, for whatever reason, that's ridiculous, and as if sensing my line of thinking, she shakes her head firmly and assures us that it is not that she has ever wished to be a man, good Lord no, but that she has other reasons for understanding what PF is saying. Hm. And her married, and all that? Here's another riddle which we'll have to wait to solve, methinks. (Shakespeare. If not others. Ta, Ms. Viner. You do come in handy at times. Though you can be a bloody nuisance at others.)

"But PF," I venture, "I'm not trying to be funny, but why are you dressed so glamorously, and the hair extensions, the nail polish, and all that? I mean, if you're going to Oz to live as a man – though I don't know why you have to go there, by the way, surely there are doctors in America? – why aren't you kitted out like a fella for this trip?"

PF regards me with something like her old disdain. I crumble.

"Passport," she utters, tersely. "I haven't even started the process yet, and of course I have to travel as who I am at the moment – which, unfortunately, is still a woman. I guess," she goes on, a little more gently, "I kind of decided that as this will be my last few days as a female, I might as well do it to the nines – the sexy clothes, the hair, the makeup, the whole works, you know? Kind of goodbye, farewell to all that, good riddance, if you like."

"I see." I do get this. I think we can all – except perhaps Ann – relate to living it up just before taking on something much more difficult and challenging. "But still," I insist, "why does it have to be Australia?"

"Um. Totally unempathic family back in US. Fundamentalist Christian and all that hooey."

PF grunts to herself, as if fighting some invisible enemy, as I guess she well might.

"I mean," she corrects herself quickly, "not that there's anything wrong with being a strong believer, but they don't understand at all, and really freaked when I told them what, at the age of thirty-four, I had finally got up the balls to do. If you'll pardon the unintended pun!"

Again, we are able to laugh with her, but this of course provokes my wayward curiosity. Will she be given the complete male works? Will she have –

"Mmm-hm." PF grins. "I'll be a fully working male once the whole kaboodle is done. I know it sounds improbable, but I'll be able to have sexual relations, and all my female bits will be gone. Oh –" she puts in, before we can ask it – "you can have various levels of surgery, some less – er – comprehensive, as you might say, but I'm going for gold here. The only thing I won't be able to do is father kids, but I regard that as a price worth paying."

Well, I think, that makes two of you, Samra and yourself; and I don't see myself churning out any babies of my own, if it comes down to it. It wouldn't be fair to Joseph. Or not for a long time, and then it'll be too late. I realise, in the same breath, that I'm not sorry about that, just as Samra wasn't. Hah. So Ann will have to make up for us in continuing the human race. With that white knitting – which has grown, by the way – it looks as if she might already have started.

There's a companionable hush now, and I for one am picturing a masculine version of PF: the strong, characterful jaw, the eyes as blue as Robert Redford's in his heyday, the blonded hair cut short, the long, shapely limbs bulked out with muscle and the toned body. Yes, she will make a handsome dude. *Buns as good as Matende's... Now, stop it, Lucy. Just stop it. This is a serious issue we've got here. Yes, really.*

"So." Ann breaks the thread of our imagining. "How are you going to live in Australia, PF? Financially, I mean? And how long can you stay? I mean – "

"Oh, I've landed a job there," says PF, nonchalant as you please. "You see, I'm a child psychologist – "

Involuntarily, I gasp quite loudly. Ann merely gives a brisk little nod, but Samra does look as astonished as I probably do. Mind you, this does explain a lot; the keen gaze, the searching looks, the silent scrutiny. I hate to think what she has really deduced about me. But PF is ploughing on, ignoring the interruption.

"– and I have made it my business to specialise in gender issues. I'll be working in a clinic for adolescents so I'll be supporting myself, for the year of what they call psychological adjustment, and I've saved up a lot of dollars and will be able to whilst I'm working – Aunt Dolores will let me live there for free, bless her wonderful heart, and then I'll be able to take time out, and use holidays, for the treatments. I mean," she says hastily, "I'm not saying it's going to be a cakewalk. It will be hard, but I'll get there, I'll get through it."

I suddenly recall commenting inwardly that nothing about this person would surprise me. I was right. She is going to do it, she is going to manage this huge and frightening thing. Like the others, I suspect, I am swept away with admiration. Awe, almost. It's going to be gruelling, physically and mentally, and I know for certain that I would never, even if had the inclination, be brave enough to undertake anything remotely like this.

But woh, Lucy girl, don't knock yourself. Not everyone would go to a country several thousand miles away and bring home, for keeps, a child that although blood related, they hardly know. And be fine with that.

All in all, each one of us has reason to be proud, to give ourselves some praise, and we should be rooting for each other too. After we hear Ann's account of herself, and that will be brief and predictable, much more mundane if not slightly boring after what we've heard today, we should have some right royal celebration. A real old *cailigh*, as the Irish one would say.

Another thought pops up, unbidden, and I stifle a laugh.

Maybe I could parcel up Stephen Foredock and send him to PF in Australia? He might not have gender issues (horribly heterosexual, he'll breed like a bunny) but she could sure sort him out...

"What's so funny, Lucy?" PF asks mildly.

"Nothing, really," I say, blushing. "Well, actually, it's the idea of you dealing with all those probably stroppy, mixed up teenagers. I don't know whether to feel sorry for you – or them."

"Touché!" PF laughs aloud, a really good, belly laugh, and suddenly I feel on even Stevens with this woman (soon to be man), and all is getting righter with the world by the moment. I also realise, in a flash of blinding insight rare in old Lucy here, that all my jealousy about PF in female terms was so off kilter as to be totally absurd, and I realise too that if nothing else, this trip is teaching me to value what I am, and what I have, appearance-wise, woman-wise, ME-wise... At which I also burst into abandoned laughter of a kind that I would severely tell my kids off if they did that in the lab. (Hm, yes. Maybe I should let up on the poor little perishers a bit? With the exception of Stephen F., of course... Oh what the fuck. Even him.)

The other two join in, Ann cackling like a chicken in a run, Samra sniggering like a schoolgirl. Amazing: out of all our stories, all our sadnesses and problems, comes this: what the text books might call *female bonding*. But you know something? It's real, and it's here.

It is evening now, and we are sitting around as usual, rather missing male company, if truth be told. So much for my erstwhile (ooh, good word on half a bottle of plonk) Who-Needs-Men stand. But Matende entertained us so well and cleverly, and Fergus was … well, just Fergus. Calm, relaxed, sociable and – there. Only now he isn't.

Oh, we're not miserable. Too much to be glad about. I guess it's just that suddenly we're at a loose end. Tales have been told, lives revealed, shocks, surprises and even some laughs. So what now? I don't even feel like finishing this half of red, and push the bottle away.

"Ah!" says Ann, promptly, spying this. "Time for some tea?"

"Well," drawls PF, rather sleepily, "I wouldn't mind some coffee – decaff if there is any."

"Me too." Samra struggles to gain a sitting position on the sofa. "And some biscuits?"

We don't need to take a vote on this; it's obviously unanimous, and we vote Ann in as chief beverage-maker and caterer. It's not that we're lazy, honest, it's just that she does these things so briskly and efficiently; that husband of hers will be well pleased. He'll never be kept waiting for good tea and coffee, that's for sure. And if I sound anti-feminist, don't you believe it. I just mean that whoever is good at a job should be the one to do it. And I hope if I ever do marry it will be to someone who loves to cook. Cos I sure don't.

Returning with the tray, Ann smiles and tells us to help ourselves, girls, and brushes away our thanks. She really is a lovely woman, you know that?

PF confers her radiant beam upon her and then, without warning, reminds Ann that she still has a second story to tell.

"Sure, now, and it's a good thing I've put that tray down or I'd be dropping the thing all over the place," says Ann with mock horror. "But as it so happens I have just a short tale I could delight you with, if you're in the mood to hear it."

We are, we say, like a chorus of three little girls from school. We most certainly are.. This will make a pleasing interlude in which, almost instinctively, I think we know might be our last night in Wonderland. Reality, the real stuff ahead, will happen all too soon. So, Ann, fire away.

And she does.

"Well, now," begins the soft, mellow voice. "This is just a bit from my own past, when I was just out of college and about twenty-one. A little more wordly wise than I had been, but still green about the ears, you'll now what I mean? " Not really, Ann, I think the rest of us were more, er, experienced by then, but never mind. Continue.

"My da was a navy man, you understand? So he was away a lot, but when he got to be First Officer he was allowed to invite his family to go with him, or to visit him in any of the ports where his ship was. Sometimes my ma would go on a trip, but not always, as she loved her house, and even though we were all away by then she liked to be there in case we needed home."

Ann looks wistful for a moment, and we can appreciate that; the warmth of one's childhood home is something never forgotten, and hard to replace. I notice that PF is looking particularly plaintive, her face shadowed, and I wonder just what is going through her mind. No matter. Let's hear Ann's story.

"Anyway," says the Irish one more perkily, "this is not a sad tale, no, just a memory of an evening that turned into a night of pure magic, you know? Just magic, as it was."

Aha! So perhaps – there is more to Ann? A *night* of illicit pleasure, then? At last…

We lean forward, and the melodic voice carries us with her.

"Well, my da was docked in Alexandria – in Egypt, you'll know, on the coast of the Mediterranean, and it was early October. My ma and my younger sister and I flew out, and we were invited on board for a party, first for the bigwigs, who were piped onto the deck, youse know, two lines of officers and ratings to greet them, and pipes played in ceremony. It was all a bit stiff and formal at first, but then the VIPs went, and the real party began. It was the party of a lifetime, I'll tell you. I mean, I'd been to college parties but at a girls' college, and a Catholic run one at that, they were pretty tame affairs. Not that I had a problem with it, since I've never been a drinker, and we were all innocent young things, but this party on the ship was a real eye-opener. Oh," she adds hastily, "there wasn't any wrong doing, nothing indecent, you mustn't misunderstand me, it's just that – well, the alcohol seemed to flow from the walls, and everybody got very happy and the dancing was wild, oh, wild – I danced with one young officer and he collapsed in a heap, sweating like a pig on my uncle's farm, and said I'd worn him out. Worn him out, girls! Me!"

And she herself collapses now in merriment at the recollection, and we also fall apart at the mental picture of Ann as dancing dervish – or try to. It doesn't quite happen.

"Well," she says more soberly, "after a while I got chatting to this lovely man." (Mm, she's warming up now.) "He was – oh, around forty-five or so, not a navy man but a friend of my da's. He didn't like dancing, so we sat and talked, and I found him so easy to get on with and he was civil and educated, so when he asked me if I'd like him to show me round Alexandria, I said yes. And then he surprised me utterly by saying, 'Right, let's go, then'. It was nearly two o'clock in the morning, you understand! Now? I said. Now, he said. No better time to see this great and amazing city."

I'm wondering – is this Mr. Right? Is this the one she married and is going out to join? Egypt, Africa... Could be. PF and Samra are looking oddly puzzled.

"Of course," continued Ann, "I had to ask my da and my ma, but they knew this man, Robert, he was called, and absolutely could trust him, and it's a strange thing but when you're in a totally foreign country and the night is still hot and all around you is like another world, you do things you'd never do as a rule."

Again, three heads nod. We all know about that one and I'm thinking – and hoping – that Ann can relate a little to my episode in far-off France, though I'm not expecting her story to be quite so in-your-face, as you might say. Though you never know with her.

"So, we walked round Alexandria till gone five in the morning – walked, and walked and walked, and Robert knew all the back streets and the oldest parts of the city, and it was truly fascinating. We trod on cobbles in some places, and in narrow alleys and on broken pavements and we talked the night away."

She smiles, the serene smile of memory. Ah! More to come...

"The air – oh, it was so soft and soothing, and there were still the smells of the day, some not so pleasant, sure, but some heavenly, like the lingering smoke from the charcoal fires in the markets, or souqs as they call them, and perfume from the perfumery quarter, and of course, food, the delicious waft of Arab chicken, spiced rice and Turkish coffee – why, there were one or two cafes still open, serving men who sat up through the early hours, and Robert knew the vendor of one of them and we stayed there for half an hour whilst he chatted in Arabic with the owner. I couldn't understand a word, but I didn't care; I was just so at ease and utterly content with the night scene, the dark streets, the glow of the braziers in the cafes, the warm wind brushing my face... I tell youse, it was the most romantic night of my life, in the truest sense of that word."

Eh? The most romantic? But nothing has really happened. Yet.

This doesn't sound like marriage material.

As if reading our thoughts, Ann laughs, mischievously.

"You'll be pleased to know there was some – contact."

Our ears prick up, as do our hopes. Or at least, mine do. Surely –

"He tucked my hand in the crook of his arm, and we walked like that the whole time. It was very gentlemanly, and I felt respected, and safe. Nothing more, girls, sorry to disappoint."

We are disappointed, naturally, but I for one can also identify with that feeling of being treated, not chivalrously as in the old fashioned sense where men had to fling their cloaks (or themselves) in the mud lest a lady get her shoe wet, but without the automatic pawing and clutching that we all seem to do as if we *have* to. When we actually don't. Have to, I mean. I like this arm in arm idea. I also recall Samra's account of how decent and respectful Faisal has been all these years. There's something in this, you know. Perhaps I should think about that when – and if – I'm next with Fergus...

"So – why did you say it was romantic?" PF asks this cautiously, clearly not wanting to offend by sarcasm. "I mean – "

"Ah." Ann sighs. "There's romance in so many things, isn't it so? Just a beautiful city for itself, the fabulous night air in a hot place, the meeting with a charming and intelligent stranger, and the fact that you know it's only going to be this one time, this one occasion, well ... such times are precious, every second an enchantment..."

Yes. Yes, we get it. We see it. And I am wondering if you can fall in love, just for a night, a day, and never forget that person, that day, although –

"You never saw him again?" I whisper, not certain whether I want the answer to be yes, or no.

Ann shakes those untamed curls, and sighs.

"No. He walked me back to the hotel where we were staying, along the sea front, and we listened to the sounds of the waves splashing ever so gently onto the promenade, or Corniche, as they call it there; and we roused the poor old *boab*, who wasn't best pleased but went away happier with his generous tip, and we shook hands and said goodnight."

"And that was that? No more contact?"

Ann lifts her shoulders, spreads the white hands.

"What would have been the point? I had my future, my career path to pursue; he was over twice my age – sorry, Samra, I don't mean to be tactless – and set in his own path in Egypt and other countries. We'd had a perfect time together – in fact, apparently he said to my da that it was the best night of his entire life. But nothing would ever have been as good, and it could not have gone anywhere."

PF and Samra are now nodding in agreement and some kind of understanding which leaves me behind. I am still baffled. If this wasn't Husband, then who was, or is? But more than that, I am moved by the – yes, the delicacy of the incident that Ann has told – different than her "pure passion", where there was unfulfilled longing, much calmer and in many ways more beautiful because of its – its quality of being *unsullied*. It takes me back to much earlier days of my own, much, much earlier, when I was capable of feeling ecstasy or joy from the simplest things, like watching the tide running over my bare toes and into the moat of the sandcastle that Mickey and I had built, or going out for a walk very early on a bitterly cold frosty morning when the fog was so thick you had to grope your way along walls, and every piece of grass, every stalk of bay willow herb was stiff and silvered, and sounds came ghostly and echoing., and the world seemed yours, and yours alone …

For a moment I feel intensely sad at what I have lost; and then I remember that it is not lost, only put on a shelf for a while, and that I can share all these things with Joseph, and show him how to get pleasure out of the good things in the world. God knows, he must need that.

I set my shoulders straight, sit up, as if putting myself on course for what I am taking on. And I thank Ann, most sincerely, for a great and happy story, and a very suitable end to our tale telling. I wish her luck for her future in Africa, and with her man.

She smiles, a rather curious humour in her eyes.

"More tea?" she says brightly, and I have the impression she is keen to leave the room.

PF and Samra too are smiling – but at each other. What in the name of Beelzebub is going on here? You tell me. Pass the biscuits.

It's another morning in Paradise. And I'm not being altogether sarcastic. This smashing hotel suite has been like a cosy cocoon, holding us and supporting us whilst we worked through our tangled webs, feeding us, keeping us comfortable and in some considerable degree of luxury. Mentally I send up a blessing to dear Fergus, though not, I sternly tell myself, of the religious kind. Honestly. Just a bit of human fellow feeling, of positive thinking.

Oh – and, guess what? After we'd exhausted ourselves yesterday evening with listening to the last of our Chaucer tales (ha! Got it right at last) and some light hearted silliness afterwards, we turned on the telly; I think we'd almost forgotten that. And there it was – the news we had waited for. Ash cloud has presumably been given a course of vitamins and some energy pills, as it's moving quite sharpish now out westwards with the strong easterly wind – probably from Russia, good old Putin must have been spouting more hot air – and should have cleared the British Isles by later today. Some flights have already been lining up, depending on which direction they're headed, so we have to keep checking the screen and not going far from our apartment. We've all done some final packing, and it looks very much as though we will be flying to our different destinations by tonight or some time tomorrow morning. Well, after all, hurrah.

"It's been great, hasn't it," I venture, "but it's time to move on – literally and –"

"*Metaphorically,*" the others groan in unison. Okay, right, so it's a cliché, I'm full of 'em, but I do mean it. We have to get our various acts together and start our real journeys, tackle and conquer what lies ahead, travel the road that life has decided for us. (I can hear Ms. Viner tutting at the banality of my thoughts, can see those thin over-red lips pursing; well, bugger off once and for all, Ms. V., I don't need you any more. I really, really don't.)

"Yes, Lucy." PF speaks more softly now. "Great is putting it mildly. Incredible, life-changing. The whole thing – meeting you guys, getting this great hotel apartment – and you must thank Fergus again on our behalf, Lucy, what a terrific fella – just time to rest, to take time out, to – to –"

Here she stops, and I see for the first time a hint of tears. Impulsively, I put my arm round her, and to my utter amazement, she flops her head on my shoulder and snuffles into my tee shirt. I really will go to the end of our road, or would if there was one handy. This person is full of twists and turns, and I suspect that within that crusty shell is a soft, pulpy being like an articulate brachipod – I.e., a mollusc that has two hinged shell sections; think big freight wagon, or – but I sense I'm being tedious. Funny, though, that I should come up with an articulated mollusc. PF is *par excellence* articulate, and she's also sensitive deep inside, just like the sea creature that anchors itself to the ocean floor.

I'm doing my old thing of going off into my own head, into rational, comprehensible science, and here's PF, bivalves at least half open, gradually sniffing herself back to self control and an upright position.

"I tell you what," I suggest now, to buck us all up a bit. "Why don't we go for a coffee in the airport? The departure announcements will be all over the place, and it might be nice to get a change of scene – lovely though it is here."

"Agreed," says Ann, briskly, and vainly attempts to scrag the wild hair into a little knot at the back of her head.

Samra looks at me teasingly.

240

"Oh, I know what you're after, Lucy. Without Matt and Fergus around, you want to put some more notches on your belt!"

"I so do not," I protest, but good humouredly. I cannot think anything ill of this young woman any more and wonder why I ever did.

Ann chuckles, and PF smiles indulgently; thus, in harmony, we make our way out of the hotel and to the airport lounge, which is now buzzing with excitement and life. I spot the family with the baby which – all those aeons ago – I carried round in the early morning; the mother looks rejuvenated, very pretty, and the baby is smiling in its father's arms. They give me a friendly wave. We glimpse others whose weary, sagging bodies were draped over the lounge floor only two or three days ago, and everyone is looking ten years younger, a lot fresher and cheerful. All at once, a queue begins to form as a flight departure is called, and travellers scurry like a column of hungry ants to be checked in. And then another. Things are happening now, and we four link arms, get our coffees and kind of glue ourselves together, very much aware that these are our final hours.

"We should swap addresses and contacts now," says Samra, sensibly. "I mean, at any moment –"

"Yes, good idea." PF brings out an efficient looking notebook and a pen, hands round a page to everyone, starts to write. "Whatever you can think of that will help us stay in touch – email, obviously, but – "

She stops. A frown crosses her forehead. We stare at her.

"Stupid, stupid me," she murmurs. "I was going to put my name as it is now. You'll need to know my male identity, won't you?"

This brings home the facts of what she's about to confront, and we are all a bit quiet as we put down all the means of contact we can rustle up . For me, it's probably the easiest – my little house in the UK, my telephone and mobile I've had for years; it's so familiar, and it comforts me to know that soon it will all be there again for me – and for Joseph.

"Hey, PF – or whatever you're going to be soon," I interject to break the awkwardness a little. "We never did judge whose story – I mean the tales we told, not our actual life details – was the best. Who's going to judge, anyhow? It was your idea, so – "

"Ah," says PF, thoughtfully, "but that doesn't mean I'm more qualified to decide. Let's take a vote, shall we?"

She brings out the notebook again, and begins to make a kind of grid; then she heads each one with the title of our little narrations, including my own revelation, albeit very personal and not really a second tale.

"Now," she announces, "let's all give stars for each story – like out of five, you know?"

"Like film reviews," says Samra. "Good idea."

"Exactly." PF nods. "Okay, then. Off we go."

And the next ten minutes are a time of hilarity and fun as we try to gauge each tale in turn, without much to base our rating on, when it comes down to it, as all were good in their own way. I only had one actual tale by the rules of our home-made competition, as by the time it was my turn for a second one I'd lost the plot (in a sense) and just burst out with the real stuff. So I don't think I've much chance of winning this, not that it matters in the least by now. I have gone beyond needing anyone's approval, even PF's. But then –

"Well," says this she-soon-to-be-he, "the grand champion of story telling is …"

We sit with bated breath. I guess it will be Samra, for her hilarious descriptions of flying G-strings and the rest. Or possibly her folk tale, which I liked very much; or –

"Lucy, with Mon Nuit Avec Claude."

The word falls like a stone on my ears. What? Me? Moi? Freckle-face old Luce from commuter-belt land, with her bawdy tale of long-ago shenanigins in la belle France? Oh, come on. Come on, here.

"Yes," says Samra. "It was brilliant, Lucy."

I have to admit, 'fess up, as they say, that I'm well chuffed, bloody over the moon at this sudden turnabout, this praise. It's almost too much to take in, but I'm beginning to glow with it, to enjoy my fifteen minutes of mini-fame...

PF, however, merely turns to me with a smile.

"So, Lucy," she says mildly, "you seem surprised. Well, let me tell you it was a story worthy of the great man himself –"

"Geoffrey Charter," I say, triumphantly. "Chaucer," mouths PF silently, and I go red again and correct myself.

"Yes, he'd have been proud of that one," continues PF. "Bawdy enough for a medieval pilgrimage and with enough of yourself in it for us to get an insight into the younger Lucy – which was, by the way, most interesting."

Hm. Well, okay then. Story teller *preeminent* (Ms. Viner now rolling in her grave) to add to my meagre CV. Maybe I've missed my calling: stand-up? It would certainly beat standing up in a school laboratory and trying to get disaffected teenagers to understand elementary chemical reactions.

"Well, thanks, folks," I mutter. "What's my prize, in that case?"

And PF amazes me once more, and produces a beautiful pair of long silver filigree earrings, which, she affirms, will set off my wonderful hair when I have it in an up-do like I did that night with Fergus. I suspect that she bought these in advance, for they wouldn't go nearly so well on Ann or Samra – or, for that matter, on her, not that she'll be wearing such adornments much longer. Hmmmm again...

I don't want to go down that route of thinking, so I just thank her once more, and genuinely, for the earrings are lovely, and all of a sudden I wish Fergus was here to show them off to, and my stomach does a funny little flip, and then I change the subject quite abruptly.

"So who got the second highest score, then?"

"Ann did. For 'Pure Passion'."

Now there's a shock. I did think that Samra deserved second, even if jointly with Ann, but apparently Ann's score was very near my own. I don't ask whose scores were the lowest, but I strongly suspect it was PF's own. Which gives me room for thought.

Viz:

I put myself down, put PF on some ridiculous pedestal, and yet when it came to it, she wasn't as effective as any of the rest of us in her own competition. Talk about having to realign your thinking. My head hurts, and I don't want to put a dampener on our coffee time or our generally relaxed mood, so I'm glad when the conversation moves on to other things – mostly to do with the latest news about flights and generally listening to airport tannoys.

These, of course, are virtually indecipherable and unrecognisable as English – "Will Mr. Bejikhglllgggghhh of Skijdghrughbh please condadtt Shiiwwer Hawksssulleer at the Gldemmart Hdel…" – and other such offerings, but then one comes through very simple, loud and clear.

"Sister Ann O'Hanlon, please go to Desk 25 immediately. Sister Ann O'Hanlon."

"Ah, sure, that's my call."

As my jaws drop with an audible thud, our Ann stands up promptly, smooths her skirt and says, jauntily,

"I'll be back soon, girls – it'll just be the convent checking on me."

The – convent? Convent, as in – as in, no, can't be, she's married, she's knitting white baby clothes – she's – *no! Not a – not –*

"A nun," says our Irish girl serenely. "Yes, an Anglican nun."

And with that thunderbolt, she whisks away, the untidy hair flying freely in all directions. I note that PF is chuckling faintly.

"Oh Lucy, didn't you guess?"

Erm, no. Am I the thickie of the gang, or what? Samra is also smiling at me, and I have a suspicion that she knew, or was onto it too. Why do I not see what is right under my nose? Why do I go on wild goose chases? But then, there were a lot of red herrings. Not least of which is –

"The white knitting?" I ask, when Ann returns. "What is that about? And your wedding ring? And the man you're joining in Africa to help with his work."

Then it the penny drops, like a lightning strike from the sky, if that's not too mixed a figure of speech. Wedding ring: bride of Christ. Doing God's work in Africa. This is what she's going out for, this is who she's 'joining'.

"But the baby clothes," I utter feebly, clinging to a remnant of dignity.

"Ah, sure," says Ann, beaming. "My sister in law. Having her first. It's something to keep me occupied, y'know? There'll be long evenings out there with not a lot to do – we're working in a kind of orphanage-cum-children's centre, and the accommodation, so I'm told, is quite basic. We'll be busy with the usual duties, sure, but there'll be time on our hands and I think knitting things for babies is a lovely use of my time."

"Yes, I'm sure," I say, uncertainly. "But why aren't you in nun's clothing? And why have you still got your hair – a lot of it, incidentally. I thought you had to shave it off."

Ann laughs. "Anglican nuns don't necessarily wear the traditional robes, and some of the old rules in some orders have fallen by the wayside. We're quite a modern order, and we just dress modestly and plainly – though I have to say, my hair gets on my nerves at times, so it does, and I wouldn't be against cutting it a lot shorter when I get to Africa, so hot it will be there."

She sighs a little plaintively, and it occurs to me that Ann, too, though I didn't expect it, is facing new challenges and has perhaps been enjoying her few days incognito, before she too gives up a lot. I also ponder on the question of her hair, and conclude that it would be a crying shame to hack it off; it's part of her simple, rather wild beauty, and Fergus, bless the man, would have a fit…

As if on cue, a text chirps from my phone. It is from the man himself, and the news is better. His father has come out of intensive care and is doing well. Fergus sounds a lot happier, as well he might, and wishes us all the best, and hopes to hear our news. He also hopes to see me back in England and to meet Joseph. This I will have to put on hold, as I'm not sure of anything right now except the next week and then the important task of settling my nephew – my adopted son – into his new life, school, and all that will go with that probably quite frightening situation. I turn my attention back to Ann, as another quite dreadful thought has crossed my mind.

"Ann," I say hesitantly, not sure how to put this, "were you not offended and shocked by some of our stories, and our language, and all that? I mean…"

There I trail off, unable to express any more of the acute self-consciousness, if not shame, I am feeling within. That story about Claude! What could she have thought?

But she laughs, and puts her arms round me lightly.

"Lucy, I have lived, you know. I'm thirty-five years old, and I wasn't always a convent girl. I'm not so easily outraged as you might imagine, and what does shock me is cruelty, violence and meanness of spirit, also the terrible injustices of the world. Nothing you have said offends me, though some of it worried me a bit for your own sake, you understand? But now I know what you're doing here, and the good and marvellous thing you're embarking on, I am content that you will go from strength to strength, and I hope very much – " she looks directly into my eyes, and I melt in the glow of her beautiful green, slanting gaze, with its warmth, its wisdom, its tolerance – "I hope you will write to me, or email me (yes, we do have computers these days!) and let me know how it goes with young Joseph and all."

"I most surely will," I say, and return the embrace, "and I will want to know how you get on with your valuable work, really, I mean it. You never know," I continue, inspired, "I might bring Joseph out to see you one day."

"You'd be entirely welcome," says Ann, "and may the love of God be with you, and may he grant you your own guardian angel to see you through."

Something weird happens here; four days ago I'd have pulled away from her and mentally asked for a sick bucket. Now I do nothing of the kind; I clasp her more closely, and accept the blessing, I think you call it a benediction, not that I truly believe in it, but because it is so sincerely meant, and it is from *her*. Well, if there ain't a God or a divine creator, Fate sure is a strange and wondrous thing; we have all of us forged the strongest of bonds, and I have a reassuring feeling that we will continue to be in each other's lives. I truly hope so.

Ann releases me, smiles at us all, and says her farewells.

"I'll just be going for my luggage, and then I'm on my way. My flight is going very soon now. God speed, and be with you all."

PF and Samra are hugged in their turn, and I see genuine tears in Samra's eyes. They have made a real connection, and I have an instinct that Samra might need to seek counsel and spiritual help from Ann in her own difficult path. PF

247

simply gives Ann the most radiant and affectionate smile, and then our Irish nun, that amazing woman who looks nearly half her age – no drinking, smoking, drugs and, one assumes, sex seems to be some kind of recipe for a long, healthy life, hm, must think on this one – this incredible person vanishes from our view, leaving the three of us to do a little quiet mourning of our own.

* * *

I am sitting with PF now in the departure lounge. It is very late, but they're getting flights out as fast as they can, bearing in mind safety and crowding of the skies, and Samra has departed through those no-return checkpoints with many fond goodbyes and good wishes. We have wished her well, and meant it; again, I wonder why I ever disliked her or distrusted her motives. She has put away her western clothes and is wearing shalmar khameez and flat, beaded shoes; her hair is discreetly wound up in a slick chignon and she wears a light head covering which she calls her 'dupatta'. She looks very beautiful, and we tell her that Faisal is one very lucky guy.

"I know!" she laughs. "I tell him that all the time."

And then – she's gone. It's like the ten green bottles now, down to just the two of us, back where we started in what feels like another lifetime. It also crosses my mind that, with Ann's revelation, this means that none of the four of us, by all accounts, will be furthering the human race; Samra and PF won't be able to, and unless Ann breaks all her vows quite spectacularly she won't be reproducing, and as for me – well, as I said, I have this strange intuition that I shan't either. Ah me, the planet will just have to cope. Although, of course, oddly enough all four of us will be working to some extent with children: PF with her troubled teens, me with Joseph and the kids at school, whom I suddenly realise that I miss, Samra with Faisal in his clinic and Ann in the convent's orphanage. This seems like a kind of completion of the circle, a binding of our different selves; and a further strong link forged for the future. PF and I sit in comfortable companionship, until I have to ask her something.

"Do you remember that first day," I begin, but PF puts a hand over mine, and shushes me gently.

"Yes, Lucy, I remember every second of our first meeting."

"Oh, the spilt coffee, the silly conversation, you mean? How arsey I must have been?"

"No. Not exactly that. I recall other things."

Now she's got me; I can't bring to mind anything particularly significant. Does she mean how dumb I seemed to her? How clumsy, gauche, how very unsophisticated and dismally English? It doesn't seem as though she's going to expand on this, so we sit quietly for a while, and then chat about inconsequential things – as you do when there are other, quite different tensions bubbling away beneath the surface.

We managed to put our heads down somewhere – back to a square of carpet, "For old time's sake", we joke – and sleep in snatches, always listening for the vital bit of news that will send us hurtling in different directions to our destinies. Somewhere around six in the morning, when I revert to habit and bounce up wide awake, PF's flight to Oz is flagged up. I rouse her, urgently, and she comes to with a rather violent start.

"Well, this is it," I say, and help her up with her bags. "The parting of the ways."

We look at each other. There is a long moment.

"But not for ever," says PF, so quietly that I have to lean in to catch it.

"No," I say, "of course not. We all said we'd keep in

touch – and with Matt and Fergus as well."

"Oh yes, the handsome, debonair Fergus," says PF, with just a faint whisper of her former malice. "You're a bit struck on him, Lucy, though I don't think you know it."

"Maybe," I say, for once willing to mull this over. "But I'm really not sure about him. I feel I *ought* to fall in love with him, fancy him, but – oh, I just can't make my mind up "

PF puts her hands on my shoulders; the grip is firm but calm. The blue, blue eyes gaze intently down into mine.

"Well, perhaps this will help you do so," she says. "You once asked me what kind of guy I went for. It's not a guy, Lucy, 'cos that's what I'm gonna be. It would be a girl."

Then, swiftly, before I know what is happening, kisses me full, and lingeringly, on the lips.

And I also can't help myself responding; feeling myself stirring and wanting to kiss her back, only not her as a woman but sensing the man that she really is. I also feel something that I never quite did with Fergus; feel myself wanting – more.

Oh

My

God

IVIE LINDIG is the nom-de-plume of a Yorkshire writer. *"Airport Reading"* is her first foray into the "chick-lit" genre, after having published numerous short stories, media articles, educational material and poetry. Born during the Second World War, 'Ivie' recalls that time of austerity which would put the present era to shame, the subsequent, wonderfully liberating decades of rock'n'roll, mini skirts, advancing freedom and independence for women – and some of the confusions that resulted. This novel has a more serious undertone than strict chick-lit, but is written both to amuse and to make the reader ponder some of the issues faced by women in our modern twenty-first century world. Now in her seventies (and still teaching part time) 'Ivie' is currently working on other forms of novel writing, notably detective and futuristic fiction.

Lightning Source UK Ltd.
Milton Keynes UK
UKOW05f0831021116
286686UK00001B/66/P